PRAISE FOR
CHRIS BAUER

"A high-stakes art sting in play and an assassination in progress. Chris Bauer humanizes unique, frenzied, marginalized characters in a twisty and timely page turner."
–Robert Dugoni, NYT bestselling Author of The Tracy Crosswhite Series

"Taut, topical, and tremendously entertaining. Important issues and a propulsive plot. A highly satisfying read."
–Jon McGoran, author of *The Price of Everything*

"Fires on all 12 cylinders with a nitro boost. A morality tale told by a kick-ass woman and her two loyal dogs. Get ready to turn some pages."
–Eric Beetner, author of *The Last Few Miles Of Road*

"An art forger, gun lobbyists, and a transgender assassin rev up Counsel Fungo's Tourette's affliction. And a guy incinerates twenty-two Mummers in Philly. Great fun. Get this book."
–Tony Knighton, author of The Nameless Thief novels

"A sticky pool of criminals. A clever bounty hunter and her canine deputies you can't help rooting for, and the best first sentence you'll read all year."
–Michael Kardos, author of *Bluff*

"A scathing takedown of the gun lobby and its less than pure motives. Will wrap you up on multiple levels."
–Dana King, Shamus Award nominated author of the Nick Forte and Penns River novels

"A heroine hard as a bag of tanks. Counsel Fungo cruises through revenge, violence, gun nuts, transgender issues, and hoagies. The blender speed increases till the top pops in a bitter twist you cannot see coming."
–Mark Bergin, author of *Apprehension*

"Bullets, banjos, and discourse on America's gun laws and the crookedness of politics. A portrait of life *in extremis*—the hard-fought plight of the few remaining good guys trying to right the wrongs."
–Joe Clifford, author of *The Shadow People*

"*The Manchurian Candidate* crosses paths with *Ocean's Twelve* while hosting the most unique characters I've ever read. Smart and relevant. I couldn't put it down."
–Cam Torrens, award-winning author of the Tyler Zahn series.

"Multiple plot lines tackle current events alongside the action. If you're looking for great characters, action, and meaningful discussions on social issues, this is the perfect book for you."
–Gary Gerlacher, author of *Last Patient of the Night*

"A multi-faceted savvy thriller. Smart, nuanced, and not afraid to shine a light on the ugliest parts of America's love of the Second Amendment."
–Brooke L. French, author of the Letty Duquesne thrillers and *The Carolina Variant*

"Authenticity and plenty of grit. A ripper of a story."
–William J. Donahue, author of *Only Monsters Remain*

"*I Heard You Paint Cowboys* offers unique characters and punchy dialogue. The writing draws you in and won't let go."
–Jeffrey James Higgins, author of *Furious, Sailing into Terror*

"A wild ride with a twisty plot that will keep you guessing. People need to read this book."
–Natalie Zellat Dyen, author of *Locked in Silence*

"A high-stakes game of stolen art and illegal arms. A timely and meticulously crafted thriller."
–Ellen Butler, International Bestselling author of the *Karina Cardinal Mysteries*

"A masterful, supercharged thriller. A curveball lurks on every page. Be prepared for a serious roller coaster ride."
–Steve Zettler, author of *Tick... Tick... Tick...*

A COUNSEL FUNGO THRILLER

I HEARD YOU PAINT COWBOYS

CHRIS BAUER

Black Rose Writing | Texas

This is a work of fiction. Names, characters, businesses, places, events, and incidents are either the products of the author's imagination or used in a fictitious manner. Any resemblance to actual persons, living or dead, or actual events is purely coincidental.

ISBN: 978-1-68513-582-9
LIBRARY OF CONGRESS CONTROL NUMBER: 2024947560
PUBLISHED BY BLACK ROSE WRITING
www.blackrosewriting.com

Printed in the United States of America
Suggested Retail Price (SRP) $21.95

I Heard You Paint Cowboys is printed in Garamond Premier Pro

*As a planet-friendly publisher, Black Rose Writing does its best to eliminate unnecessary waste to reduce paper usage and energy costs, while never compromising the reading experience. As a result, the final word count vs. page count may not meet common expectations.

AWARDS

I Heard You Paint Cowboys—"Best First Sentence" Award, International Thriller Writers 2024 Thrillerfest Masterclass

Cradle—#1 Thriller 2024, Digital Book Today; #1 Thriller 2024, Critter Awards Readers; #1 Suspense 2024 and #2 Thriller 2024, Firebird Book Awards

". . . Oh, better to be anything than America as a gun."
—from *America is a Gun,* a poem by Brian Bilston

I HEARD YOU
PAINT COWBOYS

Wissinoming String Band Social Club, Philadelphia, Pennsylvania

The glass front door to the club was tinted none-of-your-damn-business black. Neil pulled it open, a banjo case in his hand. The string band's social club headquarters shared storefront space on a four-lane city street in the Frankford section of Philadelphia. Eye level on the door in yellow hand-painted letters was an admonishment that Neil Sullivan paid no attention to: *MUMMERS ONLY*. The second line read *Plus friends and family*. The third, *No Mets or Cowboys fans.*

"What do you want, Neil?" Walt said.

Walt sat in a high-top chair nursing a beer, the open space of the club's interior behind him. It was barely a civil greeting, and not a question Walt Grantham wanted an answer to. If Neil wanted in, he'd have to go through Walt.

Forties, scruffy beard, baseball cap, and sunken, late-night eyes, Neil Sullivan was a tool-and-die-making machinist, an urban farmer, and a Philly Mummers string band musician who had expected to perform with the rest of his social club in the traditional Mummers Parade in Center City Philadelphia on New Year's Day. Until the ATF raided his urban farm.

Neil lifted his banjo case to a café table and laid it flat. "It's busy in here," he said to Walt.

"Yeah, packed. All here for band practice in the park, under the lights." Walt further evaluated him and his banjo case. "Again, why are you here, Neil?"

"I just need to clear up a few things. Where's Dominic?"

The string band's headquarters storefront was the width of two Philadelphia row homes, its interior decorated in the colors of Philly's pro sports teams: red and white; midnight green, black, and white; red, white, and blue; orange and black. The faded wood paneling's best days were a memory. The club's bar was noisy, members priming the pump for a full walk-through with musical instruments and costumes as soon as the band's captain called things to order in the small parking lot out back of the club.

"Dominic's here somewhere, but I can't let you in, Neil. You clean up your rep, maybe they reinstate you. Until then, no."

No chance that would happen. Multiple complaints from neighbors about midnight rifle bursts on his small farm property in a quiet section of the city had prompted the raid. The Alcohol, Tobacco and Firearms Bureau turned his house inside out, the visit yielding illegal long guns and other banned military weaponry, plus a small cache of explosives. The charges escalated after the ATF finished with his computers: alleged child endangerment and possession of child porn. Neil was out on bail. On the Philly streets, illegal guns were one thing, kiddie porn was a whole different story, and "alleged" wasn't part of anyone's vocabulary.

Neil listened to the cacophony of a social club in full weekend stride behind Walt, bottles and mugs clinking, shot glasses trip-hammering the mahogany, voices raised.

Walt took a smooth, unthreatening sip, his eyes on Neil. He lowered his glass to the table and left it there, freeing his hand. A common knowledge thing about Walt: On his hip, under his Hawaiian shirt, was a holstered handgun.

A retired cop, also a musician, he was the string band's unofficial security officer. In that capacity, Neil knew, Walt had a feel for things: the unease and tension of a situation, and when something might get out of hand. To Neil, Walt was in that zone already, predisposed.

Neil unlatched his banjo case and flipped the top open, its hinges creaking. Inside the case, a banjo.

Walt's drawn handgun made Neil raise his hands, Walt's eyes drilling Neil's.

"Easy, Walt. I'm just dropping this off and solutioning through a coupla things. I sold it to Dom to pay back some of the bail money the band put up."

"Leave it, Neil. You need to go."

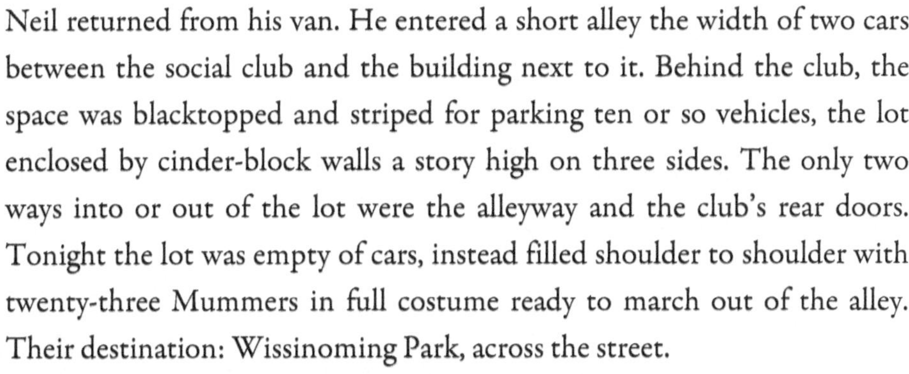

Neil returned from his van. He entered a short alley the width of two cars between the social club and the building next to it. Behind the club, the space was blacktopped and striped for parking ten or so vehicles, the lot enclosed by cinder-block walls a story high on three sides. The only two ways into or out of the lot were the alleyway and the club's rear doors. Tonight the lot was empty of cars, instead filled shoulder to shoulder with twenty-three Mummers in full costume ready to march out of the alley. Their destination: Wissinoming Park, across the street.

Neil's long guns were gone, all confiscated in the raid, four AR-15s modified to be fully automatic, which made them illegal. He had only one gun left, a legal semiauto handgun he kept in his van's glove box. It was now tucked into his waistband. For after.

He exited the shadows into the floodlit parking lot noisy with banjos being tuned, honking saxophones, and excited voices. He raised the long black wand of his brush-clearing flamethrower waist high with both hands, its hose connected to the fuel tank strapped onto his back. He squeezed the fuel discharge valve. The tip of the commercially legal XL18 flamethrower's wand ignited.

A half-gallon of burning napalm per second streamed over a hundred feet, a dripping clothesline of fire moving left, right, up, and down. Panicked Mummers in flammable costumes ricocheted off the walls and each other with nowhere to go inside this cinder-blocked death box furnace, crumpling to the blacktop in smoking, melting flesh, all of them screaming, writhing, and busy with dying.

The flamethrower spoke for Neil and his disappointment, his despair, his depravity, and his disillusionment. It also spoke for his online presence, his pro-gun voice and persona.

He drew his handgun, and with a single trigger pull, he solutioned the last of it.

ONE

Two months later, Lake Harvest, Pennsylvania, in the Pocono Mountains

Counsel Fungo owned more than enough guns. Enough to do her job plus a few extra for home protection. Did she need to buy a semiautomatic assault rifle? Sure, for when the zombie apocalypse hit, or if she decided to unretire and return to active duty in the K9 unit of the Pennsylvania State Police. Or maybe to prove to herself again that gun control in the United States was porous as hell, which was why in late January she was outside a gun show in the Poconos in her van, in a parking lot, the engine running for heat.

Ken Duke, Frankie Dolphus, Brad Spilvey. Banjos.
Cook Tinker, Bernard Shanahan, Taylor Mitchell. Accordions.

These names and more. In her head, in her heart, and so she'd never forget, on the backs of her business cards a few names at a time, too many to fit on a single card. The Wissinoming String Band, all of them gone.

"The gun lobby can kiss my ass," she said, her only audience her canine deputies.

Tess, a brindle bull-terrier mix, and Fungo, her namesake black and tan German shepherd, the best four-legged bounty hunters and listeners a person could ever have, sat at attention on their haunches behind her in the van. This culminated her rant against Arms Equal Freedom, or the AEF, a large gun lobby in the US, its membership in the millions.

Ernest "Buddy" Masusock, Preet Mhangor. Banjos.

A Philly string band could never have enough banjos.

Counsel slipped a baseball cap over her espresso-colored pixie cut, pulled the brim down onto her forehead, and turned off the van's engine. This time of year in the Poconos, it was still well below freezing. Cold enough that if she peed outside, she might be able to sit on the stream.

"You guys have your orders. I won't be long. Cuddle up." She left the windows open a touch and slid her long, toned, athletic frame out of the van.

Today's indulgence was to recon a gun show run by Regal Eagle Protection Inc., at Split Granite Lodge resort. Ski season. Little snowfall so far this year, way below average yet again, but this visit wasn't about global warming.

Inside the lodge's large, well-lit convention center were seven hundred tables with over five hundred exhibitors, and on nearly all the tables, guns. After going a few rows deep, Counsel picked up a pamphlet from inside a large carrying case now empty of its Bushmaster AR-15, a semiautomatic rifle.

Austin Fevering, Chick Wolson. Fiddles.

"Got two for sale," the gun show guy said, nametag Dave. Older guy, seventies maybe, seated, chunky, and his double chin in need of a shave. His gray-blond comb-over sat atop a Jabba-like head mounted directly onto his shoulders—someone Counsel wouldn't have expected by his age and appearance to have his own website, yet he did. *Gunshowdave.com.* Gun-Show-Dave was seated behind the middle of his three tables.

"All my prices are up, sweetheart," he said. "Inflation and, you know, the crazies." His bulbous, Rodney Dangerfield eyes smiled.

Of course the prices were up. A recent mass execution had come at the hands of a wronged gun owner, his published manifesto a rant against liberal-backed government overreach regarding long guns. Another validation that guns don't kill people, people kill people, with other means available that could guarantee the same outcome, like a commercial flamethrower.

Counsel mumbled something off-color that wasn't in response to Dave's opportunistic capitalism and tone-deaf antifeminism.

"—here we go round the mulberry Bushmaster, eeny, meeny, miny, cunt."

A minor Tourette's episode, in public. Her subconscious knew no shame, was usually as inappropriate as hell. Part of her nursery rhymes repertoire. Then again, sometimes the affliction told it like it was.

Corky Sampson, Mike Heller. Mandolins.

Slap McFarland, Jack Ballard. Saxophones.

Gripping the furry keychain attached to her belt loop eased her tension. Animal fur, real or fake, like magic it spoke to her and could blunt the severest of her Tourette's lapses. She and her disease had an arrangement: She took the meds, so she got a pass on many of the episodes. The meds, plus her dogs, plus her furry talisman, all worked together to get it done. Usually. But when the disease did speak, she was stuck dealing with the blowback. Just another day in her vocally diuretic life. Thirty-five years of this affliction had desensitized her.

The outburst did nothing to dissuade Gun-Show-Dave. He beckoned her forward with upturned fingers, his face registering a been-here-done-this-a-*lot*-in-the-past-few-hours kind of boredom, with folks maybe crazier than you, sweetie. On his feet now, Dave one-handed a long gun from under the table and laid it out for her to inspect.

"She's a beaut, ain't she? 'Course if you want it, I'll need some ID."

Gun condition, meh. The collapsible stock needed lubrication, was hard to slide. The magazine release button was stiff. The barrel was notched. Someone had recorded kills on it. Seventeen notches. Seventeen what, she wondered. The rifle was legal, not full military, so she wanted to believe the kills were animals. Which didn't sit well with her either.

"And you, Gun-Show-Dave-Dot-Com, shall have some," she said.

Counsel produced her wallet and laid out her driver's license, also her license as a Pennsylvania Fugitive Recovery Agent, aka bounty hunter, and her concealed carry permit, plus a business card with a Pennsylvania State Trooper insignia watermark and the silhouettes of two at-attention dogs.

They completed some paperwork. Counsel, on purpose, didn't answer a few questions on the ATF form.

"So. It's Sergeant Counsel A. Fungo, then," Dave said. "Thank you for your service to our fair state, Sergeant."

"Former state cop, not active," Counsel said.

Dave had one, and only one, question about her personal history, addressing the info on the ATF form that Counsel had chosen not to provide: the answers to the mental health and criminal convictions questions.

"You're not crazy or a crook, are ya?"

"No."

And that was the background check. No validation with any database. No way of finding out about Counsel's early brushes with the mental health system, like the time she was 302'd for a Tourette's-fueled incident when she was a teenager, aggressively flipping off an Ivy League college admissions director, the gesture continuing nonstop until she needed to be physically subdued. The latter was the copropraxia—the physical tic—part of her disease, although the incident did sum up her feelings about her father's wishes that she attend the University of Pennsylvania.

Dave served up a box of rifle cartridges. "You get fries with this," he said.

Chipper Chamberlain, Chris Beauregard. Percussion.

All Counsel needed to do was plunk down six-fifty in cash—seven hundred, including tax, if she paid by credit card.

"What's that?" Counsel asked, pointing at a gun accessory. She knew full well what it was. She just wanted to hear Gun-Show-Dave legitimize its existence.

"A bump stock." He leaned forward and raised his hand to his mouth like he was about to tell tales. "I was selling them when they weren't legal, and now the Supreme Court made 'em legal again. It makes an AR-15 more like an automatic M16. For whenever you need to lay down some rapid fire."

"I see. And when might that be, Dave?"

"Urban strife episodes. PCP users. Rioters. Hey, you never know. They became a collector's item after they were outlawed; now they're back on the market. I can't let it go for anything less than one-fifty."

Laid out here on the counter was the entire debate about personality disorders and mental health testing and their relationship to the purchase process for semiautomatic assault rifles in the US: weapons that auto loaded their ammunition, making it faster to deliver a round each time someone tickled the trigger.

Her reason for her gun show visit: the recent massacre of twenty-two adults at a Philly social club and Mercer Crawford's antagonistic response to it as CEO of AEF, him reveling in the fact that the slaughter was not at the hands of a semiautomatic rifle. Insensitive comments made at the expense of the folks of Uvalde, Las Vegas, Sandy Hook, Columbine, San Bernardino, Aurora, Colorado Springs, Charleston, and more. All the victims, according to Crawford, were "naïve greenhorns responsible for their own deaths" because they hadn't armed themselves.

Counsel wasn't mentally compromised, but to the uninformed, her outbursts might have indicated otherwise. Not an issue for Gun-Show-Dave. Counsel knew that Dave saw in her an attractive, white, female buyer who no doubt had mowed down dangerous perps as a state cop, and who would do the same to troublemakers and undesirables as a civilian, hallelujah, if she had the right firepower.

Hallelujah this, Dave: Counsel Fungo was pent-up vengeance personified, looking for a release. Hers was a passionate itch in need of a way to scratch it. She knew her personal mission's *what*, and was in search of the mission's *how* ever since the Mummers slaughter and the vocal gun activists' stock, in-your-face, screw-you comments about them.

She would drop all pretense of civility toward knuckle-dragging assault rifle lobbyists, but she had no intention of going after other firearm types, nor the Second Amendment. Too counterproductive, considering the business she was in. She'd instead go directly after Mercer Crawford, looking to kneecap him and his organization. As soon as she could figure out the how.

As the load-bearing beam falls, so too shall the barn. Counsel had no idea whose quote it was, but it fit.

The US gun show loophole was the size of a canyon. Law-abiding gun owners needed an alternative to the AEF and the NRA. They needed to follow, and be part of, a group that was less militant, less paranoid, and less interested in attaching gun liberty to the ownership of military-grade, assault-style weapons capable of slaughtering civilians in mass quantities.

Enter GAS, short for *Gunowners Against the Slaughter,* a new agency. A startup that supported responsible civilian gun ownership and weaponry, more effective background checks, and the creation of a national gun database. It advocated that sales of military-style assault rifles to civilians should be discontinued, and that a percentage of its membership dollars be funneled to families of gun violence victims. Promoting GAS had become a large part of Counsel's *how.*

Walt Grantham. Fiddle.

The last notation on the back of Counsel's business card, below other names: *Dominic Lucatelli. Tenor sax, Band Captain. Wounded survivor.* The only person to have survived the attack, and Counsel's close friend since kindergarten. Dominic was alive, but he would never be the same.

"So, whaddya think, miss? You can put away a lotta PCP users with this baby. Make you a hero."

She'd shot, killed people before, PCP and bath salts crazies included. It never made her feel like a hero. It only made her sad.

"Here," Counsel said, and she handed him a few more business cards. "Turn them over. The names of members of the Wissinoming String Band out of Philly. Musicians one day, innocent victims of the gun debate the next.

"Here's what I think, Dave. I think you should cut this assault rifle into pieces, melt them down, then shove them up your ass."

Counsel's parting words for Gun-Show-Dave, her Tourette's masking most of her anger: *"Old man Crawford lost his arms, E-I, E-I, cunt."*

Mercer Crawford needed to go down. His barn, too. How to make this happen had yet to manifest itself, but she was working on it.

TWO

Mid-September. Tonight their plan was to check out Longwood Gardens, a thousand acres of horticultural bliss two miles from a pet-friendly bed and breakfast where Counsel and her significant other, Andy Prudhomme, had stayed the night before. A short-notice thing, the tickets a treat, sort of, because it was also business-related: Longwood's annual chrysanthemum festival included an art exhibit that Vonetta Posey, her bail bonds employer, hoped would draw a certain human bounty out into the open.

Vonetta's text to Counsel: **Odds are Mr. Leone will show. My cop contacts are calling it**

Mr. Sebastian Leone. Vonetta's art-forging, art-thieving, bail-jumping client was a fugitive who could cost the bondswoman her business if he wasn't caught and returned to the judicial system.

More texting from Vonetta, setting up her request:

Mark my word Counsel he'll be there. Scout's honor

So you're a girl scout now?

Yes ma'am. Truth justice and the American way

Wrong motto bozo

Hell if I care. This is red meat for a sticky-fingered guy like Leone. Just get on it, Sarge

Woo-hoo, Counsel thought, but in small letters only, her sarcasm showing. She wasn't much of a flower and garden person.

It was different with Andy, an unlikely ambassador for horticulture and the visual arts, and Longwood Gardens in Kennett Square, Pennsylvania, was gardening at its grandest. If physical appearance could telegraph fervency, Andy's appearance didn't. Tall and lanky, his arms were toned and long and more compatible for working farmland or coal mines than flower beds. An angular face with beard stubble the color of coal dust, his dark hair had less gray than his age, late fifties, had earned him.

"Magnificent American art on display," Longwood's classy website boasted, including the work of some of the Philadelphia area's finest artists, past and present. Counsel could handle the flower exhibits and the art if there was the prospect of a bounty waiting for them somewhere nearby.

They presented their passes to the admission attendant at the visitor center. The attendant stopped them.

"Sorry, ma'am, your other guest isn't allowed."

Leashed and heeled behind her, Counsel's German shepherd Fungo sat on his haunches, his tongue out, his short, ratty leash in her hand. The leash was ever present; her K9 deputy's security blanket, whether or not Counsel held it.

"Longwood Gardens' policy is no pets," the attendant explained.

Counsel liberated three cards from her wallet, her business card with the Pennsylvania State Police watermark, her retired state cop ID, and her Psychiatric Service Dog card.

"Here. Check these out, please."

The service dog card was good for trains, planes, and whatever the hell other gatherings and/or methods of public transportation Counsel thought she might need to abuse when she wanted one of her dogs with her on a case. Yes, she had PTSD, some from a traumatic childhood, some from her K9 assignments. Yes, she had Tourette's, and she took meds for it. She kept a keychain clipped to her belt just like her similarly afflicted older brother did, for whenever she needed to feel fur while her dogs were otherwise preoccupied. And yes, Fungo, her German shepherd, was good at intimidating bounties just by showing up, even the tougher ones. Was Fungo needed to subdue an artist? Probably not. Counsel had never met an artist she couldn't push off his or her feet with a finger. Yet some of them—those starved, rock-star thin, street-hustling types—looked like they could run really, really fast. Her deputy Fungo could run faster.

Counsel and Andy entered the grounds, Fungo alongside. Water fountains in multiple colors and shapes danced in rhythm to music by Miles Davis, Charlie Parker, Wynton Marsalis, and John Coltrane, piped throughout the gardens while she and Andy walked. The fountains were synched, swaying to their mellow accompaniments, the jazz cajoling the lazy, wind-kissed flora, sprucing it with be-bop and swing. The exhibition of all these flowers and fountains in such coordinated, cool, finger-snapping abandon was something Counsel could get used to.

So what did Sebastian Leone look like? His mug shot wasn't flattering. Slicked, oily black hair. Long face, beaky nose. Big front teeth, which he proudly exhibited for the police photo, and inky but bright eyes to match. Height, short at five-five, body type, slight. Latino. Anywhere from thirties to fifties, Counsel guessed, when she first saw the picture online. Vonetta's text had confirmed it.

He's 44. Likes to play dress up when he's on a scam. A chameleon. Only other identifier is he gestures a lot while he talks. And if he's talking, his mouth and his hands are lying

The original exchange that got them where they were, which put them knee-deep in the art world, began like this:

I'll give you 10% to bring him in. That's cause I love you sweetie

A payout on someone who had jumped bail in Allentown had left Vonetta on the hook for the $100,000 she'd bonded for him. A large amount, even for Vonetta. Ten grand would come Counsel's way. Big-time bounty money. But Counsel was still picky about the cases she took. Given her large inheritance, she didn't need the money.

That much bond, who's the competition?

Other than the Feds, you and only you my friend

Dude. That's BS. You had to lay some of the money off. Too much risk

Nope. Sorry to say I got greedy and it's gonna cost me. He put up way more than he had to. On paper at least

On Counsel's face, a smile now.

Let me guess. He gave you some expensive paintings as collateral

No. He's an art thief remember? Jewelry and cash. Problem was the jewelry had been stolen, and . . .

Counsel hadn't been able to see the phone to respond, she'd laughed so hard. Enough texting; she rang Vonetta up.

"You accepted jewelry as collateral from a conman?" Counsel said, still chuckling.

"I had a jeweler friend appraise it. Worth every penny. It just wasn't his. Law enforcement came after it. And some of the cash was counterfeit."

"Stop it, you're making my sides hurt. Oh my. You, ah, say he's Hispanic? Sebastian Leone sounds British."

"Not with his accent. I think he's Bolivian."

"An alias then," Counsel said.

"Maybe. Who cares. The guy's a scam artist. He bilked some art investors out of a few hundred thousand in Salvador Dali art. *Alleged* Dali art."

"Wait. If the jewelry he gave you was stolen, where's my ten grand bounty coming from?"

"Who said anything about ten grand?"

"Vonetta, you SOB, you said ten percent—"

"Of what he put up. That's about—well, let's see. The jewelry was confiscated, so right there, that's ten percent of zero. The cash—what wasn't counterfeit—amounted to about three thousand bucks. So you, my hard-ass, canine-cop sergeant best friend, would get three hundred."

And Counsel had agreed to it. She'd had the best friend part of it right, and Vonetta would have done the same for her if Counsel ever got that temporarily stupid and greedy at the same time. What else were friends for?

Their destination after the dancing water displays was the Peirce-du Pont House, where the art show would still be in full swing on the first and second floors. Long and stately, Peirce-du Pont had a white, high-arched conservatory that connected two red-bricked, bookending, three-story colonial structures. Inside the conservatory was a smorgasbord of art media. Naming names unfamiliar to her, here was the work of Charles

Willson Peale, Cecilia Beaux, Dox Thrash, Howard Pyle, and Maxfield Parrish. Familiar to Counsel was, however, the work of Ethan Bowen, a photorealist painter whose piece on display here captured the infamous 1968 Philadelphia Eagles Santa Claus snowball-pelting incident at a football game at Philly's Franklin Field. After some arm-in-arm browsing, Andy strolled one way while Counsel and working dog Fungo strolled another, toward the portable bar.

The art hung on seven-foot temporary walls erected wherever it made sense in the conservatory. Elsewhere were easels behind cordons, all displayed under LED lights. Visible through the glass roof was a clear night sky and, as luck would have it, an in-progress meteor shower. A heavenly exhibition.

"Sparkling wooder," Counsel heard a man say to the bartender. *Wooder* was fractured Philly parlance for *water*, in this case a bottle of Perrier. Money changed hands at the bar cart near the Ethan Bowen painting of football Santa, titled *You're All Getting Coal: Philly 1968*. The bartender handed the water requester his bottle. Mr. "Wooder" was short with dark hair, wore a tan blazer over a thin physique, with large-framed tortoiseshell glasses. He took a pull from the bottle then got busy, interesting himself in the Bowen painting. Out came the man's phone, but it never made it to his ear. He instead lowered it to his side, his hand and the phone poking out from inside the sleeve of his sport jacket. He sipped his Perrier.

Counsel strained, listening for the shutter to the phone's camera, heard nothing, but Mr. Wooder's busy index finger gave him away: He was taking pictures. So much for observing the *No Photography, No Video* sign on a nearby easel. Discreet photos taken from all angles, right, left, up, down, then moving behind the tripod that held the painting, more of the same photo-taking of the back of the canvas.

Counsel's assessment: Here was not your average, selfish, rules-don't-mean-me jerk. The short guy, dark skinned, maybe Latino, was hiding his fascination.

Engage him, Counsel thought. Ask him something, anything, about the painting. See how he pronounces *Eagles.* Counsel's own Philly accent had diminished, but it wasn't gone.

Screw it, Counsel would follow her hunch.

"The guy who played Santa that day, in the painting," Counsel said, pointing with her chin at the pictured figure, "he's gone now. His name was Frank Olivo. A barber from Delaware County. That football game made him famous. So, how about this year's Eagles? They gonna do as well as the Phillies? Maybe make the playoffs?"

The phone disappeared farther up the sleeve of Mr. Wooder's jacket. "Never heard nothing about no Frank Olivo," he said, "but yeah, how about them Iggles, and the Phils. Both lookin' good. We'll see what happens this season. A bowl game for the Iggles maybe."

Iggles. Two for two in the Philly accent department, like a real Philadelphian. Counsel's true sports passion was baseball, and the Phillies were hopefully going to make this year's postseason again. But WTF, a *"bowl"* game for the Eagles? There was only one real "bowl" game in pro football: The Super Bowl. Not labeling it as such was odd. And did she detect a slight Hispanic accent underneath his *wooder* boy persona?

Here, maybe, was an imposter. Maybe even an art forger, or an art thief casing the exhibition. And maybe Counsel's bounty.

"Good-lookin' dawg," Mr. Wooder said, eyeing Fungo while still playing the part.

"Yes, he is. Tell me, why the interest in this painting, Mister—?"

The guy's hand went up, an open-palm, *no mas* gesture, the phone no longer in it. "Whoa. No need for swapping personal info, ma'am. 'Scuse me, I wanna get a closer look at a few other paintings before the show closes."

Counsel and her K9 deputy backed off. Mr. Wooder went left and began discreetly snapshooting another painting. Counsel crossed the length of the conservatory, where she found Andy. "See that short guy over there, near that painting?"

"Maxfield Parrish's *Mother Goose.*"

"Sure, whatever, yes, that one. The guy looking at it, in the tan sport jacket. He's sneaking phone camera shots of all the artwork. He's doing a poor job of hiding his interest. I think he's my guy."

"Look, Counsel, let's not make a scene over this, okay?" Andy said, looking worried. "There's original art in here and some great flower arrangements and all. Not a good place for a takedown. You sure?"

"Maybe. Not yet. But he's looking good enough for me to have an extended discussion with him."

They wandered through the crowd hand in hand in leash, working their way across the open space of the conservatory, back toward the suspected bounty, but they were too slow. An on-duty art curator with a grim face moved in, gripped their target's elbow, whispered into his ear, then escorted him away from the exhibits. In seconds, the curator's contact escalated into a bum's rush with the indelicate help of two security guards, their target squawking about the manhandling but unable to keep himself from being led out of the building.

Counsel and Andy followed the procession. The guards and the curator reentered the conservatory and brushed off their clothes, the curator offering a generic apology for the ruckus when he passed them. Counsel and Andy ambled outside in time to catch Mr. Wooder gesturing at the door they'd just exited, fingers, fists, arms, his smallish pelvis, his body speaking volumes at his rude dismissal, his mouth spewing obscenities a little less in blue-collar Philly English, a little more sounding like the Hispanic accent Counsel thought she'd heard. The guy was looking better as their Bolivian target. Counsel called to him. "Sir, you have a minute?"

"No, I don't," came the rebuttal with a chin thrust and a tug at his blazer's lapels, both righteous, then an about-face. His brisk walk toward the rear of the visitor center escalated to a trot then an all-out sprint, sneaking a look over his shoulder at Counsel as he ran.

Counsel leaned down and spoke softly to her canine deputy. "Fungo, you're up, dude. Go." She let go of the leash.

Fungo was off like an arrow from a crossbow. Big dog, small man, in a few seconds it was over, the man on the pavement, his tan blazer sleeve the only thing protecting him from a broken wrist or losing a pint of blood or both. Fungo's mouth surrounded his clothed forearm, maintaining pressure like a snare on a rabbit's leg.

"Not the wrist or the hands! Call him off! I will have it returned. *Owww*."

Counsel found her cuffs, snapped one onto a wrist, heeled Fungo, snapped on the second one. The target was now seated on his butt on the walkway, his cuffed hands resting in his lap.

"See, all better now, Mr. Leone," Counsel said to her captive.

The bounty raised his head. "You are mistaken. I'm a Philly longshoreman—"

"Spare me, asshole. If you're from the Philly docks, I'm from Shanghai. My employer wants you back so she won't lose her bail bond money. Get up. We're leaving."

They escorted a mildly protesting Mr. Leone, alleged, out through Longwood's entrance to Counsel's van in the parking lot. Counsel belted him into a secure leather harness in the jump seat behind Andy. She tucked Fungo safely into his crate. She let her other deputy Tess out for a quick pee before Tess curled up behind the van's floor console between the front seats. A thick chain hanging from the ceiling rattled as Counsel let it drop into her bounty's lap. She attached it to the man's cuffed hands and the leather harness. Plenty more chains hung in the cargo area, plus leather straps, leashes, and muzzles, and an out-of-reach unloaded shotgun clipped into a gun rack on the wall across from him.

"Comfy?" Counsel asked.

"Um, no, thank you for asking, the seat isn't—"

"I don't really care. It's either sit there or inside the crate with Fungo. Fungo's not fixed, by the way. Your choice."

"Since you put it that way—"

"Glad we cleared that up."

Counsel pulled herself into the driver's seat, leaned over for a peck from Andy. She turned on the ignition, checked out her bounty in the rearview mirror, then addressed him.

"Some introductions. I'm Counsel Fungo. As a heads up, I've got Tourette syndrome, which may or may not expose itself on our trip. It's medicated, so my disease and I do a decent job of coexisting. This is Andy Prudhomme, my life partner until, I suppose, I do something major to piss him off, my affliction excluded. Love you, Andy sweetie."

"Back at you, hot shot," Andy said. Air kisses.

"Up here also is my working dog partner Tess, a retired state cop like me. You already met my German shepherd Fungo. That should catch you up."

Counsel continued, pontificating. "So in our midst we have the legendary Sebastian Leone. Bolivian art forger, con man, and one of the best art thieves out there, or so I hear. And you're a bail jumper."

"Outrageous! Mr. Leone would not frequent so petty a gathering. He's not simply *one* of the best, he is *the* best, but *I* am not *he*."

Small man summoning a big, blustering denial. Counsel put the van in gear. "Give it a rest, Leone. Fine, you wouldn't be caught within miles of so folksy an exhibit like this. Except you were."

Counsel waited for a rebuttal. Their passenger was preoccupied with a long look out the van's rear window, the well-lit visitor center getting smaller in their wake. Their alleged bounty finally broke the silence. "I might know this Mr. Leone you are after, or some other people who might interest you. Perhaps we can work a deal—"

"Save it, sport. We're on our way north, to Allentown. We'll be there in a few hours."

In the rear-view mirror Counsel noticed what Mr. Leone had found interesting: A hundred yards back, a frenzied crowd converged on Longwood Gardens' entrance building from inside the grounds. Security guards, and the curator who had confronted his bounty in the conservatory—they were all in a hurry, entering the rear of the shop. Counsel's passenger seemed as interested in the activity as she now was, maybe even more so.

In Counsel's head, a replay of their bounty's words during his takedown: "*I will have it returned.*"

Counsel hit the brakes, the van stopping short. She leaned over her seat. "You stole something back there, didn't you? Where is it?"

"I most certainly did not. You may even search me. I took snapshots of paintings that interested me, that is all. But the staff, shall we say, were all kept very busy, were they not, watching me take those photos?"

"Sonovabitch. A diversion. Somebody else—"

"I strongly suggest we get moving, Ms. Fungo, otherwise you might find yourself relieved of me, your prisoner, in short order."

The van started up again in a hurry, Counsel watching in the rear view as the activity spilled outside the front of the welcome center. She studied Mr. Leone, vocally accosting him again. "Tell me what you took."

"Nothing," he said, speaking low, interested in his cuffed hands, his look despondent.

"Your accomplice, then."

"Nothing of consequence. A trinket. On commission."

Counsel then saw the light bulb go on in Leone's head, his face lifting. He met Counsel's gaze in the rear view.

"We take things for other people. The pieces we're commissioned to acquire may or may not be of significance, but for the people we steal them for, they are of high significance."

Counsel stopped her questioning. Leone wanted to talk, and she would let him.

"Fine. If you must know," he said, unprompted, "it was a cameo. Our client wanted an expensive antique cameo created by a well-known Philadelphia carver. Few in the art world will even miss it. Perhaps we can work a deal. I give you some names, you let me go."

"I'm not a cop, Leone, at least not any longer. Tell it to the Allentown Police when we get there. Maybe they'll go easier on you."

"But there is reward money. The stolen pieces, many of them have substantial reward dollars attached. Substantial *names* attached to them."

"Not interested."

Leone rubbed his cuffed wrists again. "Actors, politicians, athletes. Hip-hop divas—"

"Nope."

" . . . monarchs, gun lobby activists—"

Counsel checked Andy's expression, hoping hers remained as deadpan as his, but this last category of clients piqued her interest big-time.

"Okay, I'll bite. Give me some names. Start with the gun lobby category."

"Well, there's Mercer Crawford . . ."

***

"You feel like Chinese, Sebastian?" Counsel said. "Andy and I feel like Chinese. My dogs like Chinese, too. It's decided. We're getting Chinese."

They cruised Hamilton Street in downtown Allentown, arriving at Lo-Phat-Chow, on the corner of Hamilton and South Ninth, a little after ten p.m. Eat-in plus takeout. Counsel parked the van across the street and climbed in back to disengage their bounty from the hanging chains and leather belt. He crept out and squinted at the bright restaurant marquee overhead. Andy sidled up next to him, put his arm around his shoulder, and escorted him across two traffic lanes toward the eatery's street corner entrance. Counsel leaned back inside the van to tend to Tess.

"Do I really need these?" Sebastian asked Andy, raising his shackled wrists.

"Pretty much. Less inclined to run, right? Which will make Counsel's deputies less inclined to shred your ankles."

Counsel attached Tess, her terrier-boxer mix, to a leash, with Tess's turn as her service dog. They followed Andy and their bounty across the street, not busy at this hour. The three of them plus her deputy paused at the restaurant's front door so Sebastian wouldn't miss the cross-corner inhabitants: the Allentown Police Department.

"I thought you might appreciate a decent meal before we turned you in," Andy said. "Oh, almost forgot. Someone will be joining us."

A woman of considerable heft, a person of color, exited a car parked in front of the police station, crossed the quiet street diagonally, the traffic lights flashing yellow one way, red the other. In a double-breasted navy peacoat with her hands in its pockets, she wore super-tight workout pants with a dark slouchy beanie above her forehead, tapered at the back of her neck. When she arrived, she and Counsel clasped hands and pulled themselves together for cheek pecks and a hug.

"Vonetta," Counsel said. "It's good that you're back. You stir up any trouble in prairie dog country?"

"Don't you know it, sweetie. Had me some good, clean, hell-raisin' Mount Rushmore fun."

"Make any new friends?"

"Indeed I did. I met a few kindred brothers at the AEF gun conference as pissed as I am with the gun lobby, all willing to listen. Be still my heart."

"Excellent. Just what the doctor ordered."

After a quick peck on Andy's cheek in greeting, Vonetta dropped her hand onto Sebastian's shoulder and squeezed.

"So. Sebastian. You remember me? Vonetta Posey, your bondswoman. You shorted me on some collateral." She glanced at the police station. "We're now going to fix that."

Vonetta, at six feet and change, was a few inches taller than Counsel and at least thirty pounds heavier. Which made Sebastian the significant underachiever, physically, among the four of them.

Vonetta guided Sebastian forward, pulling open the restaurant's glass front door. "But first, let's get inside and have some chow mein, shall we?"

***

Sebastian looked uncomfortable in the booth, him in a valley between the comparative mountains that were Vonetta on the right and Andy on the left. Counsel sat alone on the other side of the booth, Tess next to her feet. It was an hour before closing time, only one other group of dine-in customers present. The Allentown Police Department loomed through the window over Counsel's shoulder, its well-lit exterior eye level with their bounty.

"Can I sit on the other side please?" Sebastian asked in Hispanic-accented English, shielding his eyes. "The lights from the police station—"

"No." Counsel folded her hands and started her spiel, speaking evenly, quietly, to avoid prying ears. "Here's where we are. You're a fugitive. You failed to appear at your hearing. A bench warrant was issued for your arrest."

Their bounty squinted his confusion. "I do not understand your point."

"The court notified Ms. Posey here that she'd need to forfeit your bail bond."

"You are telling me what I already know. I'm still not understanding."

"Ninety days from the order, the bond will be forfeited, which means the Court's not ready to take Ms. Posey's money just yet, Sebastian. She has another eighty plus days or so to produce you."

"So why doesn't she just walk me across the street tonight and turn me in? What am I missing?"

"We have a suggestion—a proposition—about how you might use your skills during what's left of those eighty or so days. It involves one of those influential people you mentioned."

Sebastian's eyes lit up, but were soon squinting again. "What is your name again? Are you a Fed or something? You would need to tell me if you were."

"Counsel Fungo. And that's only true in the movies. I'm not a Fed, just a concerned citizen. For now, all you need to know is we've got time, and we've also got you. You'd get a reprieve from going to jail for a few months. If you cooperate."

His hands were in his lap. He raised them to the table and nonchalantly unfolded his salmon-colored cloth napkin—a nice touch for the restaurant, the color matching the walls. He separated his chopsticks and set them out in front of him. When he finished, he smoothed the tablecloth and raised his eyes, looking askance at Vonetta and Andy, then at Counsel. "Which means just under the wire for Ms. Posey to avoid the bond forfeiture," Sebastian said.

"Now you're getting it. A couple of weeks to spare, yes," Counsel said.

Their food arrived, filling the table with rice, chicken, pork, and steamy chow mein and moo goo dishes, interrupting their exchange. Counsel uncuffed one of Sebastian's hands.

Sebastian picked up his chopsticks. "But I still go to jail, to await trial. It would be a shame for that to still happen if I do whatever it is you want me to do, wouldn't you say?"

Counsel stared him down. Her glare then detoured for serious glances at Andy then Vonetta, then back to Sebastian.

"You scammed wealthy, influential people, right?" Counsel said. "They're out how much—a few hundred thousand? And these people can physically harm you, as in do nasty things to your body? Your hands?"

Sebastian tucked a piece of cubed chicken into his mouth with his chopsticks and chewed, turning pensive. "I admit to nothing, Ms. Fungo. Like the law says, innocent until proven guilty. Whatever you have in mind will probably be too big a risk for me."

Vonetta put her large black hand over Sebastian's lithe fingers, pried his chopsticks loose, and brought the chopsticks to within an inch of his nostrils, adding her big, toothy smile.

"You ever pick your nose with these, Sebastian?" Vonetta said. "I've seen it done by the Chinese mob. We can poke around back in there, pull out whatever we find, maybe poke inside your other orifices as well, add it all to your dinner, then make you eat it. What say you simply answer Counsel's questions and spare us the BS, hmm? You might learn something."

Counsel's squint at Vonetta said *What the hell was that?* Her return shrug said *I dunno, but it sounded scary, right?*

Sebastian eyed the chopsticks close up. "Erm, ah, there are, I suppose, a few intimidating people who entrusted me to acquire some valuable pieces at below market prices on their behalf."

"How much do you owe these people?" Counsel repeated.

"Again, that's presupposing a crime—"

"How. Much."

"All told," more tablecloth preening, "they're out four hundred thousand, maybe four-fifty."

Counsel studied this short man with long, delicate fingers and restless hands. She said nothing, deadpanning another stare at Andy.

Sebastian broke the silence. "You are wondering if I am that good at what I do, and if I'm worth that much in commission. I am."

"And humble, too," Counsel said. "Supposing that's true, just how much money do you currently have, to put toward your restitution?"

"Well, see, that's the thing. I have some expensive habits. And my cash, it is all tied up in long-term investments and the Bolivian Stock Exchange."

"Ah-h-h," Counsel said, mocking her understanding. "Which means you're broke, then."

"Basically, yes."

"What if I told you," Counsel reached over, took Sebastian's hands in hers, sensuously massaged his fingers with her thumbs, "we could help you prove to the court that you are sorry for your criminal behavior, plus help you with restitution? So you'd maybe avoid having to do any real jail time?"

Sebastian's eyes softened, absorbing the attention. This was more than a good-cop bad-cop routine on Counsel's part; it was more like flirting.

Then, suddenly, after Sebastian took too long to answer, it wasn't. His eyes widened in pain. Counsel's fingers dug into his palms, his shoulders slumping with the increasing pressure. "We *really* need your help, Sebastian sweetie. What do you say? Are you out, or are you in?"

He squirmed, trying to pull away. "Ahm . . ."

"In?" Her grip changed, Counsel bending his fingers backward a bit. "Or out?"

"Okay. OKAY. I'm in. Just how might that be accomplished, Ms. Fungo? *Owww*, not the hands . . ."

Counsel loosened her grip. "Very simple," she said. "First, you agree not to run. And to help you abide by that agreement—"

Vonetta slapped a GPS electronic anklet on the table. "This jewelry will let us know where you are day and night," Vonetta said. "Not police issue, so you won't show up in any law enforcement system. Just on my phone. It's commercial, but it will do the job."

Counsel continued. "Second, by working with us, the court might show leniency with your sentence if you earn enough from this arrangement to pay back what you owe."

Sebastian's dark eyes narrowed, some from skepticism, some from excitement. "It all sounds wonderful, but how do you propose to make this happen, and for that much money? Who would be the mark?"

Counsel found her fork and twirled some lo mein around it. "Tell us what someone in your circles might do to engage a person like, say, Mercer Crawford of the AEF."

THREE

September 13
State Correctional Institution (SCI) at Muncy, Pennsylvania

Days before the final US Presidential debate: 33

Aaron Pappas and his escorts neared the inside of the prison's front gate on foot, the morning crisp, the horizon a pre-dawn glow, expansive in a yellow gold below indigo blue and a few swatches of white. A light jacket zippered to his neck did little to lessen the chill, the prospect of warmth distant. At least there was no gray. Aaron hated the gray. He could kill the gray.

Stop. You can't kill a color.

Galvanized steel fencing below prickly coils of razor wire jammed the brown-green lawn separating him and his escorts from an exterior parking lot. On this side of the fence, incarceration. Freedom, and maybe Aaron's fragile sanity, somewhere out there on the other.

SCI Muncy resembled an early nineteenth century college campus. Fifteen permanent and two modular inmate housing units that fit inside the fence's perimeter on thirty acres. Buildings, plain and impersonal, had been added over the years, amounting to seventy-six structures spread over 800 acres. The state prison's street address had never seemed real to Aaron: 6454 Pennsylvania State Road 405. Numbers only, attached to a road not good enough to bear its own name, just like the inmates.

Natural light and distinctive countryside aromas enveloped him: creosote from a nearby railroad tie company, and decaying, decapitated cornstalks closer in. A rising sun would soon chase away an early morning chill. To Aaron, it was all so wonderful.

"Good luck, Miss Pappas," the prison's superintendent said. "You'll need it."

Miss Pappas. A slur regarding his gender dysphoria, unrelenting, right up until the end.

The gate buzzed open. Once through, Aaron, hands in his jacket pockets, slow stepped into an about face while the gate rumbled closed between him and the superintendent. Black moussed curls above Aaron's forehead didn't offset the severity of the rest of his short-cropped, military-style haircut. He stepped closer to the fence, willed away the elation of his release, and turned stone-cold serious. Aaron and Superintendent Smythe had disagreed on many topics over the years, one topic in particular.

"It's *Mister* Pappas," Aaron reminded him, looking down at this tiny prison jockey of a man one last time. At 5'4", the superintendent stood half a foot shorter than big-boned Aaron, 5'10" and a solid one seventy. The size difference pissed Superintendent Smythe off from the first day they'd met at the beginning of Aaron's sentence, and all through the many years of hormone therapy the court had awarded him when he first entered prison, which the prison staff was forced to administer. That, and Aaron's facial hair. He could grow a beard, the superintendent couldn't.

The superintendent thinned his lips. This one dehumanizing topic continued to transcend all others. "Not yet you are."

Karis Ophelia Pappas, now going by Aaron, identified as male. Muncy was a women's prison. His sentence had to be served according to biological, birth-assigned gender. Prior to the murders, University of Scranton college student Aaron, as Karis, had started hormone therapy for gender reassignment. Reassignment surgery? Not a chance while incarcerated. Exiting the prison system at age fifty-three, Aaron could now finish the gender change he'd started over three decades ago.

The gate locked with a buzz and a snap, leaving Aaron on the outside, unchaperoned. The superintendent thrust out his self-righteous chin and straightened his necktie, then he led his staff back to the administration building.

And that was it. No apology. No acknowledgment that the past thirty years, four months, sixteen days that Aaron, as inmate OV1497, had all been an unconscionable overreach by the judicial system. There would be no financial compensation for the misjudged exoneree; Pennsylvania had no such statute.

On another level, Aaron knew the felony conviction had not been a mistake. There'd been a purpose to it, a design of the worst kind, public and conspiratorial, on the part of a prominent northeastern Pennsylvania district attorney with political aspirations.

For too many of those thirty years—eight years off and on, the longest stint nearly two years—Aaron spent all but two hours a day in a Special Treatment Unit, or STU, which meant that for more than a quarter of his incarceration, he was in brain-scrambling, solitary confinement.

Solitary did things to a person. Almost all these things were bad.

Outside the gate, Aaron's son Linus Pappas, age thirty-one, greeted him with a warm, square-jawed smile above a rugged chin with black stubble. His words included something Aaron thought he'd never hear again. "We're going home, Dad."

Wide, charcoal eyes—his mother's—and the strong Pappas chin. Aaron took his son's head in his hands and pulled him forward. Their foreheads touched, and the hug that followed was long, tight, and magical. Aaron breathed deep, absorbing what he could of what he'd missed over the decades. Baby powder, dirty diapers, crib bedding, formula. Dog fur, cat fur. Baseball glove leather and Boy Scout campfires. The aromatic Pappas Greco-Italian Bistro restaurant during its happier days before the decline. Before the carnage. And, more recently, hospital antiseptics, urine, and everything else that came with Linus's mother's chemo. Dying cells and mothballs.

He drank in these aromas in a rush, most of them imagined, but all feeling so real. Linus wrapped his arm around his father's waist and ushered him toward the parking lot. Sunrise broke as they walked. Warmth, finally.

Dad. The word sounded better, so much so, today. Hearing Linus say it while Aaron was incarcerated had always felt inappropriate, unsatisfying. His son used it all the time now when they spoke, his infrequent visits to see Aaron over the years dictated some by prison administration, but mostly by Linus. Lately, however, Linus had made more of an effort regarding visitation. Hearing him address him now, on the outside, with no bars between them, where father and son could share the personal contact he thought he'd never experience again, was heaven.

Aaron raised his stooped shoulders, strode proudly at his full height, the two walking arm in arm toward Linus's car. Prison had taken his freedom. It had robbed a son of his father and vice-versa. It had also deprived Aaron, formerly Karis, of Lena, his college sweetheart and soulmate, who'd been unable to hang on. Lena, gone ten months, had died at age fifty-two. Karis, as a biological female, had met her in college at the University of Scranton. The two became a committed couple after graduation. They wanted to start a family, which meant artificial insemination. Karis had a sympathetic cousin who agreed to the sperm donation. The rest of the Pappas family was to learn about this loving gesture from Aaron when the time seemed right. The right time had never materialized.

"We'll be home in a couple of hours, Dad. Push the seat back and get some rest."

No one else was there at the prison to greet him because there was no one else. No parents, sisters, aunts, or uncles, and no loving life-partner Lena, who had died in hospice, peacefully, in her sleep. Compared to the ravages of Lena's prolonged fight with cancer, Aaron's family members, all of them save one, him, had been lucky in a sick, twisted way. For them, their lives were over before they knew what had hit them.

Karis had grown tall for a woman and was thick-waisted. Her mother called her husky. Her father called her *choiros,* Greek for pig, had called her this often, and not fondly.

She had come to the family restaurant that day looking for her father's blessing. The restaurant was in trouble, crippled more so because its patriarch and head chef, her father, was dying. She'd expected her family to be underwhelmed by her announcement that she was transitioning from her biological gender, but she thought they'd be excited by her partner's pregnancy. She hadn't expected these announcements to be the tragedy they became. In a most violent, gruesome fashion, that day at the restaurant had ended the lives of nearly everyone she loved. Linus, her baby boy, was born during the murder trial. He would have had, should have had, a great life, part of a happy two-parent family, had Aaron-as-Karis not been convicted of the carnage.

Linus and Aaron drove east, into the sunrise, onto Pennsylvania route 118 toward Wilkes-Barre, then they would head north into Scranton.

"I'm a monster, Linus."

Solitary confinement. Gray walls, gray floor, light gray ceiling overhead. A ten-by-twelve-by-eight-foot-high cell, containing metal, clothing, bedclothes, and vinyl. To Aaron, it was all in different, penetrating shades of gray. Nine hundred sixty cubic feet of gray, all smelling of painted cinder block.

Smelling gray, hearing gray, watching gray, touching gray. So evil a color.

Some colors needed elimination. Gray was one of them.

Solitary. It did things.

He *was* a monster, but not because of his inconvenient gender and his unresolved need for reassignment. It was what had built inside him during three decades of reality-bending, mind-screwing prison: a need for revenge that required satisfaction.

"Dad, stop thinking that way. The DA was mistaken. The medical examiner's office screwed up. If everyone had done their job . . ."

. . . whirr, whirr, hum-a-chink, hum-a-chink . . .

. . . one victim, one mound of pulpy flesh and bones, multiple trips to the industrial-strength garbage disposal. Aaron's mentally compromised father had hacked his way to victim number five. This one, by process of elimination, was his mother . . .

"Dad? Hello?"

Every day for the past thirty-plus years, Aaron's mind paid a PTSD visit to the blood-spattered restaurant. "Sorry, Linus. What were you saying?"

"What I was saying was, who knows how your life—or Mom's, or mine—would have turned out if the prosecutor hadn't rushed to judgment."

It had been too horrific to be believed. The multiple murder case solidified Lackawanna County's young District Attorney Quinn Hudson's reputation as a tenacious prosecutor and tireless overachiever, and soon after the trial, he became a national media darling. After the 1986 verdict, the aspiring local DA reportedly found his current job unfulfilling. Great press, smart public relations, and upward mobility had solved that for him.

"You mean Senator Hudson," Aaron said.

"Yes, I stand corrected. District attorney then, senator now. And come January . . ."

Linus, against all possible ironies that Aaron could have ever considered for his son, was now a Senator Quinn Hudson supporter, and part of the senator's campaign.

" . . . the next president of the United States."

"That won't happen," Aaron said.

"Don't be so sure, Dad. Folks are behind him, and they absolutely adore Iowa Congresswoman Mary Inkster, his running mate. And I know this might sound flippant on his part, but he's sorry, you know, about your conviction and incarceration."

A hollow hearsay apology not worthy of a response; something Aaron considered insincere. He watched the sun finish its rise above the trees. So glorious. How long had it been since he'd last seen a sunrise, a sunset, or the moon? He knew how long. Ten months and eight days, when the guards gave him a surprise early morning walk in the yard. Superintendent Smythe had been there to greet him, and he let Aaron feel the sunlight on his face for a few minutes, just before he took the moment away from him by revealing that Aaron's life partner Lena had died.

Overhead and in the distance, in the direction they were headed, thunderheads gathered.

"He won't be the next president, Linus. I can feel it."

"Hope you're wrong. He's a good man, Dad, you'll see. He and Congresswoman Inkster make a great team. Sorry. I suppose we shouldn't be talking about this now."

The epitome of gray. This was Senator Hudson. Graying head of hair, groomed facial hair streaked with gray, gray suits. A gray soul.

Kill the gray.

The thunderheads rumbled, moving swiftly toward more clouds on the horizon, soon leaving only a sliver of light as their car drove toward the sunrise.

Aaron felt the gray again, could feel it building overhead, its suffocation, the clouds bringing the menace of their grayness.

. . . can't kill a color . . .

He would prove them wrong. He would kill what couldn't be killed. But first he would need a gun.

FOUR

September 13
Thunder Wonderland Lanes, Rancor, Pennsylvania, near Scranton

Days before the final US Presidential debate: 33

Counsel pulled the van through a break in the stand of Pocono pine that lined the road, took a right onto fifty yards of mottled blacktop that bounced the van's frame and made Andy grip the seat. The short entrance road emptied into a parking lot. Directly ahead was Thunder Wonderland Lanes, an all-corrugated bowling alley with a Vegas-like flashing marquee across its flattop roof, the lanes busy every day and much of every night.

"I hate those owls," Counsel groused.

"*Who?*" Andy said, smirking.

They'd stayed together last night at Andy's B&B, in his owner's residence. Vonetta took Sebastian Leone home with her to her family in Bethlehem, and was expected to deliver him here today, to this bowling alley, ninety minutes north. They would all meet over an early lunch of burgers and beers with Dody Heck, the town's retired sheriff, also Rancor's Town Watch coordinator.

Counsel adored Andy's B&B, Willow Swamp Farm Bed & Breakfast. A restored Victorian on three acres. Wraparound porch with plenty of wicker and tall ladderback rockers. A two-person swing. Full homemade breakfast, afternoon tea. Pets welcome. A move to Scranton or thereabouts for a living-together arrangement could be in the offing for her, something Andy had suggested more than once. She heard about it again last night.

"I said, if you want me to move up here, you'd need to do something about those owls. Worse than cats in heat."

Multiple species of predators roamed the Pocono woods and patrolled the mountainous airspace. Conversely, Counsel's little farmette in Willow Grove, Pennsylvania, two and a half hours south, had cooing whippoorwills, beautiful songbirds, and the therapeutic sound of trout chasing mayflies in a calm lake. Not Pocono birds of prey screeching and mating outside her window.

"They weren't mating," Andy said. "I found a dead raccoon this morning. Her body was shredded. It was too large for the owls to carry off. They probably fought over it. A raccoon mother."

"Were her babies with her?" Counsel said, her look squinty, wounded.

"They watched from the underbrush while I stuffed what was left of their momma into a Hefty bag. It was gruesome. And sad."

Counsel spoke under her breath into her hand, emoting a Tourette's mini rant about body bags and screeching owls mating, her subconscious telling her she hoped the raccoon daddy would step up. A grip of the furry keychain on her belt settled her anxiety. She repeated her complaint, her head shaking in agreement. "I am so hating those owls."

"Survival of the fittest," Andy said.

"I'm familiar with the phrase," she said, her heart aching for the raccoon kits. "Still, predators suck."

"You know raccoons are predators, too, right? And they eat cats."

"Shut it, Andy."

They cruised in closer to the building, were entertained by left-to-right illuminated animation along the roofline: a ten-foot-tall coal miner rolled a flashing chunk of bituminous down a short alley where it exploded into the tenpins in the one-two pocket, the pins crisscrossing into a sexy dancing X, signifying a strike. Sequential lights signified another chunk of coal taking the same path with the same outcome, then another, then another.

Bowler porn in coal country, USA. Mesmerizing. Counsel grunted, narrowing her eyes while watching the flashy marquee in action.

Andy, observing her: "At Christmas they reconfigure the lights on the miner's helmet into a Santa hat and change them to red and green. Clever."

"Whatever."

Counsel followed the path of each successive rolling chunk of coal, stayed stoic when they concussed the pins, their chaotic dance reflected in her eyes. Working dog Tess snorted and got to her feet, on alert. Fungo, her shepherd, remained crated in the rear of the cargo van while Tess pushed her nose against Counsel's thigh, making sure she noticed her, a response to Counsel's discomfort. The van slowed, drifting past the alley entrance and the animated coal miner sequence overhead. She found a parking space five rows back from the building entrance and backed the van in. She grabbed a backpack.

Eleven o'clock on a Monday morning, and the bowling alley lot was nearly full. This was upstate Pennsylvania, where entertainment staples included hunting, fishing, bowling, gambling, shooting, bowling, hiking, bowling, boating, bowling, skiing, and bowling. And alcohol consumption during most of it, no matter what the clock said.

A few steps inside the building, the noise enveloped them. "Look for Dody," Counsel said, checking her phone texts. "I'll wait here. Vonetta just pulled into the parking lot. Tell Dody that Vonetta and I will catch up in a minute."

Forty hardwood lanes with spinning bowling balls scattered the wooden bowling pins inside each rectangular crash box at lane's end. The pinbox: a no-man's-land of crisscrossing tenpin chaos violent enough to injure young "pinboys" in the days before pinsetting machinery. The lanes ran along the left side of the building, the other side lined with kids' amusements, video games, an indoor playground, and a café. The middle of the right wall was where the counter for distributing bowling shoes started. The counter's distant end was spliced with a stocked bar and a kitchen menu, with café table seating out front and carpet underfoot, a lot of it stained. TVs filled the wall space above the bar and the shoe counter.

The exterior door to the bowling alley opened. Vonetta entered first, held the swinging glass door open wide for her timid charge Sebastian Leone, his entrance tentative until she gripped his shoulder and pulled him in. Sebastian's face was pained.

"Wonderful," Counsel said to herself. "Probably his first time inside a bowling alley."

Sebastian tiptoed forward under his own power, no cuffs, no leg irons or chains. Vonetta's heavy hands on his shoulders gave him a rocket assist from behind to speed him up. They arrived alongside Counsel.

"Seriously, Vonetta, you couldn't dress him in something a little less . . . cultural?"

Sebastian's hooded sweatshirt read *FUBU* across the front in sewn gold letters, an acronym for an urban clothing brand meaning *"For Us, By Us."* Big in the nineties, but not ever big with short, middle-aged Bolivians.

"It's what he picked out of my son's closet," Vonetta said. "Vintage. A fashion statement, right, Sebastian?"

"I like being noticed," Sebastian said.

"Yeah, well, you might have to temper that from now on," Counsel said. "Are you feeling refreshed? Have a good sleep at Vonetta's?"

"It was okay. A little noisy maybe."

"You'll love prison then." She chin pointed, changed topics. "See that shoe guy, Sebastian? That's Floyd. He's also the bartender. Floyd's an acquired taste. So, considering his temperament, why don't we do this."

Counsel pulled a red wallet out of her backpack. "Here's sixty bucks. Hit Floyd up for three full orders of onion rings and three draft Yuengling Porters. Tell him to put the change in the Robbie Fund. You'll sound like a local. So it's three orders of rings, three Yuengling Porters, the Robbie Fund. Got it? Vonetta and I need to find Andy. He's wandered off somewhere."

"Sixty dollars?" Sebastian looked at the cash in his hands. "That much for beer and onion rings?"

"Breakfast of champions. A delicacy for the locals. It'll be around forty and change. The rings are incredible. Battered in beer, heavy on spicy ranch seasoning. The Robbie Fund is for widows and orphans of coal miners and their descendants. No shortage of them in these parts, sorry to say.

"Look, Sebastian, trust me here. Floyd's a good guy but he can also be a dipstick. Do as I say and you'll stay on his good side."

They reached the shoe counter together. Sebastian surveyed the clientele, lowered his hood, and hand-combed his dark Latino hair into place. "An educated guess says he won't think I'm local."

"Just order what I said and you'll be fine. Hang near the bar, where we can see you. We'll be back."

Vonetta used a restroom while Counsel headed to the last two lanes. She leaned over the molded plastic seating, a speckled Art Deco salmon that looked slippery from its contour but wasn't. A whispered promise of something naughty with a colorful Tourette's chaser let her invade Andy's space and stay there, where she planted a light, sensuous kiss on his neck behind his ear, his essence quite pleasing. She swung around the seats and squeezed in between him and one of his teammates.

She gave Andy a cheek-peck then scanned the bowlers in their red silk shirts, the team name inked above the shirt pocket in a dripping black script that mimicked blood from a wound. These were four former female doctors who were Andy's teammates from a different hospital team, him a part-time psych nurse. Counsel quickly scanned the lanes nearest them, looking for other familiar faces.

"Dody here?"

"Lane twenty-eight," Andy said. "They finished their match. One more frame for these guys here. They need at least a rhino or they're toast."

Counsel didn't ask, already understood: two consecutive strikes was a rhino, three was a turkey. Bowlers. Who knew the rationale?

She retreated behind the lanes where she could view the last frame of this match and watch Dody and her team collect their personal things a few lanes away, all while keeping an eye on Sebastian. Dody Heck, the anchor for her bowling team was, at one time, Rancor's top cop. She now ran the town watch with no interference from local law enforcement. Its mission statement, posted on signs throughout the borough, was a warning: *"Protection however necessary."* An admonishment came in smaller print and a smiley emoji: *"Nothing's ever been proven. Rancor Town Watch."*

Voices sparked up over Counsel's shoulder, Sebastian's then Floyd the bartender's.

"I do not believe this is Guinness," Sebastian said, seated at the bar.

"Don't have Guinness," Floyd said.

"Why didn't you say that, sir, instead of trying to pass off this retromingent raccoon urine as good stout?"

A wary Counsel left her vantage point and sidled up to Sebastian.

Floyd dropped his hands flat onto the bar in front of his customer and leaned in to make himself clear. "You ask for Guinness in here, you get Yuengling Porter. From the oldest and best brewery in the U-S of A. A beer my coal miner daddy loved, so that means it's way past being good enough for you." He eyed Counsel. "Straighten this rude crap weasel out before I show him the hard way that I know what retromingent means." Floyd leaned in closer to Sebastian. "And 'retromingent raccoon urine' is a redundancy, runt."

"Sebastian," Counsel moved into Sebastian's line of vision, "I gave you one job. All you had to do—"

"Yes, but all *he* had to do," Sebastian whined, raising his mug of beer, "was say he didn't have any Guinness, not try to pass off something inferior."

Floyd wheeled and relieved Sebastian of the frothy mug with a malicious grab as it neared Sebastian's lips; Floyd finished by spilling the mug in the sink. He about-faced, leaving Sebastian to stare at Floyd's chunky butt on his way to taking an order from another customer at the end of the bar.

Sebastian raised his voice to a retreating Floyd: "A Perrier maybe?"

Counsel moved a mug of Yuengling from in front of her to her bounty. "Drink this and shut up, and pray your onion rings don't have any piss in the batter, retromingent or otherwise. I'll order another beer for Vonetta."

The three heaping orders of onion rings arrived at the bar, as did Dody Heck, fifty-ish, salt 'n' pepper hair, her full body cornerstone solid. A moment later Vonetta rejoined them, grabbing the extra beer. Dody pointed at a table. "How about the three of us sit so you and Vonetta can tell me more about your art guy?"

The bowling alley's sound system blared rock 'n' roll and pop favorites in a near-deafening loop, some hip-hop mixed in. Counsel, Dody, Vonetta, and now Andy surrounded a café table. Sitting at the bar alone, Sebastian used a knife and fork to cut up a second plate of onion rings.

Counsel riffed to her audience about Sebastian, using terms like sneaky, maybe Bolivian, untrustworthy, electronic anklet, high roller, chameleon, art connoisseur, thief, scam artist, and desperate, considering he'd jumped bail and was now Counsel's bounty.

"He's a fugitive, and the talents that made him one are what we've been looking for. And he needs us, considering his list of creditors. If we keep him on a short enough leash, we'll do fine."

They eyed Sebastian, watching him daintily cut and eat his food at the bar. Counsel paid him a compliment, out of his earshot. "He has a plan. An approach that's ingenious but simple. We just need to entice the right players. As far as I'm concerned, Sebastian needs to be a part of this. Andy?"

"He's eccentric, but I think he can deliver. I'm good."

"Vonetta?"

"A sophisticated little loudmouth," Vonetta said, "who talks a good game. And he has some art world contacts, even local. I grilled him about them last night. I think he's the real deal."

Dody sipped her beer, eyed the maybe-Bolivian who was balancing himself on the bar stool while he ate. To Counsel: "You sure he won't try to run?"

"He owes too many influential people a lot of money. Plus he's already had a taste of Fungo, or I should say the reverse. To answer your question, I don't know. Is there anywhere we can put him where we can keep an eye on him, but still give him room to do his thing?"

"As in paint, like a studio?" Dody said.

"That would be the plan," Counsel said.

Dody and Andy shared head-scratching facial expressions. Then, from Dody, "Saint Possenti's."

Andy nodded. "Saint Possenti's would work."

Saint Possenti's Bingo Hall carried a saint's name but had no meaningful affiliation to a religion, and never was, never would be, a bingo hall. Named after Saint Gabriel Possenti, the patron saint of hand gunners, as an inside joke, in one previous existence it was the Rancor Police Station. Now it was a membership-only gun range.

Counsel digested this. "I see the incarceration side of it, but it can get busy in there, and loud."

Dody was able to speak with authority about police station jails. "We'll make him comfortable. It's been remodeled in the back, for short-stay guests, with bathroom privileges and privacy. For the locals if they get too rowdy when they come back from downtown Scranton. I'll set it up."

"He'll need internet access, some art supplies," Counsel said, "and maybe no bingo during the off hours?"

Bingo was code for target shooting. Dody shrugged. "All doable. We'll get him some peace and quiet. How long, you think?"

"Through October sixteenth. Until the debate."

"He'll be good with that?"

"He has no choice otherwise. Look, we won't need to handcuff him to the toilet or anything," Counsel said. "Just feed him and have someone keep him company and let him get some daily outdoor exercise. He knows what the alternative is if he doesn't cooperate. Our mark is driving the timing. Crawford plans to be at the presidential debate. Or so say the media."

"Supporting candidate Hudson," Dody said, "in an official capacity as AEF CEO."

CEO Crawford's timeline for his activities around that date weren't known. Some things would never be made public, media snooping or not. Clandestine, personal things. They'd tried to learn more but had come up empty.

"Hell, we sound like we almost know what we're doing," Dody said. "Anything else?"

Counsel strained her neck looking past Dody, at the bar. She jumped to her feet. "Dammit—!"

Empty glass of beer, empty plate, empty barstool. Sebastian was gone.

Vonetta quick-checked the electronic anklet security app on her phone. "He's still in here somewhere." She started walking.

Counsel sprinted toward the bar. *"Fuckety-ass-pounding-bastard-fuck-fuck-fuck damn it—"* A grip of the fur on her belt loop shut her up. "Floyd! *C-c-cunt,* where is he?"

Floyd leaned over a plate of food and noshed, unimpressed by her rant. He raised his hand, gestured at the restroom while his eyes stayed glued to the TV.

Vonetta followed Floyd's thumb. Counsel's talisman choked off her testy language. She and Dody waited outside the restroom door. "You said some of Saint Possenti's cells were converted," Counsel said, out of breath. "That means some weren't?"

"Some can still function as jail cells."

"Good. Saint Possenti's it is then, when Vonetta finds him. Carrot and stick for this guy, all in the same building, in case he doesn't *d-d-dickedy-dick* want to stay with the program."

Vonetta exited the restroom, ushering Sebastian forward with a meaty fist on his shoulder, him complaining. "Have you no decency, Ms. Posey, that's a men's room—"

"Shut up."

Counsel relieved Vonetta, put her arm around her bounty's shoulder. "Look. You can't scare us like that. You said you'd work with us." She pointed at the café table. "Sit."

"Fine. Yes," Sebastian said. "I want to help. I am on board with your passion for this heist. It could be epic."

"Epic is good. Super. We'll spend the rest of the day working out the details, whatever you'll need, whoever you'll need—who does what—to make it work. People on the inside and out. But you disappearing like you just did while we're out here in public . . . that makes us really *d-d-d-doggie-dick* nervous."

"I had to relieve myself . . ."

"Of course you did," Counsel said. "Maybe we overreacted. So I've come to a conclusion. Today we brainstorm a plan, and when we're done," a look toward Dody for validation, "help me out here, Dody. When we're done . . ."

"So it's like this, Mr. Leone," Dody shook her head in agreement with herself. "When we're done here today, you're going to jail."

FIVE

September 17
Brandywine Museum of Art, Chadds Ford, Pennsylvania

Days before the final US Presidential debate: 29

Four stories of red brick, battered, but in a chic way. A former gristmill the width of a drive-in movie screen and the height of an IMAX. At cellar level, below where Counsel stood with Andy, crusty, jagged chunks of rock and stone had been cemented randomly into a peeling limestone base. Dried rainwater streaks stained the exterior, and small black metal plates stamped into the grout dripped brown and black rust from their edges. This was Counsel's first visit to this art museum. For Andy, it was anywhere between his tenth and twentieth. An impressive structure with easy-on-the-eyes character, and that was just the exterior.

The same could also be said of Andy, Counsel thought, a few years her senior, Andy still with all his hair, brown streaked with gray.

"I always forget how charming this building is," Andy said, raising his phone, moving it for a better angle. The smartphone photos captured the magnificent combination of the old gristmill and the newer wings of glass and steel and concrete awash in natural sunlight, and following alongside the gentle sway of the Brandywine River.

Counsel grunted a yes, removed her hands from her pockets and pulled Andy toward the end of the line leading to the museum entrance, she in tapered jeans and heels, he in jeans and hiking boots. His long legs loped up the paved incline in stride with hers, his arm remaining around her waist after they were in line.

To correct any misconceptions, Counsel in tight jeans showcased how hot she could be if she wanted to be, eventually having bought into this as Andy's frequently voiced assessment of her. In his words, standing next to her upped his standing big time. But what few observers could see in them as a couple was the damage they'd each experienced during their lifetimes, individually and together, which led to something else not visible, when they carried them: their concealed handguns. Counsel's two handguns were a nod to her work as a bounty hunter. Andy's one handgun was his equalizer as part of Rancor, Pennsylvania's well-organized town watch.

But today there were no guns on their persons, their pieces needing to remain in Counsel's van, along with her dog deputies Fungo and Tess. Museum protocol, unless Counsel wanted to push it from her therapy dog angle, which she didn't.

"I want your ticket to the presidential debate," Andy whispered into Counsel's ear.

"I earned it fair and square. No."

"Earned it?" Andy pulled back in full mock-indignation mode. "You were in a campaign donor lottery. You didn't earn it, you didn't even get lucky. You cheated by sending the election debate committee a picture of you and Tess in state trooper gear. How could they not pick you? You'd look great in the audience. You don't even live near Scranton. Cheater."

"Yeah, how about that. The final debate. I am so stoked. President Lindsay and that local Republican poseur."

"You can't say his name? Really? Quinn Hudson, our senator. Former local DA. The Republican Party's nominee. C'mon, he's not such a bad guy."

"Whatever. I'll make the trip north so I can watch our incumbent president have him for lunch. And shut-uppa-you-face about my good fortune, you sore loser."

They were at this wonderful museum because *a)* art was cool, and this setting was a cool place to house it; *b)* a new exhibit had opened here recently, and it included a nostalgic piece Counsel was partial to; and *c)* museums had a calming effect on her . . . usually. There was also a *d)* but Counsel had initially given it only limited credence, chalking it up to an ambitious boast by her bail bondswoman buddy Vonetta. Still, Vonetta's boast, gleaned from friends in their respective law enforcement backgrounds, was that a person of major interest would make an appearance here today, and this was the largest reason for their visit. And now, behind them, the boast was being validated.

Two men in suits bulky enough to conceal hardware exited a silver Bentley. They jostled their way up the sidewalk incline.

"Excuse us. Pardon us. Excuse us . . ."

When a few folks didn't react quickly enough, their bluster turned into barking and heavy-handed shoving. "Move or be moved, *now.*"

Counsel held her temper seeing this. This was neither the time nor the place. She and Andy gave them a wide berth.

Following quickly in their wake, another bodyguard and a female staffer-type ushered their charges forward, two men in their sixties. Counsel recognized one of them.

Multiple appearances in front of the US Senate. Speeches against government gun control. A perverse enabler of violence against innocent people who continued to die in large numbers executed by long guns— semiautomatic rifles—capable of rapid-fire, mass execution. Mercer Crawford was here, in the flesh. Whispers ricocheted throughout the small crowd.

Counsel's temper sparked. *Screw the AEF.* Still, she knew better and stood down, managing her anger. Andy, his dark, serious eyes on Counsel's balled fist, wasn't buying it.

His hands surrounded her clenched fingers. He pried them open, intertwined them with his, and stepped into her line of vision to take measure of her, to be in her path if she tried something stupid. Crawford's entourage continued its march past the crowd of ten or so people lining the inclined walkway. When the procession reached the museum entrance, Andy's apprehensive face relaxed. They'd weathered a potentially severe storm. He moved out of Counsel's path.

But Counsel's forever companion, her Tourette's, had missed Andy's efforts.

"*. . . dickhead—penis—eatshit . . .*"

The verbal salvo was loud, launched past Andy as Counsel's blood pressure rose, which meant her subconscious was gearing up for more. Crawford's procession halted. Andy moved Counsel's hand to the fuzzy keychain dangling from her belt, closed it over the fur, then closed his fingers over Counsel's.

"Fight it," he said into her ear.

Mercer Crawford turned, adjusting his glasses for a look in their direction. Tan summer suit, a deeply tanned white face, and a conservative haircut, his reddish gray hair parted on the right. His wide mouth was closed, expressionless, him assessing his audience. He faced down the small crowd, all of whom had retaken their places in line, but whose heads turned and were now keying on, outing, the last two people to join them in the queue, Andy and Counsel.

In Counsel's hand—

Nice doggy fur, soft doggy fur . . .

Crawford's female staffer, in a business suit that flattered a full, hourglass figure, leaned into her boss and whispered in his ear. That restarted their procession, but it was minus the two goons who were bringing up the rear. The bodyguards visually canvassed the line behind them, their heads swiveling, their hands covering earpieces. Their glances converged on Counsel. They were on the move.

When they arrived, Counsel gave them a pat answer: "It wasn't me. Sorry."

A half-truth, considering her affliction had a mind of its own, but they had no choice other than to accept it.

***

Counsel and Andy passed through a metal detector. The Mercer Crawford procession hadn't needed to, the museum guard removing a silk cordon rope to usher the group through. Andy went for his wallet at the museum's admission counter. "Two."

Counsel, her skin smooth, her dark hair short, became the wise-ass she could occasionally be. "Senior discount for him, right, miss?" she said, straight-faced. "Show her your driver's license, Andy dear."

The woman at the counter balked, her look at first confused then expectant. This was the part of Counsel's age shaming she knew Andy liked, when theater or other events cashiers did double takes. Counsel herself was good for a double take when people learned she was in her early fifties, but Andy was an age-defying marvel.

"You can ignore my girlfriend here," he told the cashier, "we're both AARP members." Andy stared Counsel down, smirking. "She's in denial."

Admission to the museum was Andy's treat. She was there not only because of Andy and a certain new Wyeth exhibit opening today; it was mostly because of the tip about Crawford.

The museum's glass and concrete rotunda had a planetarium feel. Counsel and Andy moved through the displays until they reached the large room housing its newest exhibit. Below a high ceiling crosshatched with glass and wood beams, the museum's maze of exhibit walls jutted into the center of the open space. They wound their way toward the rear of the room, past forty-plus Newell Convers (N. C.) Wyeth illustrations and paintings, some moved here from elsewhere in the museum, others on loan from private collectors, including one new piece, its owner remaining anonymous.

Artist N. C. Wyeth was born in 1882, had died in 1945, the patriarch of a family of world-famous artists. His demise was tragic, deemed a freak accident by the authorities: He and his three-year-old grandson Newell were killed at a railroad crossing near this museum, a freight train crushing them and their Ford station wagon.

N. C. was consumed with the American West. Cowboys, Native Americans, horses, lassos, and cattle, plus their guns, which fed Counsel's childhood interest, and now, apparently, the serious interest of one Mercer Crawford. His ensemble had formed a semi-circle around him as he, his female staffer, and the other guest who'd entered with him, a man in a western bolo tie, stood inside the stanchioned area between the rope and the exhibit wall. Crawford's glasses were off, a magnifying glass replacing them, as were the glasses of the man in the bolo. The two examined one painting with the seriousness of art authenticators. On the wall farthest from the room entrance hung *Wild Bill Hickok at Cards,* a 1916 oil on canvas, 32 x 40 inches, signed upper right with "N. C. WYETH / to ELVA CORSON / 1921 / from / N.C.W." Counsel had studied up on the history. Elva Corson was Wyeth's fruit orchard caretaker. The painting last sold at The Coeur d'Alene Art Auction at Reno, Nevada in 2007 for $2.24 million, to an anonymous buyer, and it was on loan here as part of the show.

James Butler "Wild Bill" Hickok. Real-life American West lawman, marksman, gunfighter, and gambler. Wild Bill was shot in the back of the head during a saloon poker game in Deadwood, Dakota Territory, holding what was now referred to in pop culture as the "Dead Man's Hand": two pair, aces and eights, the fifth card not shown.

Counsel and Andy squeezed in closer to the front of a small group rebuffed by Crawford's protection, some of the crowd grumbling before growing impatient and moving on to other museum displays.

Counsel, too, was pissed, except she was vocal about it. "You guys need to move your boy along. You're blocking the view."

Andy squeezed her arm. "Counsel, no. Relax."

All the goons stayed in position, but their goon eyes turned to face them. Laser beams, X-ray vision, and other if-looks-could-kill stares, all were now focused on Counsel. This time, out of necessity, Counsel sized each of them up. Three men her size or larger, two smaller, the suits on all five of them tight, hiding some well-toned bulk. The one closest to her spoke, his sun-bleached blond hair slicked back and long enough to need tucking behind his ears. A puffy, baby face. He remained civil and kept his distance, but Counsel could tell he didn't want to do either.

"He'll just be another minute, miss," the baby-faced goon said.

Saturday morning TV reruns of *The Adventures of Wild Bill Hickok* had helped define Counsel's childhood, along with cartoons and Philly sports teams. Horses, dusty roads, rattlesnakes, ranches, saloon poker, and gleaming six-shooter gunfights. Sexy Guy Madison as Wild Bill, "the law in these here parts." Andy Devine played Jingles, his capable but whiny 300-pound deputy. Wild Bill wore his guns butt forward, two Colt 1851 Navy Model percussion revolvers with ivory grips and steel frames. He drew his pistols using a reverse, or twist draw. As a kid, Counsel wore her holsters, all leather, no studs, the same way, which made her different from her kid friends, especially her kid girlfriends, who had no time for playing Cowboys and Indians.

Unique. Counsel liked unique. Unique defined her.

Behind them, she heard the clickety-clack of high heels in a hurry on the hardwood floor.

"'Scuse me. 'Scuse me . . ."

Thin and energetic, with short auburn hair above stylish horn-rimmed glasses, the woman hustled her way to the perimeter of Crawford's cone of protection.

Andy whispered to Counsel. "Christine Adamsky. Curator. Don't look at me funny. I met her years ago, at a coalmining art exhibit."

Ms. Adamsky rippled her way to the front of the crowd then turned to address them all while catching her breath, looking stylish in her gold blazer with the museum's orange logo. "So sorry for this inconvenience, folks. As a new member of the museum's Trustee's Circle—I won't embarrass our patron by mentioning his name or how generous he's been—our newest VIP donor asked for a quick examination of this wonderful piece, and we always try to accommodate our major patrons when and where possible. He'll be finished shortly. Thank you so much for your patience."

Crawford neither flinched nor gave any other indication he was being acknowledged. He kept his nose buried against the magnifying glass that was inches away from the painting, or rather inches away from the only gun in it, Hickok's Colt, which Wild Bill pointed at the card player sitting across from him at the table. Counsel held up the museum's literature for this piece and reread the description:

The man with the hatful of cards picked a hand out of his hidden reserves, put the hat back on his head and raised Bill a hundred. Bill came back with a raise of two hundred, and as the other man covered it, Bill shoved a pistol into his face, observing, "I'm calling the hand you were dealt. The one in your hat."

Big, hairy balls on Wild Bill's part. Back in those days, guns settled most arguments. It was easy to understand why Crawford loved the painting. Tough-guy swagger, a time when "men were men," fortified by the romance of the Old West, and a drawn gun.

Ms. Adamsky strode toward Andy, grabbed his hand and shook it. "Good to see you, Mr. Prudhomme," she said. "So, what do you think?"

"Not as popular as *Dogs Playing Poker*, my all-time favorite," Andy said, "but it'll do for an afternoon diversion."

"Ah," she said, smiling, "you're talking about Cassius Marcellus Coolidge's *Poker Game*. Another oil on canvas. Sotheby's auctioned it for big money back in 2015. Maybe someday we'll exhibit it here. Excuse me, but I have to go."

She eyed Counsel, taller than her, slipped a wink in there somewhere to Andy, then click-clacked her heels out of the exhibition room.

"What the hell was that all about?" Counsel asked Andy.

"What?"

"The wink."

"She thinks you're hot," Andy said, loud enough for other museum patrons to hear.

No reason to argue with her, Counsel thought, so she'd go with it. Otherwise, it was the lamest signal she'd ever seen.

***

Fifteen minutes later, the Crawford parade finally moved out of the way. A few patrons originally waiting to see the painting were still there, Andy and Counsel included, the others having moved to other pieces in the Brandywine's collection. Counsel hadn't budged, still inspecting each of the bodyguards closely, for future reference. With Crawford leaving, the vacated area in front of the painting quickly filled in again. Counsel and Andy would join the next wave.

The baby-faced bodyguard trailed the Crawford procession, his shoulder invading Andy's personal space on his way past with a shoulder bump, the physical equivalent of *Up yours, pal,* made minor only because Andy moved to avoid the brunt of it. A mini game of chicken, and Andy had wisely lost. The procession made its way around a corner. The bodyguard delivered his parting glance with a snarky smile that said *Thought so, wimp.*

Not so fast.

"Philly string band massacre," Counsel called at the Mercer Crawford procession in its wake. "Thoughts and prayers my ass, you enabling SOBs."

This was all Counsel, no Tourette's, and not a shout, but rather a statement with feeling. A taunt loud enough for Babyface to hear, prompting double takes from nearby patrons.

Babyface reappeared from around the corner in a hurry and strode toward them, or rather Counsel, with resolve. He arrived, the two of them toe to toe, nose to nose.

Onions, the man had onions for breakfast.

Andy nudged Counsel aside, replaced her menacing face with his. Phone cameras were out, the bystanders ready.

Someone had to speak. "I'll give you that bump, champ," Andy told the bodyguard, "but don't embarrass yourself and your boss with an assault and battery charge."

"And you need a Tic Tac," Counsel added.

"Renner!" Crawford's female staffer arrived behind the laggard bodyguard. "We're done here. Let's go, Renner. Now."

"Bye, Renner," Counsel called past Andy's shoulder with a wave and a smile.

Seething, the bodyguard straightened his tie and did an about-face, following the staffer.

Counsel 1, Babyface Renner 1.

Somewhere down the road, she expected there could be a tiebreaker.

SIX

September 22

Days before the final US Presidential debate: 24

The front parking lot was empty at eleven p.m., the Brandywine Museum of Art closed. Lighting for a smaller side lot encircled a cluster of cars: one security vehicle, two beaters, a late-model Cadillac, and now a Chrysler minivan coming to a full stop behind the other vehicles. The driver and the front passenger of the minivan climbed out while the side door slid open for the other occupants to exit.

A humid day had turned into a cool night, the Brandywine Creek gurgling nearby, sparkling in the late-summer moonlight. A hefty bodyguard stepped onto the blacktop, followed by Mercer Crawford in a black turtleneck and slacks and a charcoal sports jacket, a cat-burglar, man-of-mystery look. Dagmar Bystrom, his female staffer, exited after him: blond hair in a bun, gray workout clothes, a six-footer in her heels. Tonight's transportation was by Enterprise Rent-A-Car. Ms. Bystrom gestured to Renner, the bodyguard, pointing to a ground-level side door with crisscrossed inset wooden planking.

"We need to use that entrance," she said. "Let's get him inside."

Their previous visit to the museum had been enlightening. Bosco Horvath, art authenticator and critic, had accompanied them. A prominent AEF member, Bosco was a Virginian like Crawford, but also like Crawford, he was not native to the state. He was a transplanted Philadelphian, a Wyeth art expert inclusive of all members of the artist-rich, talented Wyeth family, and an N. C. Wyeth biographer as well. After they'd finished their reconnaissance work on the previous visit, they had folded themselves back inside Bosco's Bentley, where Bosco had given his feedback.

"It's authentic," he'd said, then added, smiling, "and it's one of my favorite N. C. paintings, too. So tell me why I needed to see it, Mercer. You, ah, looking to steal it?"

Crawford blanked his face in response. "Maybe."

They both chuckled, squeezing out the momentary dead air.

Crawford stifled himself, then clarified. "Seriously, I'm just getting ready for the next time it goes up for sale. I want it."

"You and me both," Horvath said. "Frankly, I know a few people who'd love to make a run at it if it were ever available again, including some of our AEF pals. But you do realize that that might not happen in our lifetime, right?"

"Unfortunately," Crawford said, adding a sigh to sell his feigned woe, "I am painfully aware of that."

What he hadn't shared was that his comical *maybe* response should have really been a *yes*, considering its acquisition was an activity already in progress. The iconic painting would trade hands again shortly, this time offered to a highly selective potential customer base, via a clandestine online community—the darknet.

Crawford had seen the Hickok painting up close in Las Vegas during its 2007 auction, but he left the bidding when it exceeded $1.5 million. The Las Vegas examination, along with this more recent one coupled with Bosco's pronouncement of its authenticity, had sealed it. Tonight's after-hours private showing arranged via a darknet contact would move things along. The price tag on the black market for the painting was an obscenely discounted $750K.

"*A steal,*" his anonymous darknet contact *vigilpokus101* had prodded online weeks back when Crawford, as *2Asammy44,* took too long—days— to respond. "*Seriously, we'll get someone to steal it for you. Put a deposit in* *your wallet on our website so we can do some recruiting. $200K will handle it. Do it ASAP. Other parties have shown an interest. Don't worry, we won't bid it up, the price is firm. First come, first served. Honesty among thieves and all that. When we deliver the product, you put up the remaining amount and we all walk away happy. Easy-peasy."*

No other details were exchanged online. The first part of the plan would begin tonight, after their meet-and-greet onsite with someone repping what *vigilpokus101* dubbed as his darknet "photographers." Meet, greet, then the museum contacts would need to respond to his assistant Dagmar's planned in-person bold suggestion regarding a certain non-negotiable requirement to consummate the transaction. To assure there could be no hanky-panky, *vigilpokus101* or his proxies would not learn of Dagmar's additional requirement until tonight.

Dagmar Bystrom. Crawford's chief of staff, and an AEF lieutenant twelve years running. A female Marine, former enlisted, now retired. Not his lover, but not for a lack of repeated efforts on Crawford's part, even though Crawford was happily married according to all public AEF information. Regardless, he intended to make another run at her, and soon.

The darknet. A lawless online wonderland that enabled anonymous communication via software called "The Onion Router," or *Tor* for short. When Crawford learned of *Tor* from a gun manufacturer four, maybe five years ago, an invitation to use it seemed as appealing as a walk in the city's sewers. So drippy-dirty-skeevy, with lowlifes and bad actors and products and services to satisfy any need, for any person, group, or species, animal, vegetable, mineral, without prejudice. He'd become a regular by having someone access it for certain business transactions. Specifically, for brokering gun sales that needed to fly under the radar, arising from these hardline conservative ideologies that were his and the AEF's both:

Freedom takes firepower.

Speaking softly works only if the stick you carry is bigger than the other guy's.

There are no bad guns, only bad people.

But tonight Mercer was mixing business with pleasure, scratching an itch, using the darknet to address one of his favorite passions, fine art that showcased the American West, and its acquisition, legal or otherwise.

The museum's side entrance opened on their approach. "Follow me," the security guard said.

The three of them plus the guard entered a curved corridor softly lit by recessed ceiling lighting. At the corridor's end was another door. The guard punched in a security code and the heavy door glided open. This process was repeated twice more, until the last door placed them inside one of the galleries.

"Glad to see you again, Mr. Crawford, Ms. Bystrom," said the diminutive curator in heels, her dark blazer crested with an embroidered museum logo.

Crawford nodded. Dagmar Bystrom spoke on their behalf. "Likewise, Ms. Adamsky." Dagmar raised her head toward a camera at ceiling level, gestured with her eyes only, then directed an intimidating stare complete with tightened jowls at the curator, who was no taller than Dagmar's shoulders.

Ms. Adamsky returned the stare. "Yes, the cameras are operational, but they're not recording in this wing. We can't shut down surveillance in this area in its entirety. Someone might try to steal something, right? Let's have at it then, shall we? Mr. Crawford, do you care to examine it again?"

The monetary details that were in play for the heist:

Anonymous security guard, ten grand.

Christine Adamsky, one of the museum's curators, reported as having a vendetta against the Wyeth family that transcended two generations, fifty grand, but not doing it for the money, she said.

The last participant—where was this broker, anyway?—would get the remaining $690K.

All of these amounts would be released when the prize was validated as having changed hands. The where and when of the prospective exchange had already been decided: downtown Scranton, Pennsylvania, in the multi-level parking garage of the Hannigan-McMaster Center, a music hall at the University of Scranton, on the night of, specifically during, the final US presidential debate. The venue and the timing were Crawford's choices. He was a strong supporter of the Republican nominee for president, Senator Quinn Hudson, and he planned to show his support by attending the debate.

They would not be so tacky as to try to walk away with the painting now, tonight. Too many people would have needed to be paid, or maybe worse yet, neutralized, and a tracking device on the painting hadn't yet been addressed.

"Where is he?" Crawford said, grim-faced. "I was told the broker would be here."

"And I *am* here, sir."

A short man exited the shadows, stopping under the circle of light behind them to effect a grand entrance. Wine-colored cape under a long white scarf that hung close to the floor, for him not a great distance. With a thin face of forty-plus years, a Humphrey Bogart overbite, and a black Bogart fedora that he removed with a flourish, the wispy guy was more wardrobe than person. Adding to his flamboyance was wild Einstein hair that could have been a wig, a bushy beard, and an untucked, open collared white shirt over jeans, the jeans' pantlegs ending short of a pair of tasseled penny loafers. Crawford remained unimpressed at so Capote an entrance.

"Ricardo Lopez, at your service," the new guest said, his accent south of the border. He bowed, then held out his hand.

"Of course you are," Crawford said, close to a sneer, his handshake less than enthusiastic. Ignoring the art broker, he returned his interest to the curator. "Yes, Ms. Adamsky, I damn well *do* need to examine the painting again. Which way?"

***

Green, blue, and smidgens of red, the rest of the painting in shades of gold, tan, black, white, and gray. Portrayed on the canvas were coins spread on a round table, the table planked, its wooden edge chipped. A hatless James Butler "Wild Bill" Hickok was seated with three other poker players. Long, chestnut brown hair hung in waved ringlets to his shoulders, was flat at top and parted in the middle. Add a mustache, a long coat, and a fluffy tie. A stagecoach flyer hung on the wall over his right shoulder; one observer to the card game stood nearby. Hickok's Navy Colt revolver, in his right hand, was about to elicit the truth from another poker player seated across from him. It was a near religious experience for Crawford, seeing the painting again.

"Ms. Adamsky," he said, catching his breath, "to get this show started, I need the painting off the wall."

"Excuse me? You *what?*"

"You heard me. Take it down."

An irate Ricardo Lopez stepped forward, gesticulating. "Absolutely not! We are not touching anything. Our photographer contractors are still in the planning stages—"

"I'm not talking to you. Renner? Handle that please."

Renner inserted himself between Crawford and the art broker. He placed his large open hand against Mr. Lopez's chest, grabbed some fluffy chest hair, and squeezed. He shushed the little loudmouth's whimpering with a head tilt and a finger pressed lightly against his own mouth.

"I understand, Ms. Adamsky," Crawford said, continuing, "that Dagmar already told you I would have a special request."

"Yes, but—"

"So here it is. Turn off the painting's tracking device, grab some gloves, remove it from the wall, and place it on that table." He pointed to a long piece of furniture with pamphlets on it. "I want it held upright, balanced on its long edge."

"But—"

"You're getting paid handsomely for this. Do it."

The curator left the room, soon returned with a box of un-powdered nitrile gloves. She laid the pink gloves end to end on the tabletop to approximate the length of the painting's bottom edge. She removed another pair of gloves from the box and squeezed her hands into them, as did the security guard. Facing the painting, she took a deep breath, squared her legs, then she and the guard gingerly lifted the frame off the wall. On steady feet they carried it to the table and set it down on the line of gloves as instructed and held it upright, on its short edge.

Crawford pulled two more nitrile gloves from the box, tugged them onto his hands. He stepped in closer to the painting, moving awkwardly close to the curator. He placed a hand atop the frame, caressed it, then addressed her. "Ms. Adamsky, let go of the painting."

"Sir—"

"This won't take long. I promise I'll be careful. Your guard can keep the other end steady."

Crawford repositioned the painting slightly to let the overhead lighting play with the precision of the brushstrokes. He nodded at the guard for him to maintain his grip, then Crawford withdrew his hand. He removed a tiny brown medicine bottle from inside his sport jacket, pulled the cap off the bottle, and placed it out of the way.

"Please, Mr. Crawford, sir, *no*, do *not* deface..."

Crawford ignored her, caught up in the magnificence of this coveted piece of art, and moved to the other side of the table, behind the painting.

Dagmar responded for him. "Relax, Ms. Adamsky, everything will be fine. This won't hurt a bit."

Crawford produced a toothpick from his pocket and dipped the end into the small bottle. Leaning down, he made a few light strokes on the back of the canvas. When finished, he nodded to Dagmar.

"Okay, that's a wrap, everyone," Dagmar said. "Ms. Adamsky, you're free to rehang it."

The curator hustled over to check the markings on the rear of the canvas.

"When it dries," Crawford said, "it will not be visible to the naked eye. Just know that it's been marked, and that only the correct chemical will show the markings. Use the wrong chemical, it will destroy the canvas. Have a good rest of the evening."

SEVEN

September 23

Days before the final US Presidential debate: 23

Day ten of freedom began much like most of Aaron's prior days on the outside, with little sleep the night before at his son Linus's townhouse condo, just inside Scranton's city limits. The nights subjected him to debilitating interruptions—taunts—that awakened him in fits and starts, the horror of an extended nightmare.

"Wake up, Pinocchio . . . Get up, you blockhead, NOW."

His eyes struggled to open, the image of the woodcarver Geppetto hovering over him, Aaron's arms outstretched, strings leading from his wrists and head up to the small wooden bars in Geppetto's hands. Not Pinocchio's creator Geppetto, but rather SCI Muncy prison's Superintendent Smythe costumed in Geppetto's white hair, white mustache, and wire-rim glasses, his hands manipulating the puppeteer controls.

"You will never be a real boy, Karis—"

Aaron bolted upright in bed, his breathing fast then evening out before calming, but with the calm came a chill that started in his back, across his shoulders. His T-shirt was sweat-soaked, and his bare arms were cold, the hair on them beading, dew-like, from the anxiety. His sweaty head, his sucking-wind chest, the damp waistband of his pajamas—they accompanied a shiver that came in waves, moving south, from head to neck to chest to stomach, then lower still—

"*. . . never be a real boy—*"

—to his vagina, cold and ugly.

Aaron very much liked vaginas, just not his own.

***

"Where to today, Dad?" Linus asked Aaron.

Aaron sipped coffee while seated at the kitchen center island. Linus's condo was spacious and tastefully decorated. The only problem was the gray, now popular as an interior color. Different shades of it persisted throughout, except for the bottom floor, a family room converted into an apartment for Aaron. Linus had mercifully repainted it in a warm colonial blue; a real color.

—a *real* boy—

His son Linus was a Villanova University Charles Widger School of Law grad, then a clerk for the local Philly courts. He'd moved north to Scranton to clerk for the US Federal Court System, the Middle District of Pennsylvania, which was how he'd met DA Hudson, now a senator. Linus was a well-educated, heterosexual single and loving it. Linus's life seemed, to Aaron, to be perfect.

"Today it will be some shopping in town," Aaron said, answering him.

"Shopping? Great. Need a ride? I can give you one if we do it first thing."

"Thanks, but I'll take the bus."

Renewing Aaron's driver's license was on the list, potentially not an easy task. It could be a challenge for government bureaucracy, considering that the felony and the gender change were things he'd need to deal with. His scheduled stops inside Scranton's city limits would be to gun shops, looking for someone to sell him a weapon or three. And soon, at some point, there'd be an appointment with a surgeon, to address his gender reassignment.

But first things needed to be first, ever since he'd made the decision. Guns.

Aaron stepped off the bus, hoofed it in the direction of Tim's Sin City Tobacco and Firearms, a storefront one block from the bus stop. The tinkle of a small bell above the store's single door sounded as sweet as the one that signified Angel Clarence earning his wings in *It's a Wonderful Life*. An empty center aisle led to a glass display case and counter combination that extended across the width of the store. The display case's content: guns.

"What can I do ya for?" the store clerk said.

Brown-bearded, maybe mid-fifties, the counter person's haystack frame was draped in a colorful bowling shirt in purple and gold. A nice offset to the drab browns and blacks and army green that decorated the rest of the shop.

"Looking to buy a few weapons," Aaron said.

"That works for me. I'm Tim, the owner." The gold stitching above Tim's shirt pocket read *The Anchor*. Appropriate based on his size, but it was also lingo for a bowling team's cleanup bowler, the captain and usually the best bowler on the team. "Have something in mind?"

"A Glock handgun, plus a rifle, a semiautomatic R-15 carbine. Ammo for both. For home protection."

"Good choices. Sure, I can help you. Some Glocks on display here, inside the case, and some on those walls over there. I've got a semiauto carbine resale that I just cleaned up in back. It's a Remington. Give you a good deal. Be right back with it."

Tim The Anchor set up everything on the counter, long gun, handgun, and ammo. "I'll need some info so we can get this moving," Tim said. "Fill out these forms. I'll also need a driver's license and a deposit to hold everything. Hey, you want a bump stock for the rifle?"

"A what?"

"Bump stock. Turns a semiauto rifle into something better than semiautomatic, know what I'm saying? They're a lot of fun."

"Sure. Look, my driver's license is, um, pending reinstatement."

"Oh. What's that mean? You got a DUI or something?"

"It expired. I'm waiting on it to get reissued."

"Huh." Tim's casual scrutiny turned more precise. "Where you been, out of the country? In the military?"

"No."

"C'mon, help me out here. Why no driver's license?"

"I just got out of prison."

"See, now that's going to be a problem. Sorry, but we can't do business." Tim The Anchor scooped up both guns and put them on the counter behind him.

Aaron pressed. "Look—Tim—I was wrongly convicted many, many years ago. It's been overturned. The reinstated driver's license, the overturned conviction, the documents will all catch up with each other in a few weeks. I'll leave you a sizeable deposit. Cash."

"Yeah, well, that's not gonna happen. Come back after your paperwork shakes out, Mister whatever your name is. No deposit until you get that all straightened out."

"Pappas. The name is Aaron Pappas. Please . . ."

"Pappas. Wait. *Pappas?* You're a big deal. The *Times-Trib* just ran a story on you. The Greek restaurant murders, back in '86. You just got out . . ."

Tim's eyes lit up, excited, but soon he was squinting, now in full reassessment mode.

"Hold on a minute. You were in Muncy Correctional. That's a *woman's* prison—"

Tim The Anchor's face drooped. His gaze moved from Aaron's unshaven face down to his chest then to his hands, both on the counter, their knuckles hairy from hormone treatments. His scrutiny turned north again, to Aaron's high-and-tight haircut, then his eyes. "Holy Jesus monkeynuts. You're a chick. Unbelievable."

Tim winced then quickly swept up the cartridge cartons, leaving nothing else lethal within Aaron's reach. "Yeah, um, no. Nope. Sorry. I got a reputation."

"Please. I've got rights—"

"Not yet you don't. You're not legal until you can show me some ID and get that conviction thing taken care of. Good luck straightening that all out. Right now, you got nothin'."

Tim's back turned but he kept talking, leaving Aaron with one final verbal indignity, not quite under the storeowner's breath. "Freak . . ."

***

There was another mom-and-pop shop, smaller than the one he'd just left, within Scranton's urban footprint according to the Yellow Pages. Aaron sat on the bus, replaying what had just happened, knew something else could have made what had just happened worse, much worse, but he'd chosen not to do it by resisting the urge to reach across the counter and grab Tim The Anchor by his double-chinned, bearded neck and choke the life out of him. Discouraged but not defeated, he chose instead to leave the store without incident. There were other gun shops, other dealers, plus there were gun shows. But hearing "no" hadn't sat well with him, so hearing it again elsewhere wouldn't make him feel any better. Hearing the "freak" comment had been the showstopper.

Tim's reaction shouldn't have been a surprise. To some, many, most, this was what he was. But after thirty years of incarceration, in the same cold, impersonal environs, inside the same four walls, with no one to impress other than his jailers, he was like a POW returning after an unpopular war. Little celebration, some discomfort, much hate.

And Tim's bowling shirt: As soon as Tim cursed him out, the shirt's color drained, turning from a lively purple and gold to lifeless, cinder-block gray. Not killing the gray right then and there—not draining Tim's face of its color with his bare hands—Aaron had restrained himself and walked away, the door's tinkling bell closing behind him, sparing Tim from earning his own angel wings, for today at least.

Aaron had a Plan B. It would require getting help with setting up an internet presence. He'd also need a credit card. Linus, knowingly or not, would help him with both if necessary. He'd order what he'd need online, and he'd look into assembling the guns himself.

EIGHT

September 26
The Annual AEF Convention, Deadwood, South Dakota

Days before the final US Presidential debate: 20

Dagmar Bystrom reached the center of the hardwood floor of the basketball court. Her denim outfit and line-dance boots, including a jacket pinched closed at the waist that flattered her full figure, projected power and pizzazz. Blond hair framed her tight, Nordic face, her cosmetics heavy enough to take advantage of the bright lights of the stadium. Some catcalls and whistles descended from the convention center crowd, with clapping and hollering that turned into a chant.

"*Dag-mar, Dag-mar, Dag-mar . . .*"

"Thank you. Thank you all so much. But as you might expect, I'm out here for one reason, and one reason only, folks."

She circled the arena floor, her voice carrying from her lapel microphone, her head raised, swiveling to appreciate the panoramic view of her audience. "I'm here to introduce the final speaker of the evening. Someone you all know very well. Our champion. And my boss. Let's have a rousing round of applause . . . for AEF Chief Executive Officer . . . Mercer Crawford!"

Clapping and cheers erupted again, moving to a crescendo as Mercer strode down one of the long aisles. Reaching center court, he and Dagmar air kissed. She raised his arm as one would a boxing champion, he in blue jeans and leather boots and sporting an open-collar denim shirt that made him look the part of a hog-caller at a county fair. Nineteen thousand plus were on their feet, joining hundreds more SRO attendees.

This year's AEF convention was in Deadwood, part of the Badlands of South Dakota, surrounded by the Black Hills National Forest. Deadwood was an intimate town, more so than any other venue the AEF had used in recent years, but now boasting a brand new, large arena. This location was something Mercer had pushed for coincident with his vision of channeling America's reputation as a country of trailblazers. He'd taken his bully pulpit to a place that had earned its reputation back when the nation was only a hundred years young and its most romantic: during the settling of America's Wild West. The birth of the American spirit. The lore of the open range and the cowboy. The first American city after Vegas and Atlantic City to legalize gambling, and the first city to make the National Register of Historic Places.

No rules, no regrets: The Dakota Territory in the 1870s was a gulch of dead trees and creeks full of gold that became towns full of hope, but for many in its small population, the hope for success had gone unrealized. Presently, for the nation, however, and for a revitalized Deadwood, more Americans were fulfilling their hopes and dreams every day. Its historic reputation for "outlaws, gamblers, and gunslingers," according to the town's online presence, reigned supreme and was a huge tourist draw. And according to the town's pitch to the AEF leadership to woo the convention to its intimate environs—so small a town with plans so large—today's Deadwood held much the same charm.

"How do you folks like this new arena?" Mercer said into his lapel mic, raising his voice. "Really something, isn't it?"

More cheers and hollers. Mercer raised an arm to point out the town dignitaries in the first row, acknowledging the men and women of the Deadwood Chamber of Commerce. The town saw its population swell to 80,000-plus during these four days of the convention, nearly overwhelming Deadwood, its sister cities and the county, and tonight, the convention's final night, Mercer intended to whip his members and guests into a frenzy.

He wasn't as passionate about the AEF as these folks were. For him it had always been more about the money. The perspective he needed to display publicly was that AEF members were law-abiding, socially conscious, good people. Each major gun incident that the great US of A had experienced reminded them how dangerous a world it was out there. During his speeches, comments, and statements to the media after each transgression, the sentiment had never changed. Tonight's words would be no different, bolstered by Wild West nostalgia and an appreciation of the icons who'd had a hand in shaping the history and the legend that was the Dakota Territory's Badlands. And it would be a speech geared to cajoling these Americans into buying more guns.

He was paid well—a few million per year—for lobbying US lawmakers in defense of the Second Amendment. The rest of the world felt he had different intentions, recognizing him and the AEF as agents for the gun manufacturers, his paid position existing to stoke the membership at times like this. "Lobbying" was too tame a descriptor. On occasions when lobbying the politicians fell short, political harpooning became the alternative.

More guns, America. More, more, more.

Cha-ching.

He raised his hands then slowly lowered them palms-down at the boisterous crowd to tamp their noisy enthusiasm. They quieted.

His mental checklist: dignitary acknowledgments, check; shout-outs to Dagmar Bystrom and other loyal AEF lieutenants, check; convention staffer mentions, check; beautiful wife acknowledgment, check. It was time to get down to the business of stoking their patriotism by namedropping America's romantic Wild West icons. He smiled for his audience.

"How is everyone enjoying the gambling here in Deadwood?"

Hoots, hollers, a few colorful rejoinders, plus laughing and cheering. He launched into his keynote.

"Outstanding. Okay, listen up. The city of Deadwood struck gold in 1874. A boomtown environment, but then it struggled some and went from panning gold to deep mining. They toughed out the fires, the smallpox, and for a while, they also toughed out a reliance on the opium trade that put too many folks in the region to sleep. But Deadwood's people never gave up, staying in the game even though they should have folded given the hand they'd been dealt, and the subsequent hands they'd dealt themselves. A lot like this great country seems today, my fellow Americans.

"One hundred years later, Deadwood struck gold again, this time with legalized gambling. And these past few days this small town of less than two thousand residents—and eighty gambling halls—has hosted the annual convention for the largest right-to-bear-arms protectors in the country! Well done, Deadwood! Well done, South Dakota!"

Cheering, whistling, hollering—Mercer raised his chin to bask in and absorb the rapture of it all.

"Let's calm it down a bit, and we'll play a little game of name-that-Deadwood-icon, to see if we as out-of-towners learned anything about our hosts these past few days. That is, aside from how a fool and his money are soon parted."

The audience laughed, the laughter soon dissipating, drifting into scattered whistles and clapping.

"After four days in these wonderful Black Hills and Badlands, celebrating our patriotism, we should all know who these icons are, these colorful catalysts of the American West experience, so ingrained in, and interchangeable with, this town's identity. Here's how we'll play. When I mention a name, you shout the person's nickname. Okay. Here we go."

This cued his staffer Dagmar, who rose from her seat, as rehearsed, to approach him at center court.

"Whoa!" she said, interrupting. She scanned the crowd à la a World Wrestling Entertainment SmackDown moment, milking the applause and catcalling. When the noise quieted some, she projected her voice. "Mercer, you old sidewinder you. You just wait a gosh-durn minute, pardner."

Laughter from the audience, her quizzical head-tilt including a hand on her hip. "What can we give our lovely convention guests here if they identify all these icons correctly? Some parting gifts maybe?"

Crawford waited for the heavy clapping and crowd encouragement to subside. "A great suggestion, Dagmar." He stroked his chin, playing his part. "Hmm, let's see. If the crowd gets them all correct, how about we give everyone of age . . . a coupon for a free shot of Deadwood American Bourbon Whiskey, redeemable at any of the city's casinos, courtesy of the AEF! And for the kids, ten dollars in Deadwood Gold Bucks, good anywhere around town. How's that sound?"

Applause, whistles, smiles, fist bumps and pumps.

"So, are you ready, my AEF friends?" He put a hand to his ear.

"READY!" echoed throughout the stadium.

"Excellent. Here's our first Deadwood personality . . ."

Mercer read from a list, describing one by one the characters who colored the town's history, keying on their wild-spirited, larger-than-life existences that transcended the hardened, mundane realities of their day. Each description produced shouted guesses, the audience eventually arriving at the correct answers, calling out names like "Potato Creek Johnny" Perrett, "Colorado Charlie" Utter, Eleanor "Madame Mustache" Dumont, and "Poker Alice" Tubbs.

Mercer paused, not rehearsed, only now noticing a phenomenon as he scanned the audience: mirror-like glints of silver and gold and pearl-handled plating in the hands of Black men and women in sporadic groupings seated around the arena, ten to fifteen or more in each group. Handguns, at rest in their laps, their hands on their pistol grips. Only a few of these shiny distractions like this were visible at the start of his speech; there were a lot more now. What in God's name was going on?

South Dakota was an open-carry state, did not require concealed pistol permits, and the arena likewise had no restrictions on open carry. Neither did the AEF, inside or outside the convention. Except open carry at an AEF event for many members was too over the top and in your face, with typically only a few convention attendees opting to publicly exercise their Second Amendment rights in real time.

He ran his hand over his mouth, swiping at his moist upper lip. There'd been no threatening movement by any of these attendees—yet. Had there ever been this many Black people at an AEF convention before?

Only handfuls, as far as he could recall. He could have been convinced there weren't this many non-white people in the entire AEF membership.

But of course there were. Had to be. The AEF did not, could not discriminate. That was the law. On paper at least.

He made a mental note. *Need stats. Learn how many non-whites are AEF members, last month, last year, last decade.* A little-known fact was, after the initial spike in overall AEF membership as a negative response to the election of a Black man as president—and then, after that election, a Black woman—the general membership rolls were declining. But what about current non-white AEF membership? Was it still a low percentage, a barely measurable minority, or was this Deadwood crowd proof that the percentage had increased?

One Deadwood historical personality hadn't made the cut for today's quiz, left off the list because the character didn't fit the white male likeness of a typical AEF member. Crawford made eye contact with a few of the gun-toting Black attendees and managed a smile. He cleared his throat.

"Okay then. Next. We have a treat for all you double entendre folks out there.

"After driving three thousand head of steer to this fair town, arriving on July third, 1876, this cowboy entered a roping, bridling, saddling, and shooting contest held on our nation's birthday, the Fourth of July, and he walked away with two hundred dollars in prize money plus a distinctive nickname. Known as the greatest Black cowboy of the Old West, who was he?"

Rapid-fire responses coalesced into one name, coming mostly from the Black people in the audience: "NAT—DEADWOOD DICK—*LOVE*!"

Raucous guffaws. Their smiles popped, and their hands left their handgun grips to give their friends exaggerated handshakes and shoulder slams, the rest of the audience not as boisterous, but still entertained.

"Yes! Deadwood and the Badlands, Equal Opportunity trailblazers in the Old West."

Perceived threat and paranoia neutralized.

"Now, folks, we have the lightning round. Because these next two heroes are more easily recognized," he wandered the stage, the audience's eyes following him, "I expect you'll be getting your vouchers in short order. Drumroll please." The drumroll queued up as a background track to his amplified voice, echoing throughout the arena.

"First, the tobacco-spitting, beer-guzzling, foul-mouthed female US Army scout who preferred men's clothing to dresses, and who was born as Martha—Jane—Cannary. Who was she?"

The drumroll continued, prompting the audience din to coalesce into an answer.

"CALAMITY—*JANE!*" Multiple cymbal splashes ricocheted.

"Yes! And now, finally," the drumbeat started out low but gathered in volume, "old aces and eights himself, shot dead at age thirty-nine in Nuttal and Mann's Number Ten Saloon by the despicable Jack McCall, August second, 1876. The bullet entered the back of his head and exited the center of his right cheek. He was laid to rest with his coveted long rifle, not his two Colts, the locations of his beloved Colts unknown. This poker-playing, gunslinging lawmaker, because of a posthumous joke, has as a perpetual bunkmate buried next to him, in the Mount Moriah Cemetery, the aforementioned Calamity Jane—someone he reportedly had absolutely no use for during their friendship! I'm talking about Deadwood's most famous resident . . ."

He coaxed the audience's response with carnival barker delivery and upturned, beckoning fingers, "the western hero known back then, as he is today, as James—Butler-r-r-r-r—"

"HICKOK! WILD BILL HICKOK!" the audience screamed.

Cymbal splashes. "Yes! Give these people their coupons, Dagmar!"

Released from high above, thousands of paper vouchers fluttered earthward, dropping like confetti onto the shoulders and heads and into the hands of the audience, redeemable for one free drink or one kids' gift per attendee only, when accompanied by their canceled convention ticket. He waited while the audience scurried about collecting them, with Creedence Clearwater Revival's *Who'll Stop the Rain* blasting the arena. The pandemonium subsided, as did the music. Crawford again addressed the crowd.

"Ah, yes, that was fun. So let's get down to business. I want to bring up something extremely important. Something we need to wrap our heads around."

He strode around the stadium's basketball court, his hardwood bully pulpit, his head down, letting the anticipation build. He stopped his pacing at center court, folded his hands in front of his waist, and raised his head.

"I'm talking about the Raging Creek Elementary School shooting a few years back."

The crowd grumbled, but soon their din was peppered with scattered booing, and shouts of "never happened!" and "liberal conspiracy." Crawford let the venting continue unabated until he gestured for his audience to quiet itself. When it was sufficiently calm—

"To address all you good folks who think this shooting was a hoax, hear me loud and clear: It did happen. I've seen the footage. I visited the town, and I visited the school. No amount of booing, and no amount of misdirected conspiracy arguments, by any well-meaning, patriotic American citizen, will ever change that fact. We need to accept it as the tragic event that it was. But we also must address this: how to keep it from happening again."

The booing stopped, the commotion reducing to foot shuffling and seat resettling. "The question is, what can be done about it? The answer is . . ."

Anticipation again squeezed out the stray voices and the wayward coughs, the near silence soon succumbing to a pin-drop version of it, the audience rapt, waiting to be told.

"The most effective approach is . . . to deter would-be actors. And how do we do that? Our schools *must—be—armed.*"

Speaking their language, the applause intensified again.

"To not arm teachers and school security . . . is tantamount . . ."

He stopped speaking, walked the floor, and waited for the applause to dissipate. When it did, he spoke again, but in a lower, more somber voice.

"Yes, not arming the schools—is tantamount—to participation . . . in the slaughter."

The words silenced the crowd, heads shaking their displeasure, their disgust.

"Those of you out there who feel we can reduce the number of shootings by reducing the number of guns . . . your thinking is dangerously flawed. And innocent people are dying because of it."

Grumbling, noisy undercurrents of anger heightened, the crowd stoked.

"More gun control? I say no! I say yes to better mental health management, and yes to more gun safety classes, for *all* Americans! I say no to *any* restrictions on your Second Amendment right to own whatever weapons you feel you need to defend yourself and your family, from Saturday Night Specials to automatics to a Big Bertha Railway Gun!"

Attendees not already standing rose to their feet, a mass of clapping hands and voices, shouting their agreement.

"And the sooner our legislators—our overtly liberal federal government—gets it into their stubborn, anti-freedom psyches that the right to arm ourselves any way we see fit is not open for discussion, the better we, the American people, the greatest nation on earth, will be!"

Crawford wrapped himself in another few minutes of protectionist dogma before ending his speech. Dagmar took his arm, led him off the floor of the arena to ear-piercing whistles and shouts, with thousands of waving, fist-pumping supporters still on their feet, celebrating his performance.

Once out of sight of the main arena, he shook himself free of Dagmar's ushering and pulled her into an alcove. His lips thinned, his brow furrowed.

"Dagmar, we have a problem."

She didn't answer, instead eyed his hand gripping her bicep. He got the message and removed it. "And what is that, Mercer?"

He continued, no apology for his gruffness. "Did you notice all the Black faces in the audience?"

"I can't say that I noticed all of them, but yes, there were quite a few people of color here. A good turnout if you ask me. It's encouraging to see that part of the membership growing."

"Not to me it isn't."

"What?"

"I want someone to give me a report showing how many Blacks and Hispanics we have as AEF members. I want these counts for every quarter dating back five years, and I want this info in my hands by tomorrow afternoon."

"I don't think we collect those kinds of statist—"

"Don't give me that BS, Dagmar, remember who you're talking to. I personally directed someone to mine that data years ago. I know it's out there. It's—you know what? Forget it. I'll get Renner to pull it together."

He'd already decided. Maybe the AEF's minority outreach campaign were a little too successful—he wanted to grow the non-white population, just not too much. Hell, they were minorities, and they needed to stay that way, in his gun lobby membership and everywhere else in this country. And when he got right down to it, in his opinion, many urban environments were only one more Black Lives Matter protest away from open civil warfare.

***

Mercer settled into the expansive rear seat of a black stretch Hummer with his laptop, one bodyguard and no Dagmar, who'd been dismissed along with his wife until later. Tricked out inside and out as indestructible as a POTUS vehicle, the armored SUV and chauffer were AEF perks for its CEO. Following closely behind the Hummer were two Chevy Tahoes, also black.

He fired up the browser on his laptop and entered the darknet through the *Tor* protocol on the deep web. One username—*2Asammy44*—and one password later, he was on a darknet chat app, soon finishing an exchange with *vigilpokus101*, looking into progress toward acquiring the Hickok painting. There'd been no issues with the monetary transfer: two hundred grand was now on account, sitting in his virtual wallet on *vigilpokus101*'s website, awaiting the night of the "photography shoot" at the art museum.

"Renner."

"Yes, Mr. Crawford."

"I need your help with something. You use *Tor*, right?"

"Ah . . ."

"The software that accesses darknet chatting on the deep web?"

"Um . . ."

"Thought so. Good. But first, a different topic. I need you to pull some data on membership ethnicities from files on the AEF servers. Pure statistics. I'll have someone tweak a few parameters from the Pew research studies I summarized, do some extrapolations, then you can run the programs. I want the results back tomorrow."

"Yes sir, Mr. Crawford."

"And after the rest of the staff calls it a night, you'll help me with something a bit more—interesting. It involves working through some contacts who need to stay out of sight of inquiring eyes."

"On the darknet, sir?"

"Exactly."

"Why me, sir, and not Dagmar?"

Cadillac Jack's Hotel and gaming resort, a well-lit, low-rise building, crept into the windshield in the distance. Mercer, his direct reports, and his bodyguard team, were staying there. Tonight was their last night in Deadwood.

"Dagmar's been a pain lately. Less beholden to the AEF, and nowadays less than thrilled with me personally. I'm thinking of terminating her."

"*Terminating* her, sir? You don't mean . . . what do you mean, sir?"

"Stop it. I mean firing her. But I need her to get me through some important transactions first, including attendance at the final presidential debate in a few weeks. I plan to give her one more opportunity to keep her seat at the AEF management table. Or else she's gone."

His gaze lost its focus, pondering the front entrance to the Deadwood Social Club as they cruised by, then shifting across the street to Saloon #10, where Wild Bill Hickok was murdered.

"If she blows this chance, Renner, I won't care what happens to her."

NINE

October 1
South Bridge B&B, South Street, Philadelphia

Days before the final US Presidential debate: 15

Counsel reached for Andy; his side of the bed was empty. She sat up, saw him tucked into a nearby loveseat, his feet on a coffee table, his laptop balanced on his thighs. The screen illuminated his face.

"Good. You're up," he said. "You'll want to see this."

She groaned. "What I want is coffee." A snort from the near corner, Tess making her presence known, Fungo quiet but also staring at her. "And my dogs need a walk."

"Fine. It'll keep. Bring me a cup on your way back up, please."

Six a.m.-ish. She climbed into her jeans and pulled on a black leather jacket, something she'd acquired when she bought her motorcycle. Still, Andy told her she looked great in leather, it went well with her Joan Jett dark espresso pixie cut, etc. After a few head scratches for her four-legged deputies, they were all ready for a visit to the dog relief area outside.

Back in the room, Counsel swallowed her medication. Clonidine, an antihypertensive agent, showed a real talent for fighting her Tourette's episodes, reducing their frequency and severity.

Andy sipped his coffee. "I'm looking at some Rancor town watch activity that I'll need to address when we get back. It interests you, too."

"Deep web crazies are at the bottom of my list."

Rancor PA's town watch was proactive. "It's always best to know who the predators out there are, Counsel."

Andy's mantra, plus, "The local population likes staying in front of things." Which meant Andy was active on this, the darknet portion of the internet, a lawless, funky place Counsel had no interest in visiting.

"Show me what you got, Columbo."

Andy turned the laptop around.

"These sad-looking selfies went through a few hands before they got to me, from a friend of a friend. Check out this guy. He likes his women busty and on the short side. He also might be into kids."

A "dick pic," but not your everyday variety, or so Counsel imagined, because it included a prop: a handgun nestled in close to, in direct competition with, the guy's exposed penis, his white erection paralleling the black gun barrel. Counsel, discomfort aside, leaned in to better view the image from eye level, that of the selfie-taker, his skivvies at his knees.

"So why am I interested in a picture of this guy's penis?" she said.

"As a front end to what went on in the chat room with a Rancor teenager."

Counsel analyzed the photo but was most interested in the gun. She was familiar with the model, a Gatling Arms PM9, its overall length about six inches, the barrel length half that. Measuring somewhere between those two lengths was the penis. So incongruous, considering the guy had toned abs, a muscular chest, and one word tatted onto his flat stomach, "ACHTUNG!"

False advertising. *Achtung,* or "at attention," in this guy's case might have been confused with the German military equivalent of "at ease." Why would a guy humiliate himself like this?

"I know what you're thinking, Counsel. How stupid is this guy. All hat, no cattle."

"What, you're a Texan now? Can you zoom in more?"

"Really? Ah, no. Zoomed in to the max already."

"I need a magnifying glass," Counsel said, squinting.

"That's just cruel, Counsel."

"I've got one in the van. Back in a minute."

"But you're missing my point . . ."

Counsel returned with a pocket-sized magnifier attached to a keychain. She sat on the loveseat next to Andy then helped herself to the laptop. She knew the gun's manufacturer, so she knew where it was made, at a plant in Agawam, Massachusetts. The *PM* designation meant it was a police and military model. Squinting again, she picked up the first three digits of the serial, all alphas, *DXV*, and wrote them on a notepad. The last four digits were blurred, the magnifying glass not helpful, the image too pixelated. Or maybe the digits were scratched off, or maybe not there at all.

Gatling Arms Limited as a corporate entity was in trouble. A less popular gun manufacturer, it was the only one Counsel knew that was in danger of going under—something she'd gleaned from reading the business pages, the manufacturer's financial condition highly irregular considering today's gun environment. Class action lawsuits were doing it, from a few state and local police jurisdictions. Cops had died on the job, in crisis, their handguns jamming. And then there was the AR-15 civil suits that were piling up, ignoring the legislation that prohibited them. The company chose to fight everything—the law enforcement charges highlighting manufacturing defects, the civil lawsuits citing innocent lives terminated by selling military-style firearms to the public. Their need to provision for the prospect of massive jury-awarded payouts had destroyed their balance sheet. News of the legal actions turned into cancellations of customers' gun orders large and small. Their stock price plummeted. Adding insult to injury, some company execs had cashed out their stock options just before the lawsuit filings were made public. Insider trading indictments helped tank the stock. Bankruptcy loomed.

Counsel read the chat between this troll and someone by the name of Nina.

"You maybe know this Nina?" she asked.

"I know her parents. She has some self-image issues, but she's a good kid."

The exchange was full of boasts and bluster by the adult, the sender calling himself *2Ap@1!Ndr0mE.*

—I can go all night honey. ALL. NIGHT. Big where it counts baby, in the pocketbook. I'm gangsta AEF royalty. No one gonna mess with your chunky little ass ever again . . .

The white man's thug bravado was pervasive, with the teen's responses offering only cursory encouragement. Then, there it was, the swagger that had most piqued Andy's interest. Counsel pulled the laptop closer, had to stay calm, had to handle the adrenaline rush, had to focus. But inside, in her throat, her disease wanted out. Her lips parted.

"*. . . cock-cock-cocktail wieners . . .*"

She gripped her fur keychain. It appeased the disease's appetite, for the moment clipping off an episode and settling her down. Counsel unclenched her jaw, then she read the rest of the online chat.

—guns. An arsenal of stolen guns. Don't you know it baby. You want one? two? ten? INFINITY? Gonna be in your neck of the woods in a coupla weeks. Let's be an item togetha you sweet thing!

"Send this to my email address," Counsel said. "The photo, the chats, all of it. I'll scrub it of all identifying info on the girl. I'll have Vonetta check into this guy's handgun, to see if he's telling the truth about it being stolen."

"Fine."

Counsel sensed Andy's enthusiasm was lacking. "What? Is there a problem?"

"It needs to go one other place first," Andy said.

Andy swallowed, blinked through some discomfort, then announced the one recipient they would both agree needed to see it more than anyone else. "To Teddy."

"Sure. That works."

Counsel knew better than to pursue that discussion. "Teddy" was FBI Special Agent in Charge Theodora Escobar, nee Prudhomme, Andy's estranged daughter. Ever-present in his life for her first twenty years on the planet, out of his life ever since, save for one very visible episode involving a bail-jumping serial killer who had binged on Andy's small town of Rancor and its aging population two years ago. The case had brought Andy and Counsel together, and it brought Teddy back into his life, but because of a few rough edges, it was too fresh an experience to talk about.

Andy did what he had to do in notifying Teddy. A second encounter in a little over two years would work from his perspective, father to daughter, but from FBI agent Teddy's side, it might push their envelope off the table, back into the abyss.

***

They hit the road after their B&B breakfast. The reason for their trip south, for this half-hour drive out of Philly into Chadds Ford, was a return visit to the Brandywine Museum of Art. The museum didn't open until ten a.m. It was now a little after eight, the interior lighting for the front entrance hall dimmed. Counsel's text to the curator got them buzzed through a rear loading dock entrance. Once inside—

"There," Ms. Adamsky said, pointing.

Six three-by-four-foot flat packages, wrapped in brown cardboard and securely taped, sat against a workbench in the dock area. Counsel lifted the corner of one package to gauge its weight, some of which came from firm, pointy-edged wooden framing, some from the packing materials, and heavy enough that it needed another set of hands. Andy grabbed the other end.

"Five extra canvases seems like overkill, doesn't it?" Counsel said to the curator.

"He asked for them. He said he needed them for trial runs before he painted on the one canvas you want. Which, by the way," the curator gestured, "is marked with an asterisk on the packing material. There's no questioning an artist. They're all perfectionists."

They walked each bundle outside and down a stand of stone steps to the van. Side-door deposits put each package flat against the van wall. They secured all six with bungee cords, there being no danger of damage due to the professional-grade packing job, as long as her canine Tess stayed away from them, and she would. Fungo, crated farther back, lifted his head with each deposit and dropped it back down to rest it against his German shepherd paws, unimpressed.

Their museum visit was over. "I guess we'll see you when we see you," Counsel said, shaking Ms. Adamsky's hand. That would be in around two weeks according to the project timetable, when they expected Counsel would need to make this trip once again, returning their payload.

"Yes, you will. Safe trip."

TEN

October 1

Linus Pappas's townhouse condo, Scranton, Pennsylvania

Days before the final US Presidential debate: 15

"First, let's get one thing out of the way. What you're about to do isn't rocket science."

From a blog post by a survivalist. Aaron had learned a thing or two about a thing or two on the internet in the past few weeks. Simple things he'd only heard pieces about before, like how to "google," and what a blog was. How to buy things and have them shipped to a residence. How to ask questions and receive feedback online on any topic, with no repercussions, no judgment.

And how to build do-it-yourself semiautomatic rifles and handguns.

"No engineering degree? Don't need one. No tools? No problem. All you need is $500. Follow the instructions. When you're finished you'll have a functional semiautomatic weapon."

And $500 was what he'd put up to get the secured credit card his son Linus had helped him acquire. He had cash in a bank account from leftover Pappas family money. Not much, but enough to channel some of it into secured credit cards that, Linus suggested, he could use to build up his credit. Credit agencies didn't know Aaron existed, and good credit was as essential to a person's long-term financial wellbeing as taking care of one's physical health, according to Linus.

Aaron humored his son, but the direction Aaron was going, credit ratings, and long-term physical and financial wellbeing, were things he worried less about.

The doorbell rang for a delivery. He accepted two packages, carried the boxes downstairs to his space, and locked the door behind him, even though no one else was home. Like a dog in his crate, after close to three decades in prison that included way too much solitary, Aaron drew comfort from certain levels of confinement. He opened the boxes.

In one was a polymer Glock handgun frame, or more specifically, eighty percent of a Glock handgun's lower receiver. In the second was a chunk of aluminum, ninety bucks worth, representing eighty percent of a different lower receiver: an AR-15 semiautomatic rifle. If fully machined, these incomplete gun parts would be deemed firearms by federal standards. At eighty-percent-milled or less, the Feds considered them paperweights.

He'd heard about ghost guns in prison. Un-serialized, unregistered weapons built for personal use from gun parts not recognized individually as firearms by the US government. "Overheard" about them was more accurate—few jailers spoke with him for most of his time in prison, years and years and years. Two women guards chatting with each other near his cell spoke one time about a prisoner they both thought was hot who'd just been newly paroled. The paroled felon, now back on the outside, bought a ghost gunner milling machine, learned how to build a handgun with it, and shot her ex-lover. Revenge, for that parolee at least, was worth the prospect of re-incarcerating herself.

Aaron felt that parolee's pain and understood her conviction.

Ghost gunners. Commercially produced tabletop machinery with a one-cubic-foot footprint capable of milling gun parts, from myriad materials, into AR-15s, Glocks, and other weapons. Slide in a block of steel, aluminum, or a polymer composite, run the robotic software for a few hours, and out came a gun's lower receiver. Affixing the rest of a gun's parts to the receiver would make it a fully functioning, unserialized firearm available to people not allowed by law, i.e., convicted felons, to purchase a gun on their own. The hardware sold on Amazon and elsewhere for around five hundred bucks. He didn't have enough lead time to learn how to use it, nor the space, so this wasn't a good solution. A better decision: find someone with ghost gunner machinery willing to mill the parts for him.

Which was easier than he'd thought in the lawless underground internet space known as the "darknet." A crazy playland that had surfaced during a discussion with Linus about Nigerian princes and Russian brides.

"Do *not* go there," his son had warned him. "It's not a good place for you to visit as a parolee, nor as a transgender person, nor for me as your son, considering my involvement with the presidential campaign. Please, *please,* Dad, do not frequent the deep web when looking to buy things. Whatever you need, I'll get it for you."

Finding someone local with milling equipment, Aaron discovered, was just as easy. Poconos and other upstate Pennsylvania hunters and trailblazers reveled in backwoods existences on the outskirts of civilization, much like other mountainous areas around the country. The Daniel Boones, the Davy Crocketts, the Grizzly Adamses, the Euell Gibbonses. And learning there was no way to trace a ghost gun's millwork back to a ghost gunner machine invited autonomy for folks who owned the device and looked to either make back their investment or glom onto the gun rights cause.

"*Sure, I can do it for you,*" was a darknet blogger's return message. "*Power to the people brother and screw that president and his bleeding gun-control heart. Hell yes, come on over and we'll get 'er done.*"

But Aaron then sent the darknet chat in a different direction. "*Is a polymer gun detectible?*"

Two minutes had passed, three, then four, with no response, not even a "*detectible how?*" or "*explain yourself*" clarification request, with Aaron thinking he'd queered the deal.

He keyed a follow up. "*Detectible by metal detection equipment, to be specific. I am doing research . . .*"

His message was interrupted.

"I knew what you meant brother. But know this: to be a legal DIY, the gun needs to be detectible. A minimum of 3.7 oz. of steel gets added to the build for the receiver for this purpose. The Feds forced ghost gunner folks to add that spec before they'd let the build plans back online. No steel, no deal."

Not the answer Aaron was looking for. *"Gets added by who?"*

"By me, your friendly neighborhood ghost gunner."

A showstopper. Damn.

Aaron's turn to slow the chat down. He needed time to think. His mouth moistened, his eyes suddenly hurt, were strained, like they'd get while driving through a snowstorm at night. The keyboard, was it white or gray? White before, gray now? What to do—?

His chat room partner blinked first.

"It can be machined so the metal can be temporarily removed, btw, and will still work without it."

An opening. Aaron stayed silent, would let him talk. One minute, two, then . . .

"I won't ask what you're trying to do or why. You got your reasons, I got mine. But there's another solution. The MP599 WonderSix revolver. Brand new all-plastic build. Guy who designed it is a genius. Look it up online and get back to me in 30 min."

It wasn't even a darknet search. Aaron found it with a simple query in the Google search bar.

"The World's first 3D printed revolver. All plastic, including the revolving cylinder. Double-action. Six trigger pulls, six .22 shots. 100 percent 3D printed except for the firing pin, which is a common finishing nail, and elastic bands in place of springs." Further info, again by way of new federal regs: *"Each build needs to include steel in the grip or there can be no deal. That makes the Ghost Gunner specs for this firearm legally downloadable."*

The knock about 3D plastic guns was the gunpowder explosion. It could destroy the layered, formed plastic, and possibly kill the shooter while delivering or attempting to deliver its single bullet. The WonderSix solution was to build the revolving resin cylinder in an upright position while the frame was built in a flat position, to distribute the pressure of the gunpowder ignition more evenly across the cylinder bore. Maybe a bit technical, but Aaron accepted the concept, as long as the engineering worked.

The steel rods went inside the gun grip. But one thing was obvious: The unit could be used without them. In its finished status, the firearm looked no more frightening than a Nerf gun.

This was the answer. No eighty percent receiver diversion, no other gun parts. He'd need none of what he'd ordered online. All he needed was this plastic gun and a box of .22 cartridges.

He got back online with his darknet chat buddy, who'd identified himself as *Doodlemy9erdandy*. He answered Aaron's most pressing question before he could ask it.

"Yes, I can build it. I already have."

Aaron had only one additional chat request. *"Build one for me."*

"Sure. As long as you promise to keep the steel rods in it so we both stay out of jail. And you give me $500 cash."

***

Aaron was on a Lackawanna Transit System bus, on his way to nearby Rancor, Pennsylvania, north of Scranton, a one-hour, forty-five-minute trip. There was some bounce to the ride and a severe lean going through each of the curves, the bus needing new shocks, the buckled patches of road needing new blacktop. In his backpack on the seat next to him were all his purchased gun parts and their accessory kits plus four hundred bucks in cash. *Doodlemy9erdandy* would accept as barter all the gun parts Aaron no longer needed plus two hundred in cash as a down payment, then expect another two hundred on delivery.

The bus dropped him at Rancor Corners, the last stop on the route, across from a bank with a breathtaking view behind it: steep drop, a valley a few miles wide, and a mountain ridge on the other side. He found a park bench, sat, and admired the panorama, his cheap, cluttered backpack next to him.

A white male approached, short, with chubby cheeks and sunglasses, plus a snapback Yankees ball cap on backward above a frayed University of

Scranton varsity baseball jacket. Aaron's alma mater, as a coincidence. The guy dropped heavily into the middle of the bench, close enough for a conversation.

"Hey. When's the next bus to Scranton?" he asked.

"Three-forty," Aaron said.

"Thanks." The Yankees fan picked up Aaron's heavy backpack with the deposit in it and swung it onto his back then stood to leave. Not a sophisticated exchange, but it was the one they were each looking for. Until the unscripted part:

"You white?" *Doodlemy9erdandy* said, serious as hell.

"My ethnicity? Uh, yeah, sure."

"You look dark for a white guy."

"Blame it on my Greek parents. Second-generation Greek American."

"That'll work. Greek probably means Catholic, too, right, or at least Christian?"

"Yes."

"Great. See you back here in a bit."

Aaron left the bench after *Doodle* did and walked to a bookshop to wait out the bus schedule, the departure time three hours from now.

He'd transcended having trust issues. Aaron would trust anyone once, and communicating with this guy online anonymously, and now in person semi-anonymously, had produced only one red flag, today's ethnicity question. Most importantly, there'd been no gray flashes for Aaron online, and none when they met. But if this darknet contact stiffed him—if he took his money and didn't deliver—someway, somehow, Aaron would find him, and he would use that indiscretion as a teaching moment that *Doodlemy9erdandy* wouldn't soon forget.

Coffee, books, anything to occupy his time at the bookshop. Aaron sipped and browsed the store's stacks, his mind hyperactive, unable to concentrate, a continuous loop of metaphors—

. . . the ghost gunner machine that was about to birth Aaron's baby, a plastic revolver, casting and assembling it from mated parts . . .

. . . creating a *real boy* . . .

. . . firearms made from plastics and resins, sexless raw materials of uncommitted purpose transformed into a new resolve, into oozing, newfound sex appeal . . .

. . . as an alternative, a rebuttal, a solution if he were unable to find someone to help him finish the process, the transition, to finish transforming himself . . .

. . . into a *real* boy . . .

. . . and not because his father had wanted a son, no, for sure it was never that . . .

. . . it was because this was who Aaron really was inside.

Aaron returned to the park bench halfway through the third hour. *Doodlemy9erdandy* arrived with Aaron's backpack.

"You'll need to assemble it," he said while Aaron peered inside the bag. "Directions included. I tested it myself already. Enjoy."

They shook hands, and *Doodlemy9erdandy* headed off with the other half of the fee, his hands in his pockets, returning the way he'd come. The Route 84 Lackawanna Transit bus appeared near the bottom of the hill. Aaron slung his backpack, now nearly weightless, over his shoulder. The bus arrived at the curb.

Doodlemy9erdandy turned and retraced a few of this steps. He delivered parting words while Aaron waited for the bus doors to open.

"Good luck. Don't end up in the news, my friend."

ELEVEN

October 1
Northbound Lanes of the Northeast Extension, Pennsylvania Turnpike

Days before the final US Presidential debate: 15

Andy said he wanted to drive. Counsel knew why: the highway traffic would keep his mind busy. An antidote for too much self-introspection.

Andy stayed deep inside himself while Counsel stroked Tess's short fur, her deputy's skin stretched tightly over Tess's muscular bull terrier body.

Enough self-pity, lover.

"You want a piece of this, Andy?" she said, her hand lifting Tess's boxy face up close to hers. "Good therapy. Better than popping bubble wrap."

"Thanks. No."

Two hundred plus pounds of pent-up, brooding tension occupied the driver's seat, not quite focused only on whatever the next mile of highway had in store, and the mile after that, and the mile after that. Counsel rubbed Tess's shoulder, was busy watching the scenery change from urban to suburban to small town to countryside, eventually turning into major hills and finally the old, round-shouldered Pocono Mountains. She lobbed a comment Andy's way, looking for a way in.

"Dominic is doing better," Counsel said, checking some texts. Her Mummer string band friend who had survived the flamethrower attack in Philly was out of the woods. "The skin grafts on his face and arms are taking."

"Good to hear," Andy said. It was a sincere comment, Counsel knew, but delivered with little enthusiasm.

"So the way I see it," she said, moving to a different topic, "Vonetta gets a law enforcement type to run down that gun with its partial serial. Then maybe we learn more about that internet troll who bothered your neighbor's kid."

It wouldn't work that way, Counsel knew, but that was why she put it out there, to get him to respond, to rebut her, to open up.

Seconds passed, Andy still one with the road. Seconds more. A full minute. A turnpike exit. Another turnpike exit.

Finally, "My daughter Teddy will find out first," Andy said, a matter-of-fact comment delivered matter-of-factly. "I know it, and you know it. That's the way the Feds work. The way Special Agents in Charge work. They'll know first, before the local cops or state police, or any town watch, or any bail bonds people who might rely on their databases. What I texted her will now be all over their systems. The Feds will look at those ridiculous pictures on the deep web, will look at him, and will decide if there's a there there. Then maybe she'll call me."

A riff chimed in on cue, a call coming in on Andy's phone, sitting in the cup holder. Tess raised her head and looked over as if to say *you gonna get that or what?*

"Leave it," Andy said.

The phone stopped ringing. No chirp followed, meaning no message.

Counsel's phone rang. She looked at the caller's name then hit the speaker button.

"'Sup, Dody?"

"Andy didn't pick up. Where are you?"

"A half hour from Scranton."

"Let me give you a rundown on our guest," Dody said.

Sebastian Leone was being a model hostage. After a continental breakfast from a coffee shop eaten in front of a TV each morning, he worked on a canvas until a late Grubhub lunch, painted some more, ate a Grubhub dinner, then had a nice early evening stroll accompanied by a town watch person. He then watched more TV, showered, and went to bed.

"His studio is a complete mess," Dody said. "I can't tell what is good art and what isn't, but who am I? I think we're in a good place with him, Counsel. Dedicated. He seems on top of his game."

"How about your call with, you know, our heavy? Still on target?"

Mercer Crawford. A major event. "Yes. Today. Can't wait. Looking forward to it."

"Good. Gimme a sec, Dody. Something hit the radar today I want you to know about." She took the phone off speaker and looked Andy's way. "You want to tell her about that darknet exchange with the teenager, or should I? We need to let her know."

Andy's expression changed slightly, a few blinks compromising his steely stare, but his eyes stayed on the road. "You do it. I just . . . I just can't right now."

On speaker again. "Here's the deal, Dody."

A gun on the darknet. A loudmouthed pervert boasting stolen firepower for protection. Maybe "AEF royalty," maybe not. Compromising pics sent to a teenager in Scranton. The wrong teenager, because she'd ratted him out.

"The FBI now knows, as do Vonetta and her cop connections. They're all running down the info on the gun."

"Why the hell did he contact someone near us?"

"Because he said he'd be there in a few weeks. He's looking for a hook up."

"Huh." A few seconds of dead air, with Dody eventually sniffing out the largest kernel buried in the newsflash. "So Andy's daughter Teddy knows now, too."

"Correct," Counsel said. "Andy sent the exchange to her."

Another pensive pause by Dody, followed by still another *huh*.

"Nothing else to add, Dody. Good luck on that call today. Enjoy yourself."

"Will do."

Teddy Escobar. Andy's, and Rancor, Pennsylvania's, prodigal daughter, but in reverse. Righteous, conservative, and by the book. Attributes that Rancor's town watch had not embraced as of late. A source of discomfort for father and daughter, and the source of their estrangement. Maybe estrangement was the only way a dedicated FBI agent from their town could function, given the town's brushes with vigilantism.

Andy's phone chirped with a text. Counsel looked Andy's way for permission to pick up his phone. He nodded.

Counsel read the text from one Special Agent in Charge Theodora Escobar.

"'Thank you for the info,' she says. 'I can't—won't—validate anything you send across,' she says. 'FBI protocol.'"

Which begot no comment from Andy.

"She signed it 'Love, Teddy.'"

Andy swallowed hard but maintained his composure. Counsel knew the signoff hit him in the pit of his stomach, but in a good way.

"You know what her answer means, don't you, you big dummy?" Counsel beamed at her badass smart self, able to read between the lines, employing air-quotes. "She 'won't validate' what you sent her. She just let you in on some inside info. *'Won't validate'* means this guy is on their radar. This is good stuff, Andy. If he's connected to the AEF—"

"It means if he's in trouble, the AEF could be in trouble, too. I get it."

Counsel commenced talking baby talk to Tess, rubbing both her ears, eliciting some bull terrier smooches on Counsel's cheek. Another text came through. She read it aloud.

"She says 'Stay out of our lane, Dad.'"

Validation of their validation. Which produced more cooing from Counsel, which led to more Tess kisses. "Yes, Tess sweetie, we'll stay out of their lane. Hopefully they know nothing about what's going on in *our* lane ..."

Coming up, the last exit to the turnpike, Clarks Summit, their destination. Counsel's phone rang. Dody again.

"What now?" Counsel said.

Counsel held the phone back from her ear because Dody was breathing so hard. She put Dody on speaker.

". . . A huge explosion in Bethlehem, like a sonic boom! In an office building. People scattering everywhere. Multiple victims. They're evacuating everyone—"

"Where? Where, Dody?"

"The National Atheists Organization, the news is reporting. You google them, you'll get the address. One whole floor of the building, gone."

Counsel did a search, found the breaking story online. The midrise in downtown Bethlehem sounded familiar, looked familiar, the video footage showing no activity at first, for three seconds, five seconds, then boom-boom-*boom*, the windows on one floor blew outward on two sides, debris raining everywhere.

Andy eased the van into the turnpike exit. Counsel's phone rang again.

"It's Vonetta," Counsel said, reading the name.

Damn it. *That* was the reason the building looked so familiar. Counsel put the call on speaker.

"You see what someone did to my husband's building!" a panicked Vonetta shouted. "You seeing this, Counsel? A bomb took out a complete floor! I can't reach him on the phone—"

Vonetta hung up. Counsel tried a return call but didn't get through.

"Andy, get back on the turnpike. We're going to Bethlehem."

***

Separation of church and state, a mainstay of the National Atheists Organization. Vocal proponents of secularization. Liberals making inroads, driving religion from the schools, from athletics, the workplace, the community. Taking the Christ out of Christmas. Such blasphemy, the argument went.

But there was more. On the other end of the same floor, a local Gunowners Against the Slaughter office. So, which of these liberal organizations was the real target, which was the collateral damage? And someone had streamed video of the explosions from across the street as they were happening. The implication of the post was chilling.

"You can stand down, Counsel," a weary Vonetta said on FaceTime fifteen minutes after her first call, her teary face onscreen. Andy and Counsel were on the Pennsylvania Turnpike, still heading in her direction, south, toward Bethlehem.

"He called? Irv called?"

"Yes," Vonetta said, wiping her teary face. "My husband is fine, there's no need for you to come. But the people in the suites above Irv's brokerage firm—"

Vonetta's eyes filled again, and this time she let it happen, let the faucets drip, even big girls were gonna cry when the road got this rough. "They're all either dead or wounded, Counsel honey. All thirty-two of them. The atheist organization and the GAS people. The floor above his is gutted. A bloodbath, Irv said. He heard multiple explosions, then the screams. My God."

Counsel teared up, launching into an empathetic cry. "The bomber, Vonetta. Anything on the bomber? Alive? Dead? Any trail?"

"A statement inside an empty pizza box, left outside the lobby of Irv's company one floor down. Handwritten. I'll read it to you.

"*'Atheism is an affront to the Lord God Almighty and must be wiped off the face of the earth. Gun control is anti-American. This was a twofer. I'm sending all your heathen neighbors to hell and my guns had nothing to do with it, except for my own deliverance to God.'*"

"What the hell. A slaughter, Counsel. He stood across from the building, streamed the explosions, then ate his handgun on the street corner."

Senseless violence. Another domestic terrorist act, like the schools, the nightclubs, the theaters, the churches, the military bases. This one, like the Mummers nightmarish executions in Philly, was accomplished without guns.

"I needed to see your face, Counsel sweetie. I just need to know that what we're doing is gonna make a difference. Maybe stop some of these bastards."

"It will, Vonetta, I promise. I love you, honey."

"Love you too, Counsel dear. I gotta go. Irv's not taking this well. Ciao."

Andy reached across the console, squeezed Counsel's shoulder, her weeping face in her hands.

TWELVE

October 2
Linus Pappas's townhouse condo, Scranton

Days before the final US Presidential debate: 14

A few taps at the basement bedroom door, sharp, knuckles-on-wood taps to rouse him. Aaron kept the door locked. "Food's here, Dad," Linus said, projecting his voice.

"Be up in a minute."

Linus had a key to the basement living space, but as far as Aaron knew, his son was respecting his privacy. Linus also respected that a person who had spent a long time in prison solitary might have a few quirks, including paranoia about wanting his space secured, even from his son. Aaron had one more thing to do before he went upstairs. Something he'd been avoiding.

He upended his backpack. A small carton of .22 ammunition spilled out. The rest of the bag's contents, the main event, were caught in a fold and didn't cooperate. He felt around inside, his fingers shaky. Maybe what he was after didn't want to be handled as much as he didn't want to handle it. He worked it free.

The MP599 WonderSix knockoff. Fat, black, revolving cylinder, squared gray frame, red trigger piece, black grip. Freakish. A cross between a graphic artist's futuristic-concept firearm and a toy store novelty. This was his first close look at the ghost handgun fully assembled, his stomach rewarding him with somersaults. He removed the resin bullet cylinder from the frame, placed it on the quilted bedspread, and laid the frame next to it on the autumn-colored patchwork.

He straightened up and would admire for a moment the simplicity of these creations, designed, and machined, in a garage or a basement. When reassembled, they would again be a handgun.

So unlike the only other handgun he'd ever handled, a commercially acquired 9mm. Thirty years ago. No matter, this one would still be capable of killing someone. He forced his breathing to stay even. No time for a flare up, not now. Linus would not need any more reminders about Aaron's PTSD.

Too damn bad, Karis, his PTSD said.

This was the gray, again talking to him, or rather talking to pre-Aaron. Unsettling business; three decades of it. It made his legs weak, collapsing them and him where he stood, him crossing them on his way down to the floor, where he sat now, almost catatonic.

So much pain that night in the family restaurant, so much deception. So much fear and hurt. So much gore.

***

. . . Muffled gunshots in the Greek restaurant's kitchen. The swinging doors slapped open, Aaron's father stumbling through them, him with his aggrieved face entering the restaurant's dining room. No customers tonight like many nights, his father weaved toward their table, approaching Aaron and other family members all seated together.

He raised the gun.

Pop, pop. Pop-pop-pop . . .

Shots fired into their protesting faces, blasting through their upraised hands and arms.

Seated were Aaron's mother plus his older sister, a party girl fresh out of rehab, his girl cousin. Barely twenty, big breasts, low self-esteem, the cousin was available to his father, they all knew, and his father hated her for it.

After the shots, after the *pop-pop-pop*, they were gone.

But not Aaron, who now stared down the barrel of the gun.

Aaron—not only gay, "worse than gay" according to his father, was *transitioning*, and this made him a freak. This visit home, Aaron was standing his ground in his gender-identity fight. He'd shared the news, something they seemed to understand and accepted.

His father? Never.

A gun trigger squeeze, but no bullet entered Aaron's head, because no shot was fired. The gun had jammed.

Aaron flipped the table and sprinted toward the kitchen. His father tackled him, hurtling them both through the swinging doors, the gun skittering ahead.

"I need to do this *now,* Karis!" he'd grunted, wrestling Aaron to the floor. "Before the cancer takes me. I need to cleanse my family of its . . . abominations! Its hypocrisy! A good Greek word, hypocrisy, a very good Greek word—"

Cancer. Liver, stomach, lymph nodes. Untreated per his father's wishes, it had spread to his brain.

His father's punch to Aaron's jaw snapped his head back against the tile. For Aaron, the lights went out.

Conscious again, his jaw throbbing, Aaron was seated on the floor underneath the butcher-block table, his head slumped, his arms around one of the table's colossal legs, his wrists drawn tight together with duct tape. Above him—

Whap, whap, whap. A meat cleaver, severing something.

Lingering kitchen aromas, garlic, wine, cooked veal, salmon . . . human blood . . .

Around him, his slow-witted uncle's body was slumped over a pot-scrubbing sink from a kill shot, the head wound draining into the greasy water. Aaron's cougar aunt, the slow uncle's wife, was dead on the floor of the vegetable pantry. Crumpled in the far corner was the fry cook Jeremy, a work release from prison, not family, the cougar aunt's young lover, with a headshot to the right temple, gray matter and blood dripping through the hairnet that contained his blond curls.

Aaron groaned, then vomited.

"Karis! Welcome back," his father said.

Whap! Another cleaver strike, pounding the table.

"God has seen fit . . . to spare you for the moment. You will now witness . . . how a God-fearing man . . . purges his own temple . . . of its sinners."

Whap!

Aaron couldn't see, but he couldn't not hear, nor could he not smell, the dismembering in progress, trying to work his hands free, the rock-hard, massive, vintage butcher block un-budging, him hearing all the blows, but seeing only the sloppy, depraved aftermath as pieces of bodies hit the floor. Above him, his father cleaved his victims, pounding, slicing them into manageable pieces, his disease-defying strength fueled by anger, him bellowing his disgust as the pile of body parts grew taller on the floor at the table's near end. Blood, urine, and feces dripped off the table, some of it streaming onto Aaron's face and shoulders as he hugged a table leg. He gagged and vomited again from the steamy effluence.

His father's supreme disappointment: All nine months his mother had carried him, Aaron must not, could not be a daughter. He would be, his father insisted, his son. The answer to the family's prayers. Their savior. It had to be that way, or the family surname would not survive.

Nature had other plans. His father's upset with Aaron's biology, and with the rest of his dysfunctional family, began the day Aaron was born. Karis Ophelia Pappas, a miracle baby, birthed by a mother deemed too old to conceive. Not the Alexander Nicholas Pappas his father had tried to will into being. The end of the line for the proud Pappas family name.

Whirr, whirr, hum-a-chink, hum-a-chink . . .

The commercial garbage disposal chugged. One victim, one mound of pulpy flesh and bones, multiple trips to the industrial-sized sink, the disposal at bottom, Aaron's ears ringing. Next victim, next pile, more *hum-a-chink, hum-a-chink.* Solid and liquid waste spewed geyser-like, violent and intermittent, above the sink's rim, a rebuttal to the wide, white stream of spigot water feeding it. No clogging, not once, during the two-plus hours since the restaurant had closed. Femurs, knees, pulverized hips, and heads, everything cleaved to fit. The restaurant's five-horsepower commercial garbage disposal was hard at work, pressed into handling the family's impromptu funeral arrangements.

On the chopping block, by process of elimination, was Aaron's mother.

His sick father had to tire soon.

Tha-thump. His mother's head thudded onto the floor, her dark eyes vacant, her face frozen in a deathly grimace. His father leaned down, meat cleaver in hand, to retrieve it. Aaron whimpered softly then cried anew, his father answering her sobbing with sobbing of his own. The blows grew weaker, his father's arms weary, his breathing more labored, his stamina almost gone.

The bloody cleaver slipped from his father's hand, pirouetted past Aaron on its way to the floor, bounced, and came to rest near him.

It had to be now.

Aaron jammed his shoulders into the table's underside. Straining, grunting like a power weightlifter, he raised his body, his calves and thighs burning under the table's weight. The monstrous table jerked up and held just long enough. He slipped his duct-taped wrists under the raised leg. In a fluid motion he grabbed the cleaver and lifted it overhead in both hands. He brought it down on his father's foot, slicing clean through the shoe leather, chipping the floor tile. He kicked the severed end of the shoe into the bloody slop-pile of human body parts that was once his mother. His father dropped to one knee in shock and agony, his toes separated from his foot.

"Karis, you are strong, like I used to be . . ."

Aaron pounced on his father's genuflection, raining blow after two-handed blow of adrenaline-fueled fury—"*Aaron . . . I am Aaron!*"—the gleaming cleaver hacking away decades of emotional pain and suffering in one violent, sickening act loosely born of self-preservation, until Aaron's fight reflex finally subsided.

His jeans were soaked with body fluids, some his own. He blinked through red-tinged sweat trickling from his scalp and forehead. The sink disposal hummed beneath the swirling faucet water then spit out another unidentified body part. It hit the suspended ceiling and stuck, puckered against its semi-smooth white surface. A viscous smear held it there until it lost suction, peeled away, and dropped to the counter. The red mark on the ceiling mimicked a child's rubber stamp version of what it was, a human ear.

"You m-monster," Aaron stammered.

He raised himself to a cautious crouch then backed into a darkened pantry on shaky legs, the swinging doors closing after he passed through them. He rose to his full height, his large body a concession to his father's dominant genes. The meat cleaver went to a shelf. Outside the pantry, and visible through the door slats, his father's body lay still, surrounded by his dismembered mother. Also in the queue for the chopping block was Jeremy, the expired young fry cook, dead but still in one piece.

The wall phone in the pantry, where was it? It used to be in here, he'd made calls on it as a teenager—he needed to dial 9-1-1—

Phone jack, but no phone. More panic, then . . . calm, coming from his deep breaths.

He reemerged from the pantry, the duct tape severed, his sore wrists free, and the cleaver again in his hand. How long had he been in there . . .?

Long enough for his hacked father to stop his groaning, mumbling, and crying, and eventually his breathing.

Long enough for Aaron to arrive at a decision.

The 9-1-1 call would wait.

The commercial disposal purred, the faucet still running. He stepped through the bloodbath that surrounded the butcher-block table.

He had the balls to do this. Not physically, but mentally. Emotionally, he'd always had them. His reason for the trip home: to let the family see his transition, the transman that he was becoming. And to tell them the good news, that his lover, partner, soulmate, was pregnant. With a boy! And while Aaron's father's blood would not live on in his grandson, the Pappas family name would. Not for placation or parental approval on Aaron's part. Far from it. In his mind, it was a byproduct of his identity as a male.

His decision: He needed to fix this. Tonight's bloodbath would create a stigma, a pox on their newly preserved family surname.

The jammed handgun. He found the release for the clip and released it. A bullet with a loose shell casing dropped out with it, the reason for the jam. He reinserted the clip.

He crouched over the dead fry cook. He would now take his chance.

Aaron's unborn son, the world, need not know about the horror perpetrated by Aaron's sick father. He lifted the cook's hand, pried open his fingers. Now work-release Jeremy's prints were on the gun along with Aaron's and his father's.

"Yes, I was lucky," Aaron would tell the police. *"It jammed when Jeremy pointed it at me. He made me watch from under the butcher block while he dismembered my family. When he dropped the cleaver, I used it on his foot, but that didn't stop him. The jammed gun . . . I pointed it, pulled the trigger. Still nothing. Jeremy laughed. I released the bullet clip. An unexpelled shell casing came out with it. I reinserted the clip, overpowered him, and shoved the barrel against his temple. This time it didn't jam."*

He stood over Jeremy's body, tucked the cleaver into his lifeless palm, squeezed and released his fingers around it, up the handle and down, four, maybe five times.

"Troubled boy, troubled past. I don't know why he snapped."

A hacked foot had saved Aaron from his father; another hacked foot would validate his story. He raised the cleaver over the fry cook's body.

Chop.

He left the fry cook's half-foot where it came to rest, on the floor tile. Aaron found the front half of his father's shoe, the hacked toes still inside. He stuffed it all into the noisy garbage disposal.

***

"Dad?" Tap-tap-tap at the door again. "The takeout's getting cold, Dad. Dad?"

Deep breath. Aaron cleared his head, cleared his throat. "Coming."

He reinserted the plastic revolver cylinder into the frame then returned the ghost gun and the box of ammo to his backpack. He stuffed his backpack under the bed. Resettling the edges of the bedclothes, he left nothing underneath exposed. Time for dinner upstairs.

"Sorry," Linus said, chewing, "but I'm about to go all legal on you. As your lawyer, and your son, you need to own your past, Dad. I'm sure your shrink says the same thing."

"Own what? My past?"

"I heard your episode while I waited up here. That's why I didn't come down after you."

Aaron chewed his eggroll, kept his eyes on his plate, rearranged his pork-fried rice with his fork, and did not comment.

"Self-defense, Dad, okay?" Linus said, a plea for a reaction. "You killed your father, sure, but poor legal counsel, and a system too willing to prosecute LGBTQ minorities . . . self-defense should have been your plea to begin with. What's important is, the crime you did commit—framing the dead fry cook for what your father did—after all these years, that debt's been paid."

Not by all the responsible parties, Aaron opined internally. One person remained unaffected and was thriving as a politician.

"So say you," Aaron said.

"So said the court, and that's all that matters."

A death penalty case, but the convictions were overturned based on re-review of the coroner and forensics reports. His father's gunshot to the fry cook's temple had produced the most blood, which pooled under the head and body. Aaron's hack of the fry cook's foot produced a lot less blood because it was post-mortem, and whatever blood was left in the foot had collected in the lowest part of the supine victim, his heel. If the order had been reversed, cleaving the cook's foot before the gunshot to his head would have produced a lot more blood.

It became a mass murder conviction instead of what should have been a justifiable homicide. An LGBTQ defendant with horrific, monstrous, courtroom images. It all translated to multiple life sentences. Revisiting the forensics had been Linus's petition to the court, and that had produced the miracle of his father's release.

"Like I said before, Dad, that's how I got you out."

A subtle distinction. His father had killed everyone else in the restaurant, and would have killed Aaron, too. But staging it the way Aaron did, and the story he'd stayed with for the trial—after all, what would a family be without its good name?—the DA had pounced. It cost Aaron thirty-plus years of his life and a chunk of his sanity.

A bite of General Tso's. Chew, swallow, a drink of water. Aaron put down his fork and composed himself. "Enough, Linus. Consider it 'owned.' Someone made sure I owned it. All of it."

That someone, a DA turned Pennsylvania senator, was now running for president, and Aaron's son, in a large irony, was a player in the man's campaign.

But why the full court press *now* to get him exonerated and released three-plus decades later?

"At some point, Dad, the senator would like to meet with you. To apologize to you personally. Maybe in a few weeks, or maybe the night of the debate. Maybe even invite you to the debate itself. How does that sound?"

A show of benevolence by a presidential candidate. A righting of a wrong. An admission that no one was perfect.

The press had jumped on the overturned conviction, turning it into a public relations coup for the senator. He became a hero for admitting he was human, and for having helped free a man who he'd wrongly incarcerated.

For Aaron, this was one of those moments where a person couldn't help but take a breath and let it just hang there, pondering the implications. Such good, opportunistic luck—luck he was owed—was now staring him in the face.

"I don't know," Aaron said, going for coy. On the outside, his was a poker face, but inside, Linus's offer made his stomach flutter in excitement. He took a bite of his eggroll. "If I'm invited, maybe."

"Super," Linus said, cracking a smile. "Seriously, Dad, super. I'll get on that."

Aaron worried about Linus. About his involvement in the presidential campaign. But it had reinforced Aaron's intention—would make it easier—for him to scratch this incredibly dark itch. This good fortune would be timely.

The gray, the deathly gray, reared itself, messing with his head again. The forces of nature—

Sometimes they presented rare opportunities. This, the gray said, was one such time.

THIRTEEN

October 2
AEF Headquarters, Bethesda, Maryland

Days before the final US Presidential debate: 14

Mercer switched off the TV. "This is a shitshow. Close the door, Dagmar."

A warm day, late in the afternoon. They were in Mercer's wood-paneled office, the kind that might boast a many-pointed elk head or wild boar or a lion or maybe all three competing for wall space, and maybe the guns that took them down mounted there, too, across from large, tufted, leather side-chair seating to admire the kills. The leather side chairs were here, but taxidermied clichés weren't Mercer's style.

With the door closed, the summoned Dagmar spoke. "You'll need to get in front of this, Mercer. You should issue a statement."

"Since when did you get so comfortable giving me orders? I'm not issuing a statement yet. We'll see what the media says about it, and the White House. We'll see if President Lindsay stays measured about it."

Yesterday produced the gun lobby's newest nightmare. After destroying one full floor in an office building, a self-anointed mouthpiece for religious and Second Amendment rights neutralized himself in Bethlehem, Pennsylvania, with his handgun. Twenty-nine dead, four injured and fighting for their lives. The bomber was Caucasian, in his thirties or forties. His three remote-controlled IEDs had two targets, the most widely recognized atheist organization on the planet, and the local Gunowners Against the Slaughter, or GAS, office, the victims all adults. The building was an hour and a half southwest of Scranton, too close to the scheduled presidential debate per the media, location-wise and timewise. This carnage would now monopolize the debate's discourse, depending on what was learned about the perpetrator.

"This final presidential debate must not be about gun control or domestic terrorism," Mercer groused, clenching his teeth but resisting a fist-pound. "Goddamn it, this guy needs to have been crazy."

"Because crazy terrorists sell more guns," Dagmar said.

"You bet your ass they do. I need a few different statements prepared, Dagmar. They should address as many scenarios as possible. The entire spectrum regarding what we might learn about him, everything from a law-abiding citizen who snapped because he was tired of assaults on the separation of church and state by liberals, to another mental patient with a stockpile of illegal weapons."

"I'll pull statements from the files," she said. "Dust them off, paraphrase them. But we can't very well go with anything that mentions prayers for people who were atheists, now can we?"

"That isn't funny. I don't care, just figure it out."

"'Our thoughts are with the victims and their families' still works. I'll get it done before I leave for the airport. Not like we haven't been here before."

"Damn straight. The price of freedom. God bless the Second Amendment," he said with feeling.

"Yes," she said, then cocked her head, "but too bad these frequent tragedies make us have to trot out that reminder so often, right? Aren't you late for your call with someone from that art museum?"

"Have Renner in my office in half an hour. I'll be done with the museum people by then."

Dagmar reached the door before turning back to face him. "Mercer, you need to be careful. If you put something in place that starts turning away new members, the Board won't like it."

His headshake was slow, chiding, a narrow-eyed response to her comment. "No legitimate Second Amendment sympathizer will ever be turned away, Dagmar. I guarantee you the Board will agree with me one hundred percent."

Legitimate. An important distinction.

His plan: Take a page from recent changes to voter registration practices on the political scene, the ones moving toward stricter eligibility. Soon it would be if a person wanted to become an AEF member, his or her US residency papers would need to be in perfect order; better order than those of previous applicants. If these practices were okay to tighten up the voter rolls in an election, they'd be okay to tighten up the AEF application process.

With Dagmar gone, Mercer went looking in his desk for a certain mobile phone, one that wasn't his, or at least it wasn't his until he'd decided he wanted to pursue the Wyeth painting about a month and a half ago, even though the painting wasn't for sale. It was a prepaid burner from a large retail store; a phone that would remain in his possession only until the painting deal was consummated. He found it, brought it to his ear while the call was going through.

"This is Two-A-Sammy-forty-four," he said to the hello on the other end. "Who's this?"

"Saloon-ten," the woman said.

The correct response, hailing from Wild Bill Hickok Deadwood, South Dakota lore, but it was from a voice he didn't recognize. "You are on a secure line, Saloon-ten?" Mercer asked.

"It doesn't work like that. You use a disposable phone and I use a disposable phone. The security's in the anonymity."

"Fine. Still, no names. A few things to discuss. First, I trust our contacts are doing well arranging things?"

"Date of delivery is confirmed per the original agreement. You still good with that?"

October 16, the night of the final presidential debate. "Yes," he said.

"Good. The location will be in the college's music hall parking garage. Easy access and departure. Give me a time."

"In a minute. Tell me about the supply end," which meant the painting's point of origin, the Brandywine Museum of Art.

"The deal is," she said, "they scheduled an after-hours photo session for an upcoming promotion for the night before the event. It happens then."

Mercer made a mental note of the date. Overnight on Saturday night, October 15.

Saloon-ten continued. "The piece will be moved from its display so it can be photographed. A common practice, so no red flags for anyone. It will return for public viewing a few days later."

This was when the swap would be made. The "it" part of "it will return" would be a forgery, returning the painting to the display case. The original would be prepared for transport north, to the University of Scranton, to complete the deal.

Mercer's mouth got moist, salivating at the prospect of owning this magnificent piece of commemorative American art and history, ignoring what had to be done for him to get it.

"Someone on my team needs to witness the photo shoot," Mercer said.

"Suit yourself. But this person gets only limited access to it. Aside from validating it, we don't need anyone else pawing at it. No firearms, either. And have him bring one camera phone only, no other recording devices. If he shows up with anything threatening, the show is over, understand?"

"I want the same restrictions for your people," Mercer said.

"Nope," Saloon-ten said. "My people will be armed. Home team advantage. Not negotiable. Do I make myself clear?"

"Fine," Mercer said, finishing with "bitch" in his head. "How good is this 'photographer'?"

"Many, many, many displays like this. Shows with big audiences and close scrutiny. A master at this, or it wouldn't work."

"He better be."

"No one said it's a man," she said. The following silence qualified this as a feminist statement, with her offering no other info.

He got the message: She was a tough bitch who would not be bullied. His mental profile had her in her fifties or sixties. Someone used to calling the shots.

"What about transport?" Mercer said.

"It'll be packed well enough. We'll provide the transport casing for it. Something standard for an art piece. Check the internet to get an idea of what to expect."

The dimensions of the oil on canvas painting were thirty-two by forty inches. A large, flat, cardboard art portfolio transport case would work fine. Regarding the trip north, Mercer had a specific requirement. "My guy needs to be with it all the way to the delivery point."

"If he has no hardware, then no problem, he can make the trip with it. But like I said, our photographers will be armed. And the prize stays in the vehicle until just before we consummate the deal. When do you want to make this happen? I need a time."

The presidential debate would begin at eight, was expected to run until ten, ten-thirty maybe, with a few bio breaks for the debaters, plus TV intermissions.

"During one of the TV commercials."

"That works. You planning to take delivery yourself?"

Mercer knew his answer, but he paused a moment. He trusted only a few people nowadays. Not Dagmar, not Renner, not his other bodyguards. Only a few of his AEF associates, plus Bosco Horvath, his Philly art critic buddy who'd validated the painting's authenticity.

Mercer had heard the metaphoric footsteps. The hints that he would be told to step down as CEO, his replacement rumored to be a specific high-profile US military type with leanings even more severely conservative than his own. Mercer loved this job, loved guiding this organization through these troubled times, and he believed he was helping citizens protect themselves against the lawless hordes and the liberals, domestic and international. He'd continue to do so by any means possible, above the radar and below. This was what drove him. Plus the money and the rock star status he enjoyed from being America's premier Second Amendment protector.

Least of all, he trusted none of these art thieves and darknet pretenders.

"Yes, I'll take delivery in person."

"Super. Something else, just to make sure we're both on the same page. Inside, or around the music building, there can be no weapons of any kind either, on any of the participants, your team or mine. This event, the presidential debate, will be so extremely visible, and its access is so restricted, if someone misbehaves, we'll close this deal up tighter'n a second coat of paint. Let's not screw this up, Sammy-forty-four, or we all lose."

No accounting for what else Mercer had planned for the evening, which was another deal to be consummated locally as well, nearby, with different, even more dangerous players. One where the money—a ton of it—would go in the opposite direction, coming to him, and where guns would be every inch a part of it. All in all, this particular evening would be incredibly productive for him. Good things came in threes: the painting, the gun sales, and hopefully a slam-dunk live TV debate defeat of a sitting US president by an AEF-friendly candidate. Mercer grumbled through his acceptance of her terms.

"Great. We're down to the last detail," Saloon-ten said.

Payment.

"After you examine the product and satisfy yourself it's the real thing—"

"It's been branded," Mercer said, "to make sure there'll be no sleight of hand. If the branding is there, there won't be any drama."

"Yeah, I heard about that little trick of yours. You pissed on the back of it or something."

"Excuse me?"

"Marked your territory, right? Look, whatever else you need to do with it—put some of your own special Sammy-forty-four secret sauce on it so you can find your mark or whatever, I really don't care—after we confirm your collateral's been released, we'll all be good to go. That's all I've got. You good for now?"

They would pass notes to each other via the darknet, arrange a further call if necessary, but right now Mercer wanted to distance himself from this conversation with Saloon-ten, fast turning into someone he'd like to forget he ever talked to.

"Good for now, yes," he said.

"One last thing. Are you a student of the game?"

"I don't follow," Mercer said.

"The way you branded that thing makes me curious. It's like you did your homework. Like you studied past deals of, shall I say, a similar nature."

She meant art thefts. His answer needed to be no. Mercer's art experience was limited to works that dramatized the Old West. He could tell an N. C. Wyeth from a Howard Pyle, but never a Rembrandt from a da Vinci. He'd needed his art expert friend Bosco Horvath at the museum for this very reason, but marking the painting, that was simply common sense. Trust but verify. And no way could he—check that, it had been Dagmar's idea— no way could Dagmar have been the first person in these circles to think of doing such a thing to keep from getting scammed. Still, his answer had to be—

"None of your business, but no, I'm not a student of the 'game,' as you call it. Just a good businessman. Are we done here?"

"You know what," she said, "I believe you." Her voice carried with it an almost perceptible nod of her head on her end. "Yes, we're done."

***

Renner sat stuffed into a leather side chair across from Mercer's desk. He placed his laptop bag across his large thighs, sitting with his shoulders squared while he delivered some news. "The membership stats have changed, sir."

"Percentages are higher," Mercer intuited.

"The percentages you're concerned about, sir, yes, they are higher."

"You sent them to me?"

"Emailed them a few moments ago, sir."

Mercer opened his laptop on his desk. "Okay, let's see what we've got." Renner did likewise with his own laptop, now open on his lap.

Mercer downloaded the files. On the screen were new Pew Study pie charts, line graphs, and bar graphs. Visible on each was the one statistic he was looking for: AEF member figures by ethnicity, based on data that new members had elected to report. Overall membership had increased. That was the good news. The bad news was the non-white percentage of the population was up even more since last quarter. Specifically, the increase in Black and Hispanic members versus the prior period was sharp, the new members not bashful about identifying their ethnicity in subsequent marketing surveys.

"Worse than I thought," Mercer said. "I'll be sharing this with the Board. Next question, different topic. Close my door." Renner did as instructed. "Our friends at Gatling Arms—are they on target to deliver?"

Gatling Arms Limited. Facing bankruptcy, cash poor, with recent manufacturing and quality-control problems, had suddenly become a desperate player in the gun industry. Mercer frequently lobbied for them with the Feds, was paid big bucks to do so, albeit with the same under-the-radar mechanism—the darknet.

"Ms. Bystrom says they can fill the order on time," Renner said, referring to Dagmar. "She wants your confirmation that you have the down payment from the buyers. You should call her or answer her text, sir."

"Is the down payment there?"

Five hundred thousand bucks on deposit from them. "Yessir, I confirmed it this morning."

Mercer retrieved his disposable phone, keyed in Dagmar's number, found her texts to him that detailed products, quantities, prices, and logistics. He called her.

She picked up immediately, no greeting, and went straight to the details for the deal.

"The buyers are good for a ten million dollar order to Gatling. AR-15s, semiauto handguns and ammunition. You want me to place the order, Mercer?"

"Do it."

The order: five thousand Gatling Arms AR-15 semiautomatic rifles, one thousand PM15-22 semiautomatic handguns, similar to the Israeli Uzi, a gun model no longer in production. Ammunition for both. Enough to equip a small army, all with untraceable serial numbers. Plus a tractor-trailer truck to deliver them from the Agawam, Massachusetts, manufacturing plant to the buyer, with all parties expected to converge on Scranton the night of the debate.

Mental note to the Board: If you want to replace me as AEF CEO with someone who made his bones by dealing in black-market guns, surprise, you already have someone like that. Me.

A million and a half in brokerage fees to Mercer. It would cover the Wyeth art purchase plus give him the luxury of looking at more of N. C. Wyeth's western art as it became available. Wyeth was a true American master, chronicling the American experience. Mercer was damn near salivating.

The price of freedom, yes indeed.

Finished with Dagmar on the phone, Mercer dismissed Renner from his office.

"One more thing, sir," Renner said before leaving. "The Bethlehem attack. There's news about the guy. He had a cache of guns in his apartment."

That was quick. Not really a surprise. The Feds did good work, especially when it came to guns and hate crimes. "Well? Legal or illegal?"

"Not an easy question to answer, sir. Some of them had lower receivers made from a plastic of some sort."

"You mean a polymer," Mercer said.

"A low-grade plastic resin, sir. All plastics are polymers, but not all polymers are only plastic. And some polymers are more resilient than carbon steel. Not so here. The receivers came from a three-D printer. Eighty percent lower receivers machined into fully functioning automatic weapons." Renner paused, then: "The shooter built them himself, sir."

Building your own guns was legal. Machining them to be fully automatic was not. New territory. The future.

"We know anything about him yet? Sane? Crazy?" Mercer switched on his TV. "Illegal immigrant?"

"White male, probably American. A God-fearing Christian, based on the statement he left behind. Nothing else released yet, sir."

The Wild, Wild West, now wilder than ever, Mercer thought. Do-it-yourself zealots, some with grudges, many with biases, all instilling fear in households across the US.

And fear sold guns.

Too bad this monster wasn't the right demographic: a minority.

No matter. *Cha-ching.*

FOURTEEN

October 4

The Office of Francine Gamorra, MD, PsyD, Scranton

Days before the final US Presidential debate: 12

Aaron's days as an enigma were, thankfully, numbered. He did the work, lived the life, was taking the medication. He was here with his new psychiatrist at her office to get his head straight and to realign himself with his goal.

The opposing brick walls of her office were painted white, the windowed exterior wall with its tall panes showing an unobstructed view of a low-rise Pocono mountain. Askew of the wall sat the psychiatrist's desk and chair, and askew of the desk, a sofa, these furniture pieces like offsetting baffles in a room-sized pinball game. An environment akin to how askew everything was in Aaron's life.

Upright on the sofa, Aaron faced Doctor Francine Gamorra, a specialist in gender studies, her thick, black, Buddy Holly glasses on the bridge of her nose. Harpo, a full-sized white poodle, sat next to Aaron, his head in Aaron's lap. The doctor's pet, but also a therapy dog. One couldn't *not* pet a dog when its head was on one's lap and feel relieved, Aaron knew.

In prison, there was never a scene like this. Any dog—a mutt with three legs, or deaf, or blind, or even with a bad temper—any dog with him in prison would have helped, would have provided some comfort against the insanity of prison life. But no; no dogs. No human friends either, demented or healthy, for those multiple years in and out of solitary. Only rats, mice, and bugs. And all of them were gray.

Such calm, Aaron felt, with Harpo next to him, helping him deal with all that was anxious about his situation.

"This is why we explore all the angles, Aaron," Dr. Francine said. "To make sure."

"I've had over thirty years of making sure," Aaron said.

Dr. Francine, the gatekeeper. Aaron was aware of her role. She was one of the mental health professionals a person with Aaron's intentions needed to visit, to double-check his priorities, to keep him from making a grievous mistake, one from which there was no recovery. Aaron was an in-between. In-betweens were in limbo. After a few more procedures, he'd become a bona fide, surgically enhanced male, forever and ever. But his positioning at the moment, with all this grayness swirling around him—he knew there was something wrong. Something wasn't normal. It was the gray. The crazy-talking gray, a color that had become alive to him. Its sooty taste in his mouth, its smell as uncomfortably breathtaking as an oven in self-cleaning mode—this kind of mental assault was not supposed to be here. And its message to Aaron was, *"Go ahead, try to kill me."*

Colors did not live. And if they didn't live, they couldn't die. But the vessels that contained a color—showed a color—*they* could be killed, except killing them wouldn't kill the gray, because a person can't kill something that wasn't alive to begin with.

Aaron was having trouble seeing this. Trouble separating the crazy from the sane.

He had no trouble separating the reality of a birthright, to be the gender he knew he was, not the one in which he'd been physically packaged. For him there was no trouble with the separation, but what about validation? Proving to the gatekeepers that he was sure? This visit to Dr. Francine could just as easily become a retreat as it could become a step forward.

Prison solitary. It did things.

The crazy needed addressing first, before the gender misalignment, which was the reason for his visit here, to see a psychiatrist suggested by his son Linus. Linus had arranged two full hours for him with this shrink today, before Linus's trip out of town with the campaign, him not returning until tomorrow. Fix the crazy whenever it reared itself, at whatever stage, with this in-between, incorrect gender status that was about to end, hopefully, after thirty years. An important pause before hitting the reset button. Get it right, or at least closer to right. That was what Dr. Francine was telling him, preparing him for a visit with a surgeon, also arranged by Linus, scheduled for tomorrow morning.

"There's nothing wrong with a woman loving a woman carnally in addition to emotionally, of course," Dr. Francine said. "And I'll reiterate that there is nothing wrong with a transman loving a woman either, or vice-versa. But it could become a disaster if the transgender person awakens to find they regret the decision they made to change. That's why it's imperative that your decision not be made under duress, or under the undue influence of any mistaken, or misinterpreted, mental gyrations."

Aaron wondered, daydreamed, whether the person who committed yesterday's anti-atheist terrorist attack in Bethlehem had been influenced by any misinterpreted mental gyrations. Had colors been alive to the bomber, too?

"So let's talk about colors, and establish one thing we can both agree on. A color cannot, technically, be alive. Are you with me so far?"

"Yes, but . . ."

In solitary, he explained, the gray had seeped in from the floor, rose above him like flooding water. It also descended from the ceiling like a spidery ninja. It surrounded him, overpowered him, bled into his pores, covered his ears, was sometimes thick as motor oil, other times as thin as plastic wrap, a film that stifled his breathing, clouded his eyes, and fogged his mind. And now, outside prison, away from his gray confinement, he had become its vessel. He'd brought the damned disease with him, and it pulsed from him in gray waves, could envelop his oppressors, could grip and hold them in place while he best decided their fate—

He folded his hands in his lap. "And that's the way it is for me, Doctor."

"So you want to hurt the gray because of what it's done to you?"

"Sometimes. Yes. More than hurt it."

Silence. Dr. Francine wrote something brief, maybe only a word or two, then returned her gaze to her client. "I think—"

She blinked, more like an eyelid flutter, a tell that said this discussion was making her nervous.

"I think now is not the time to make this life-changing, no-turning-back decision, Aaron, in my professional opinion. We need more time to evaluate your mental condition. You should wait. No gender reassignment surgery yet, please. No surgical consults yet either. Get yourself mentally healthy first.

"Once you've wrestled these and your other demons into some semblance of submission, I'll help you in any way you want."

The "other demons" related to the loss of his family and the horror surrounding it, and Aaron's role in ending it. He'd been completely honest with the doctor regarding what he witnessed in the family restaurant, what his father did—the gore, the carnage. How defenseless Aaron was during the slaughter, up until that moment when he wasn't. His complicity in the aftermath that put him in prison. Bona fide PTSD from all of it, for thirty plus years. He'd addressed it all and had done his best to compartmentalize it.

"Your present psychological makeup appears capable of supporting your transition. But we need to look at your blending of reality and fantasy, and the feelings that cause the manifestation of these vengeful impulses. And recognize that once you finish the transition, you will have joined a courageous, but marginalized, population. One that doesn't need the negative sensationalism your inclinations could cause. Let's meet three times a week for the next month and dig deeper, to resolve these unhealthy perceptions about colors. Can we do that?"

This time, the fluttering eyelids were Aaron's, eventually surrendering to a stare. After a moment, he answered yes.

Dr. Francine scribbled more notes.

Aaron made mental notes of his own. He had a competing solution. His original solution. One he would not mention to the doctor.

Should all else fail, the other way of handling this debilitating deference to the gray was an easy default: destroy its host, its personification, no matter the celebrity. Destroy what couldn't be killed by murdering the vessels that carried it.

Senator Quinn Hudson was one such vessel. Aaron's accuser. His enemy. The embodiment of the gray. Gray on gray, in gray.

Based on Aaron's personal timetable, he and Dr. Francine had only twelve days, maybe five more visits, for the two of them to resolve this thing in a non-malevolent manner. Otherwise, the way he'd originally imagined fixing it, his original plan to fix *all* of this should his efforts at transitioning fail, would be to surrender to the violence. Now that he was no longer incarcerated, and was this close to his goal, his life, plus the life of another, were hanging in the balance.

"I know I've asked this before," the doctor said, "but I'll ask it again. Are you any danger to yourself?"

More eyelid flutters for Aaron. He willed them away, then answered: "No."

With more to be resolved, and the prospect of a positive outcome, he was not a danger to himself, or to others.

He'd answered truthfully, as in for how things were for him.

At this particular moment.

***

Inside a Scranton coffee shop, Aaron sipped from a disposable cup while watching the local news on an overhead TV. He needed one more stop in town today, to a music store. His reason, on the surface, was that he might want to take trumpet lessons. A skills refresher.

From his phone conversation with the music store's proprietor regarding Aaron's influences: "Dizzy Gillespie, Wynton Marsalis, Herb Alpert, Doc Severinsen. Plus a long time ago, my college jazz band, here in

Scranton. I've been away a while but now I'm back, and the jazz is calling me. My son is telling me to go for it. Never too late, right?"

But his music store stop would need to wait while he absorbed what was on the coffee shop's TV. The male reporter's voiceover had every customer at the counter on the edge of their seats: "The Bethlehem bomber's name was Wilson Link, age thirty-six . . ."

Location and timing per the screen's news banner was *Downtown Bethlehem, Pennsylvania, live*, some of the windows of the third floor of an office building boarded up already. Then the screen split. The other half showed the FBI at an apartment building, agents leaving it with evidence bags and boxes in tow.

"Here is footage from Clarks Summit, Pennsylvania," per the same reporter. "The FBI is at the alleged bomber's apartment. What is known is they confiscated what appear to be multiple three-D printers, some computers, weapons, and parts of weapons. Tune into our special report tonight, 'D-I-Y Semiautomatic Weapons: Is your neighbor building his own weapon of mass slaughter?'"

Words from a few days earlier, an admonition, slammed Aaron like a brick to his head.

"Don't end up in the news, my friend."

From Aaron's internet hookup in Rancor, at the bus stop. Snapback Yankees cap, Scranton baseball jacket. A 3D-printed ghost gun revolver named WonderSix. Facebook user *Doodlemy9erdandy* had not followed his own advice.

Aaron's takeaway, still gawking at the TV: They took the guy's computers. Darknet or not, how long before they identified his contacts? His customers? How long before they identified Aaron as one of them?

Back at the scene outside the alleged bomber's apartment, an FBI agent made a hot mike comment while handling one of the bomber's modified assault rifles: *"These godforsaken killing machines . . ."*

Aaron sipped and watched the interview this law enforcement type gave, the agent decrying semiautomatic assault rifles and their indiscriminate killing power in the hands of civilians. A devastating military solution in search of a nonexistent civilian menace.

He left the coffee shop and walked. If he hustled, he could get to the music store before it closed.

FIFTEEN

October 5
AEF Headquarters, Bethesda, Maryland

Days before the final US Presidential debate: 11

The AEF's Board of Directors numbered seventy-six. Among them were current and former lawmakers and government officials, law enforcement officers, ex-military officers, employees of gun manufacturers, and a few high-profile actors and athletes. Ninety percent men, less than five percent non-white. Like the AEF's general membership population, minority AEF directors were also in the minority.

Here, for this meeting in one of the headquarters media rooms, a small auditorium with stadium seating, were forty of these directors. A simple majority, thirty-eight plus one, of the seventy-six directors, was what he needed. All men, all white, all handpicked by Mercer Crawford, plus a recording secretary, also a white male, there to memorialize the meeting. Ex-Senators, ex-Congressmen, retired police chiefs of major urban areas, a comic book superhero actor, and corporate CEOs. And Colonel George Jammer, a retired Marine officer with an ugly secretive background that started with a felony conviction, eventually overturned, for supplying terrorists with funds to perform the US's bidding in other countries. Colonel Jammer, a presumptive successor, was the AEF director whose footsteps Mercer had been hearing behind him.

The AEF dealt in fear, appealed to it, stoked it. But fear wasn't exclusive to the Joe Lunchpail American public or the membership rank and file. It permeated the AEF leadership as well, and Mercer Crawford was about to exploit it.

"Gentlemen, please take your seats. You too, Colonel Jammer," he said. The joke and the smile he lent to it both fell flat. "Wow. Tough room. Okay then. Thank you for attending on such short notice. I trust each of you has had time to absorb the emailed material, so let's get to it."

A screen descended from the ceiling. Mercer's slideshow began. PowerPoints with charts, graphs, and statistics about new membership demographics that reached back to 1999 and the Columbine High School massacre, Littleton, Colorado, showing increases in membership numbers coincident with heightened concerns about the public's ability to defend itself. A good news story for the AEF, and it was met with reaffirming headshakes. No surprises here.

"Now let's look at the overheads for more current data on new membership, this year compared to prior years," he said. "These charts were not in what I emailed to you."

On the screen now were pie charts for 2023 and prior periods, side by side. Recent non-white membership applications had increased significantly versus the past decade ending December 2023, from three percent non-white on average of all applications submitted, to a solid fourteen percent non-white for the first quarter of 2024, and for the second quarter, a whopping twenty-three percent of the total. In absolute numbers of members, the magnitude was multiples of a thousand versus multiples of ten.

The information on the charts sucked the air out of the room.

He let the vacuum remain while he paced in front of his audience, a slow walk so the message would sink in. After a pregnant ten seconds, the one person he did not want to hear from fired the first salvo.

"How were these statistics compiled?" Colonel Jammer said. The colonel spoke from a seat that barely confined him. "Who even keeps these parameters?"

"They're from the surveys we send to all new members after they've joined. Buying habits, income distribution, home ownership, personal interests, hobbies. Plus a question identifying ethnicity that is clearly labeled as optional, yet most applicants respond to it. A wealth of info that we mine. Then there's Pew study detail, plus algorithm extracts from our databases, some cross sectioning of the demographics—"

"Junk metrics," the colonel said. "I don't believe in that crap."

"Far from junk metrics, Colonel, yet in a way you are right, this chart is *not* accurate." Mercer continued pacing, the eyes of his audience following him.

"And here's why. We're not successful in bucketing the *entire* new member population by ethnicity. But where we've been able to mine the data, those minority counts have increased dramatically from prior periods. So if anything, this thirteen percent new non-white applicants in the recent quarters," he removed his glasses for emphasis, "is probably low."

The audience spoke amongst themselves. Mercer lowered his eyes to a white-haired man seated in the front row, the man's laptop open, his fingers keying. When Mercer spoke again, the din quieted.

"Which brings me to our recording secretary, Mr. Keaton."

Mr. Keaton raised his head, puzzled. "Yes?"

"First, I want you to delete that I called your name just now."

"Excuse me?"

"Please remove the notation from the minutes where I called your name."

Mr. Keaton did as directed, his finger holding down the delete key, his eyes on Mercer. He awaited further instructions.

"Now close your laptop."

The laptop secured, the recording secretary folded his hands on his lap.

"Thank you, Mr. Keaton. Gentlemen, we are now off the record. So let's look more closely at how our membership population is changing, shall we?"

Mercer clicked to a new chart that showed drilldowns on new member stats. The largest increases came from people the data mining had identified as Black, the second largest from those identified as Hispanic.

The fear of lawless hordes of bad guys and urban thugs and illegal immigrants with guns roaming the cities and the 'burbs—a tenet of AEF marketing—surpassing this was the fear of these hordes attempting to gather *inside* the AEF membership ranks.

All those Blacks and Hispanics at the convention, brandishing their guns—it was an image Mercer would not soon forget.

"I have a proposal, gentlemen." He turned off the overhead and stepped closer to his audience.

"We need to strengthen our membership application requirements. We want true Americans as our new brothers and sisters in arms. Citizens able to prove who they are and where they live. I therefore want your support in convincing the Board to agree to revise the membership application. It should no longer be as easy to join as plunking down your forty-five bucks for guaranteed acceptance into our esteemed organization. We'll pull together some revised application formats including a new questionnaire and survey requiring completion with each new application, and we'll send them out for your perusal."

Colonel Jammer folded his arms. "Revise the application how, Crawford?"

"Similar to what you've seen making the political rounds among the states nowadays, Colonel. A need for up-to-date IDs like drivers' licenses and passports. To ferret out the pretenders. Lowlifes who steal this country's goods and services.

"Fewer deadbeats, fewer illegal immigrants, and no Middle Eastern terrorists." Then, his hands raised palms out, he spoke to all the directors in attendance. "What say you, gentlemen?"

An awkward silence, then a few nervous nods in agreement, then a few more, then came multiple thumbs up, and finally the din of a roomful of spoken yesses, which was the way Mercer expected this suggestion would break. Excellent.

Save for one Colonel George Jammer who remained rigid in his seat, with a laser focus on Mercer. Mercer knew Jammer wanted to agree, good ol' boy that he was, but he also knew the colonel wouldn't give him the satisfaction.

The info was accurate, which to Mercer meant the AEF was being assaulted from within, overrun by too many undesirables. It was time to close the ranks.

And you can shove your disdain for junk metrics up your ass, Colonel Jammer.

"Thank you all, gentlemen. Meeting adjourned."

***

His presentation had surfaced a concern that this group of AEF directors hadn't known they had. Mercer beamed through the glad-handing and backslapping in the hallway. He excused himself, needing to get back to his office. A few steps into his exit, he rounded the hallway corner.

Colonel Jammer was in his path. "An impressive show, Crawford."

High and tight haircut, with sharp, clean-shaven facial features. Zoot-suitable shoulders, tapered tree trunk for a waist, a military crease in his charcoal pants. Taller, wider, and more muscular than Mercer.

"Thank you, Colonel," Mercer managed, skeptical. They assessed each other, Mercer resettling his glasses, the colonel's jowls tightening a tad.

"Problem is," the colonel said, "it's too little, too late."

"And by that you mean what?"

"Vietnam." Colonel Jammer narrowed his eyes. "Your history. Your birthday put you at number four in the Selective Service draft lottery, remember? Sure you do. A number that low, you'd need your student deferment to keep you from getting called up."

Mercer was intrigued. "Me and a million other college students. What's your point?"

"No shame in that, Mercer, but that wasn't your only deferment. The clincher is the one you got for mental instability. Major anxiety, depression, suicidal thoughts. It earned you a stint in an institution. The stint was short, but that doesn't matter, the damage was done. Crazy once, maybe crazy again. Something the Board hadn't known about."

"Now wait a minute—"

"They know about it now."

"You sonovabitch. How the hell—"

"Friends in high places. But there's no shame in that either, Mercer, and just look at all that you've accomplished since then. Your wealth. All those paintings and artwork you own by the American masters. Your uninterrupted career. No blemishes, with no nerve issues surfacing. So far. Good for you. But unfortunately there's one lasting repercussion from that time you spent in the bughouse."

Mercer's nose twitched, his lips curled. One hand closed into a fist, but it quickly opened again. For him to be goaded into a visceral reaction here, incented like this . . . the colonel, he was sure, could physically crush him. But Mercer was less upset about this allegation, and more upset about what he knew the colonel was about to reveal.

"I've been to your house, Crawford. Met your wife and family. I know there are guns in it. Why wouldn't there be, right? If ever there were a family that needed protection, it would be the family of the AEF's chief executive. But something bothered me. After all these years of you leading this organization, I never saw you at a firing range. Never actually saw you shoot a gun. In person, on TV, or in the newspapers, or online. Nowhere. Not. Once.

"The reality is, the guns at your house are all in your wife's name. Why? Because of the Gun Control Act. As an adjudicated 'mental defective' per the law's language, your time in the bughouse means you can't own a firearm.

"Many directors on the Board are now reevaluating your future as president and CEO."

The colonel dropped his hand onto Mercer's shoulder, squeezed it like he'd just done all the heavy lifting that Mercer had never been able to do for himself. "Keeping that secret all these years, Crawford—it must have been horrible for you."

Mercer yanked the wrist off his shoulder, stepped into Colonel Jammer's face.

"You smug, jar-headed moron. Who'd you pay off to get the Feds to overturn your felony, hmm? Up yours, Contra-Boy. I've got work to do."

Mercer plowed past his antagonist, the colonel needing to give ground.

Colonel Jammer barked at Mercer's back. "I'll give you that one, Mercer. After the presidential election, the Board will meet. Enjoy these last few months of your contract as CEO. After that, you're gone."

SIXTEEN

October 5
Linus Pappas's townhouse condo, Scranton

Days before the final US Presidential debate: 11

Aaron removed the trumpet, a rental, from the carrying case and placed it on a towel on the floor of the bathroom. The music storeowner had given him a no-risk deal on it, accepting cash as payment.

"Try it for a month. If you don't like the action, timbre, or valve response—anything—bring it back. I also know people who give lessons. How's that sound?"

There'd been a change of plans. Instead of spending his day at a surgeon's for a *pre-pre* op discussion, at Linus's expense, he'd be here, in Linus's luxurious master bathroom suite, re-learning how a trumpet made music. Trumpet, a carrying case, music teacher business cards, a snake brush, pipe cleaners, a bottle of valve oil, a small tin container of slide grease, and polishing cloths: He laid all the cleaning incidentals on a towel on the tile floor next to the large Jacuzzi. Not something he could do in his tub-less, shower-only bathroom in his basement efficiency. He started the tub water and left the bathroom. He returned with a laptop, set it up on the floor, sat cross-legged in front of it, and got online. After a few hit-and-miss internet search attempts—

The YouTube video he looked for queued up: "*How to clean your trumpet,*" four and half minutes. Its narrator was female, a cute, thirty-ish redhead with a midwestern radio voice. He'd liked this video and this one narrator, and would again let her school him on this, especially after he'd watched her lips kiss the trumpet's mouthpiece the first time he watched it, brief as the lip encounter was. Seeing her and her full lips in action again, even in an instructional capacity—it was good to know his libido was still functioning through all this.

He disassembled the trumpet, began working the pipe cleaners and the snake brush into each of the curves, the lead pipe, the valve casings. He lay the pieces carefully on the rubber mat in the tub, underwater, remembering his high school days, how gentle he'd been with the instrument when cleaning it, careful not to scratch or dent the brass. Respect the instrument, and it would treat you well. Good band director advice from a long ago, less confusing time.

Now for the main event, the finger buttons and their valves. He unscrewed the three valve caps and pulled each piston from its casing along with the short spring it rested on. He studied the silver-colored metal springs in the bright bathroom light. Coiled symmetry that surrounded so short a length of nothing. Yes, there was exactly one-point-seven-two inches of hollow, empty space inside the spring. For Aaron, this small bit of emptiness was where the action would be.

He retrieved a .22 cartridge from his pocket.

Shorter than the coil by half an inch, it moved freely up and down inside the spring when he shook it. Enough room for the trumpet's finger button to act like a finger button when reassembled, allowing finger pressure to depress the spring a bit, which meant someone, a security guard-type screener, or, say, a Secret Service agent—hopefully one who wasn't also a trumpet player—could depress the valve and accept that the restricted amount of play in the spring was normal. Excellent.

Three valves. Three hollow, empty spaces he would utilize by putting cartridges in them.

He undid his modification and finished cleaning the trumpet the way the rest of the video instructed. Maybe, if things turned out okay, he'd contact the video teacher, learn more about her, friend her. Maybe re-learn the trumpet and practice, practice, practice, to impress the hell out of her if they ever met.

Those music teachers' business cards the storeowner had given him . . . where were they?

He picked them up from the tile floor, studied them until his malignant conscience did its thing.

Who am I kidding? Trumpet lessons? Her, with me, and me not a real man?

Colors drained around him, the checkerboard tile bathroom floor, the soft green tile walls, the wall art, the special soaps, the soap dishes, the bottles of shampoo, the stacked towels—

The gray, the malevolent gray, invaded his thoughts, was coming at him from all angles again.

No chance of that, Aaron. Get back on message. You've got a score to settle. People will understand.

Aaron balled up the business cards and crammed them into his pocket for disposal.

He finished his work on the trumpet, let the water drain from the tub, then repacked the instrument in its case.

Slam. It was the condo's front door. He hadn't heard it open, but he sure as hell heard it close, with feeling. Linus? But he was out of town, not due back until tonight . . .

Aaron left the bathroom, moved across Linus's bedroom to the door to the hallway, opened it a sliver and peeked out. At the bottom of the two-story foyer Linus and a woman, a business-suited blond with a dark skirt that finished just above the knee, were locked in an embrace, with her visible from the back only, pressing him against the closed door. The embrace turned passionate, frenzied, the two of them in need of finding a soft landing.

"Not here," she said. "Your father—"

"Screw my father," Linus said, which gave them both a chuckle, Linus laughing longer at the tasteless joke than he should have. Linus nuzzled her, speaking into her creamy white neck above her creamy white blouse.

"Sorry for that image. Not possible, not yet at least, maybe not ever. He's at a surgeon's office for the day. Plus I'd rather *you* and *me* . . ."

Linus tugged at the woman's jacket, pulling it off her shoulders, she doing the same with his, the two cooing sexy sweet nothings about ignoring campaign work that needed attention in favor of taking care of other needs. The door's sidelights to the left and right of the threshold gave up a straight reveal of the parking lot, evident to Aaron from his upstairs vantage point. In Linus's parking space, visible through bunched lace curtains, a supremely polished black Chevy Suburban sat idling, its heavily tinted windows mirroring the sun.

Not Linus's car. He drove a Volvo.

Aaron looked more closely at the blond pressed full-bodied against his son, his eyes darting between their embrace and the parked Suburban, the SUV looking so solid, so black, so official, so . . . high-profile governmental. And so Secret Service-like.

Wow. This was Congresswoman Mary Inkster, the Republican vice-presidential nominee, here, in Linus's condo, and she was about to give Linus a passionate ride. Parked just outside the condo was her Secret Service protection.

Aaron needed to get out of this bedroom with the trumpet and its incidentals.

The VP nominee caught her breath, took Linus's hands in hers, pulled him with her, and backed the two of them away from the door. She turned, her hand tugging at his. "Upstairs now, lover, Momma wants to play."

Twenty years Linus's senior, married with two adult children, and oozing pheromone power both political and sexual, Ms. Inkster led him to the steps that would take them upstairs to his master bedroom. She tugged at him again, Linus hurrying behind her, his hands now massaging her butt cheeks, making her scurry up the steps faster, the giddiness in her voice schoolgirl-ish and naughty. The bedroom door burst open and she spun around, pulling Linus against her. She backed toward a stretch of wall on their way to the bed, each of them losing pieces of clothing on the way. Linus lifted her onto him, the coupling subjecting, in succession, the bureau, the TV stand, and the armoire, to a sexual pounding, the VP candidate's back rocking each piece against the wall behind it, her whimpers punctuated by short, surprise bursts of primordial pleasure. The last hurdle before reaching the bed, the bathroom door with Aaron behind it, was now inching closed.

Pound, pound, ooh, ahhh, AHHH . . .

The bathroom door was taking a beating, Aaron on its other side, him so S-O-L if the door opened. He backed away, scanned the bathroom— clean enough, no stray trumpet parts—then looked over his shoulder. Here was a convenient condo design feature: entrance doors on each end of the master bath.

He slipped through the other door into the hallway with the trumpet and its supplies safely in its case. He descended the stairs on quiet feet to his basement apartment.

***

Next to the condo kitchen was the dining room, where Linus and the congresswoman had spread out their work, eating and reviewing mounds of paper at the same time. Aaron entered the kitchen, rounded the refrigerator, opened it, and grabbed a bottle of beer.

"Sorry, don't mind me. I'll be out of your hair in a minute. Hi, Congresswoman Inkster."

Linus's chopsticks stopped in midair, noodles and all, adding a barely noticeable glance at his dining partner. She, however, didn't flinch, acknowledging Aaron with a nod while she chewed, ignoring Linus's glance at her.

Smooth, Aaron thought. Grace under pressure. She'd done this before.

"Dad. Hi," Linus said. "We, ah, didn't hear you come in."

"Been here all day, son. A shrink visit then a music store visit early, then a dead-to-the-world nap this afternoon. I took your advice, by the way. I picked up a trumpet. I'm going to learn again."

The congresswoman kept eating. Linus continued playing through his surprise. "Super, Dad, super. But I thought you would be with the surgeon all day . . ."

"Nope. Change of plans short term. Going to wait a bit."

Surrounding Linus and his guest were stacks of paper on the table, with charts and figures, political mailers, posters, two laptops, and multiple Chinese food containers, plus bottled beer to wash it all down.

"Your son and I," the congresswoman volunteered, her mouth finishing a chew, "we're prepping for Senator Hudson's debate in a few weeks. I'm glad we didn't wake you. Care to join us? Plenty of food here."

The mark of a good politician: not breaking a sweat while caught in a compromising situation.

"No, no, you two stay with whatever you're doing," Aaron said. "Thanks. But if you don't mind, I'll make a plate and head back downstairs."

Aaron helped himself to a spring roll and some General Tso's. Linus caught up with him at the center island and spoke in a low tone. "Why no visit to the surgeon today, Dad? I had it lined up. Something wrong?"

"A temporary hold," Aaron said. He pulled some silverware from a drawer. "I'm working out some issues with the psychiatrist. Don't worry, I called the surgeon and canceled and explained why."

"Should I be concerned with those issues? Is it the Senator Hudson thing?"

Thing? As a district attorney, the senator had had Aaron sent to prison for thirty years on a wrongful guilty verdict.

"Nope. We're getting to the bottom of some things, that's all, then we'll get back on track. The endgame's still the same."

"Good. Glad to see you're covering all the bases, Dad. Super."

The congresswoman wiped her mouth, picked up her bottle of beer and took a gulp. She studied Aaron before he could leave. "Mr. Pappas—"

Father and son both looked up; she smirked at her oversight.

"Sorry. Mr. Pappas *senior*, I want you to know how committed the senator's campaign is regarding marginalized persons of all shapes, sizes, and orientations. That, and prison reform. In technical politics parlance, and pardon my flippancy," she smiled at where she was going, "you check off two of the boxes. Add to that twofer the senator's heartfelt need to atone for what he, and the justice system, did to you thirty years ago, these are some of the reasons you've been invited to the debate as the senator's guest. We're thrilled you'll be able to make it."

Aaron nodded. "I understand. Much appreciated, Congresswoman."

"'Mary,' please. Excellent. I'll add this. I'm a staunch conservative from Iowa, considerably right of center. God knows how much 'stauncher' I am compared to Senator Hudson," she said, air-quoting the word. She eyed Linus. "I'll include your son here too, who might well be even more right-of-center conservative than I am. My point is, Senator Hudson is a moderate, and he fought the Party to keep these platform planks, and when we challenged him about them, he would not give an inch. You, personally, and your story, had a lot to do with his new viewpoints. This is not just a veneer. He's no longer the ruthless DA you remember from years ago. He's a very kind and decent man, Mr. Pappas.

"So you should be prepared for some notoriety at the debate. I have it on good authority the TV cameras will find you more than they find the other guests of each of the candidates."

Aaron had had enough. She was a married mother of two, might become the next vice president of the United States, she was hot for his son, and they'd had a laugh at the expense of Aaron's marginalized status during foreplay. And now she launched into a PSA about a 'reformed' Senator Hudson, a person not long for this earth.

Her conservatism, his son's ultra-conservatism, their fake sincerity and spin . . . as a politician, she was a pro at this. So, too, Aaron now accepted, was Linus. Both seemed better at it than the candidate they served.

He'd need to process this.

Food, beer, napkins, fork, not chopsticks, he was never good with them. He had what he needed, raised a beer bottle in salute before he headed back downstairs. "Thanks for the dinner, ma'am. See you at the debate."

***

Aaron needed to walk off the Chinese. He also had an errand to run in downtown Scranton. He slipped past Linus and Ms. Inkster and out the front door, not needing to be secretive, but it was easier that way.

Baseball cap, short leather bomber jacket for the autumn night air, and sunglasses in his pocket. He slid the backpack over his shoulder. Inside the bag nestled in protective padding was his trumpet, pipe-cleaned, polished, clean of prints, and loaded. He headed to the bus stop outside the condo complex, his destination the Hannigan-McMaster Center, University of Scranton, on the corner of Mulberry and Jefferson. An old haunt in his younger days as a Scranton student as part of the university's undergrad student jazz ensemble. Many, many years ago.

He entered the baroque building, a former Baptist church the college had bought and transformed into a musical performance venue. First up on the main floor was the atrium, configurable into a recital or lecture hall, then the Aula, the center's concert hall. In eleven days it would host the final US presidential debate. The hall could seat 650 in its church pews. Behind the stage, a gargantuan organ loft held a restored chamber organ.

Foot echoes outnumbering and noisier than his own followed him past the Aula. He found the stairwell that took him down to the ground floor. When he exited it, his jacket collar was up and his sunglasses were on.

The stairwell opened into a large, bright, rehearsal hall. Farther into the bowels were ensemble areas, a musicians' lounge, practice rooms, a music library, and the center's musical instrument storage and repair area. Storage area access was through side-by-side swinging doors restaurant-kitchen style, and at this moment it was just as busy. He pushed through them.

Workbenches, vats, tables, like in the old days when he was a student. Musicians of different sizes, sexes, and ages wandered in and out with instruments in various stages of music preparedness. Woodwind, brass, percussion, strings, keyboards. Lockers occupied the middle of the room, some with doors open, most of the lockers appearing empty. Perfect. He set his gig bag on the bottom of an empty locker, then he laid out a few standard finishing nails on the top shelf in haphazard, inconsequential fashion. He produced a combination lock, closed the door, snapped the lock shut, and admired the secure locker, which was now his.

"Hey. You coming or going? Needs to be one or the other."

Behind him an older woman with straight auburn hair that ran halfway down her back, no makeup, and a concert outfit blouse and skirt that smelled of camphor, wanted past him. A folksinger type, but without the warm disposition, carried her clarinet case on her way by. Behind her, another musician; guitar. Then another. Evening concert band members. Aaron was in their way.

"Sorry. Not coming, going." He squeezed past them, furtive glances over his shoulder as he left the storage room, to make sure no one screwed with his locker. He found the stairway, hoofed it up the steps, and left the building.

At some point closer to the debate, the Secret Service would sweep the area and practically dismantle this building as a precaution. They might snip the locks to inspect all the lockers. They would find instruments. They would visually inspect them then wand them, looking for anything unusual.

In his favor, the cartridges would be camouflaged by the brass of the instrument. There was no one-stop national database of musical instrument serial numbers attached to their owners. He'd left no fingerprints. And the rental transaction was in cash, the customer name involved in the transaction, *A. Horne*, fake.

Regardless, he was still taking a chance. If they found the bullets, all they would need to do was wait him out, then pounce. It was an all-or-nothing proposition, and he might well be caught.

If things got that far, he wouldn't care. He just wanted it to be after the debate, not before it.

SEVENTEEN

October 5
Saint Possenti's Bingo Hall, Rancor, Pennsylvania

Days before the final US Presidential debate: 11

A cinder-block fortress with bars protecting thick, murky, bulletproof block windows, and two black oak front doors abutting each other: The single-story structure didn't look like a bingo hall or a church or a school or any other building that should be named after a Catholic saint, save for two rustic crucifixes made from deer antlers nailed to the front doors. Counsel, a gym bag in hand, left her two canine deputies to hang out in the van, engine running, windows ajar. Too noisy inside Saint Possenti's for them.

The front door to the gun range sealed shut behind her.

She produced her wallet, flipped it open to her membership card, and showed it to the elderly couple seated in the glassed-in booth. They handed her a permission badge and nodded her forward through a door.

The noise inside was piercing, immediate, gunshots bunched together like competing drum solos, their echoes deafening. She found her noise-canceling headphones in her gym bag and put them on.

Inside one of the booths, she costumed herself for a few rounds of "bingo," the synonym for target shooting in Rancor. Bright vest, pinned permission badge, and safety glasses, all in addition to her ear protection.

Thick, bullet-resistant glass separated her booth from the one next to her, Andy occupying it. He blew her a kiss, assumed the stance, raised his handgun toward a target and emptied the clip into it.

Dody, next booth beyond Andy's, leaned back for a gander at them both. Other shooters were dressed similarly, remaining silent as the gunshots echoed throughout the indoor range. With people to see, things to do, yada-yada, Counsel wanted to log about twenty minutes of target practice. One yada was to check in on Vonetta, still reeling from her husband Irv's near-death experience at the hands of a bomber.

Counsel squared herself, raised her handgun, squeezed the trigger, and began obliterating the head and the heart of her paper target at twenty-five feet. Andy practiced his usual: target decapitation, shots that evened off at the neckline. Dody, a retired cop, for her round of bingo got no farther north than the crotch, which was where she emptied her clip with no expression, no malice, all business. After twenty minutes, Counsel ended her session. She rounded the partition and entered Andy's booth.

Andy inserted a new clip. Counsel raised her voice to him. He moved one earmuff out of the way to listen. "I'll check in on our art broker," she said.

Andy nodded. "Dody and I are heading out in a few. We plan on grabbing some Earl Grey and finger sandwiches at a new teahouse near the college campus."

"So you guys are going to a bar to get drunk."

"There is that chance. You wanna come?"

"Sorry, can't. After I check on our guest, I'm off to see Vonetta."

She stepped in close for a parting kiss, her free hand cradling the back of Andy's head, lending feeling and substance to her embrace. Her dark, naughty eyes sparkled as she disengaged. "Made it move a little for you, didn't it?" she said, grinning.

Weak-kneed, Andy rammed the clip into his .38 as a response, spread his feet, and recommenced his target-shooting, which made it move a little for her, too.

Counsel followed a corridor adjacent to the shooting range and found the large workspace abutting the rear of the target area. On the other side of a cinder-block wall Sebastian Leone, short, thin, and sloppy in another hoodie, stood addressing a painting on an easel. Counsel entered his periphery, pointed at the man's headphones snugged against his baseball cap under the hoodie, and mimicked their removal. Sebastian liberated one ear for Counsel's benefit but continued working.

"You're looking festive today, Sebastian."

He grunted.

Multiple easels, a workbench, a desk, and an open laptop with shifting images. Paint graced the canvases, speckled his brushes, face, hoodie, loafers, and the floor, but his hands and arms looked clean. The snapback ball cap in place under the raised hood had him channeling his inner street artist, a Bolivian version of Banksy at work. Iron bars crossed the rear of the room north to south, serving as the painting space's back wall, separating the work area from a small living/sleeping space tandem to it. Beyond the living space was another walled area that Counsel knew was a utilitarian bathroom. Whites, tans, grays, and the glossy black of the iron bars rounded out the area's color palette, with slivers and drips of stray paint on the walls and floor. Spotlights on retractable arms lit his work area, softer lights from table lamps beyond it.

"I am hungry," Sebastian said, not taking his eyes off his work in progress. A computer-generated image of the N. C. Wyeth *Hickok* painting was projected onto the canvas. The magnified photograph was also next to it, his eyes darting between the two. "No one has ordered my lunch."

"Poor baby. How about pizza, or maybe a cheesesteak or a hoagie? I'll get it delivered."

"A hoe-what?"

"A hoagie. If you don't know what a hoagie is, your Philly longshoreman scam needs a lot more work."

A hoagie was a.k.a. a sub, submarine, hero, or torpedo, depending on what part of the country you were from. Italian deli meats, cheeses, peppers, onions, tomatoes, and lettuce, in a long Italian roll dripping with hoagie oil.

"I know a local place that does a decent job with it," Counsel said.

"Sounds delightful. But no oil, please. I'd rather have mayonnaise."

Four empty art canvases, the same shape and size as the one on the easel, leaned upright against the wall behind the painting he was working on, which appeared less than half finished. Wild Bill Hickok's eyebrows were almost a straight line on the work-in-progress canvas, his eyes dark, intense, serious. No arms, no painted gun yet, no other card players, no table. Just Wild Bill's hatless head, his shoulders, his brown hair parted down the middle, and his white face visible as far south as his nose.

"The hell it'll be with mayonnaise. It'll be with hoagie oil. Olive oil with a little oregano, basil, salt, and pepper. You'll thank me."

Counsel's Tourette's meter clocked in, went on overload, rattling off sandwich ingredients and condiments until segueing into a forty-plus-year-old jingle for fast food.

"Twoallbeefpattiesspecialsaucelettucecheesepicklesonionsonasesameseed . . . shitshitSHIT . . ."

She grabbed a bottle of water from her bag and took large gulps while wrapping her fingers around her fake fur keychain. The calm resurfaced after some deep breaths, allowing her to call in their lunch.

A calmer Counsel checked out a completed canvas off by itself on a workbench and under a lamp, a piece that looked like the finished product they were going for. "This one here. What's wrong with it?"

"Practice. Not up to my standards. Let it be." Sebastian pointed to the laptop computer on the desk. "I have a favor. Please find some cowboy music on the radio for me. I need some motivation."

The laptop streamed a national news station. Before Counsel could change it, a mug shot of a disheveled woman popped up, with video; it halted her search. The reporter's voiceover gave a recap. Counsel tapped at the keyboard to increase the volume.

"No, please, not more news, I need musical inspiration . . ."

"Hold on."

"Presidential nominee Senator Quinn Hudson's front-row guest at the final presidential debate will be Aaron Pappas, the transman whose conviction and life sentence for murdering his family was overturned in August. Thirty years ago Senator Hudson, then a young district attorney, convicted Aaron Pappas of murder while Pappas was known as female college

student Karis Pappas. In a remarkable development this summer, the moderate Republican senator helped orchestrate Pappas's release . . ."

Counsel was mesmerized. A police photo showed a dark-haired woman, full faced, with eyes distraught, near panic. "Christ. I remember her. Or him. That mug shot. I often wondered what happened to her. Him."

"Prison's what happened to him," Sebastian said, still in front of the canvas. "Thirty plus years."

On the laptop now, something only Counsel could see, were newly released photos of Aaron Pappas, telephoto stop-motion shots courtesy of clandestine paparazzi snapped somewhere in downtown Scranton according to the news crawl, without the subject's knowledge. Quite a different appearance. Definitely male, definitely older, Aaron Pappas leaned into a lonely gait on a city sidewalk, his jacket collar turned up and his hands in his jeans pockets. Black and white photos worthy of a 1960s Bob Dylan record album cover.

Sebastian lowered his outstretched arm and looked sideways at his work in progress on the canvas, assessing it. At the end of his breather, he arrived alongside Counsel in front of the laptop.

"Such sensationalism," Sebastian said, looking at the screen. "I wonder what will go through Mr. Pappas's head while attending the debate. The crime, the conviction, the time in prison—it is all going to come up. Some good TV drama, don't you think, Ms. Fungo? Ms. Fungo?"

Counsel concentrated on the black and white photos, staying with them until they left the laptop screen, the reporters moving onto another streaming news story.

Yes, some TV drama. It was premature, Counsel thought, to say that it would be good.

She keyed, looking for more info on this transgender person who had spent more than half his life behind bars—a large chunk in solitary—for a crime now considered a justifiable homicide. In a few weeks this ex-con would be feted in front of a national live TV audience by the person who put him in prison. Counsel pulled up a decades-old news report about the Greek diner murder-slaughter, a crime that featured gunshots, hacked bodies, and an industrial-strength garbage disposal. There were photos of the kitchen crime scene. Bona fide PTSD material. The photos silenced Sebastian.

Counsel found her voice but shuddered as she spoke. "This debate is going to be a circus."

A question now on Counsel's mind: Could a person ever really forgive three decades of wrongful incarceration?

Counsel paged past the grotesque images to other thirty-year-old photographs, finding those of the former felon as a female college student with her significant other, the mother of their son together who, by the way, grew up to become a lawyer and part of the Hudson-for-President campaign. Remarkable. The circus aspect dissipated, replaced by what Counsel now thought might become transgender exploitation.

But transcending the horror was something that hit Counsel right in the feels: the mother, Aaron Pappas's significant other, had died just before his conviction was overturned. Just before he was released from prison. Her death and its timing had to have left a mark.

"Look, Ms. Fungo—" Sebastian said.

"Counsel. Call me Counsel."

Where that familiarity came from, Counsel didn't know. A weak moment maybe, with her getting too maudlin perhaps, from seeing Pappas's tragic story. No matter, she wouldn't retract it.

"Well. How nice," Sebastian said. "Counsel it is, then. Can we talk about our time together, here, me behind these bars? Do you know anything about the Stockholm syndrome, Counsel?"

Of course she did. "Look, we didn't kidnap you, Sebastian. As a fugitive recovery agent I arrested you then simply reinforced our need for your cooperation by slapping a tracking device on your ankle until we turn you in. We're doing you a favor. We're giving you more time on the outside be delaying your incarceration, and a means for you to settle your debts. This is a cooperative arrangement."

"It doesn't matter what you call it," Sebastian said, "you coerced me. I'm being held against my will. But please, I'm just making a point. I'm good with it, good with being here. Doing this work. I hold no grudge. I, too, hate how the AEF is perverting your country's gun laws."

A con from a conman? An attempt to soften his captor, maybe so she'd let her guard down?

Counsel decided no. Sebastian was part of their cause now and he was close to delivering on their deal. It was all good.

A text arrived on her phone. Food was here.

***

Next stop, Vonetta Posey's Allentown place of business, a ninety-minute ride.

Vonetta opened the door to her bail bonds storefront. Her jowls tight, her eyes hard, Vonetta faced Counsel but had no words for her, and Counsel had none in return. They hugged in the doorway, Vonetta crying hard into Counsel's shoulder. When they separated—

"Get inside, lady," Vonetta said and swiped away her sniffling.

It was a fine line, Counsel knew from personal experience, the very close personal experience of Counsel having lost her ex-husband for real, that not being what this was for Vonetta, this being only a close call. Counsel had loved her husband when they were together, of course, but he was someone she'd still loved even after they'd divorced.

Counsel entered the bail bonds office, a hole-in-the-wall storefront half the size of the check-cashing bodega next to it. Vonetta's one-person shop had a desk, side chairs, a coffeemaker, and a micro-fridge. State cop memorabilia and photos hung on walls and shelves, plus a framed FBI's Most Wanted poster from the fifties, plus family pictures.

"Sit," Vonetta said. "Want some coffee?"

"No. What you serve isn't coffee."

"Stuff it."

"Back at you."

Small talk, or their version of it, but it wasn't working for either of them. Vonetta swallowed hard, her hands folded on the desk. She added a hard look at her friend. "Counsel, my life sped past my eyes when I saw what those IEDs did to that building. Those defenseless people never knew what hit them."

"I know."

"I know you know. My husband also knows, for sure, because he knew those people. He could have easily been upstairs with some of them. He could have been there . . ."

Then came the piece that Counsel didn't want to hear but had prepared herself to hear it, because Vonetta was her best friend from back in the early days, from state cop boot recruit forward, and Vonetta had seen the best that fate had had to offer Counsel, but also the worst.

"These wounds cut deep, Sarge. Ones I never want to ever feel again. I am so sorry you lost your ex, Counsel. And right now I'm feeling guilty as all hell from having been delivered from that pain. For being relieved . . . that you're not here to say those same words to me."

The two retired state cops both teared up again and needed a moment to wipe their eyes on their sleeves. Vonetta composed herself. "Back to business. I've got news about that handgun."

The one that showed up in the disgusting picture-chat between someone named *2Ap@1!Ndr0mE* and a teenager on the darknet.

"Make and model are confirmed. Gatling Arms PM9, police and military issue. An incomplete serial. Not scratched off, Sarge, *incomplete*. It means someone or something interfered with the manufacturing process then put it on the street. Complicit or not, Gatling Arms is gonna be screwed. Andy's Special Agent in Charge daughter sent us the info."

"So his daughter is adding this info to a case she already has open."

"Apparently. That darknet scumbag adding his boast about side-door gun-maker exits and him being AEF royalty made them really interested in him. They have an identity."

"Did they—she—share?"

"Teddy? Not Teddy. Another agent shared their code name for him. They're calling him 'Little Big Man.' But his full identity, no."

Counsel leaned in, folded her hands on her side of Vonetta's desk, the mental tumblers turning. "Interesting. Anything else?"

"I re-upped my membership to the AEF. I sent their Board a letter, telling them I want all semiautomatic rifle sales in the US banned. New sales, resales, semiautomatic rifle gun parts—all of it banned, and I want them to lobby legislatures to make it happen. It won't ever happen if members don't talk back with some real truth-to-power language, honey, know what I mean?"

"You let them know you're—"

"A person of color? I made a point of it. And that a lot of my P-O-C AEF member friends feel the same way. They copied me on their letters."

"Did you work Gunowners Against the Slaughter in there?"

"Oh yeah. 'Straighten out your story, Mr. Crawford, or me and my friends will straighten it out for you, everywhere possible, inside the AEF and outside it, at the polls. And if that don't happen, there's always GAS, your new competitor.' But Counsel, about the Feds . . ."

"What about them?"

"The agent told me to stay out of their lane and let them make their case. To let this whole other thing happen."

"Fine. Sure. Let's hope they and everyone else stays out of ours."

EIGHTEEN

October 13

The Office of Francine Gamorra, MD, PsyD, Scranton

Days before the final US Presidential debate: 3

"I've been doing the exercises, Doctor, and they've been helping."

"Excellent, Aaron. Tell me about them."

Aaron lay on the psych couch in his analyst's office. Dr. Gamorra guided her black-rimmed glasses back atop the bridge of her nose, snugging them up, something Aaron knew she did when preparing for a bumpy session. Her glance at the notepad in her lap followed by her focus on the reclining Aaron, said she was ready. Harpo the therapy poodle lay on the floor next to the couch, there for support if needed.

The prescribed at-home exercises addressed Aaron's PTSD from his days in prison, specifically his days in solitary. Those endless moments day and night, often not knowing the difference between the two, when he'd been overwhelmed by bursts of orange jumpsuits that came at him from more than one angle once they were let inside his cell. The blandest of colors, the gray, had been his only refuge during the assaults, the color's dull vibe numbing, comforting, but soon morphing into what became his worst enemy, a living, hovering, talkative gray entity, still dull in color, but loud in temperament.

"Transcending my body was the only way I had of surviving. I'm doing a better job of coping now, without needing to dissociate."

Dissociation equaled old news for his doctor. Many patients experienced it. The new territory the doctor would hear about was Aaron's more recent method of coping with it.

"In my bedroom at night, I close my eyes, put myself back in my bunk in solitary, to fight the demons. I've seen, felt, what that manipulation, this lack of freedom, did to me. What it makes a person willing to do to avoid the loneliness.

"I was so bereft of any semblance of life in those long stints in solitary. No human touch, limited human scent, no smell of sunshine on another person's skin, no faint scent of a summer day in their hair, or a winter chill reddening their cheeks. No prison food flavors mixed with the sweat from their pores. No closeness with anyone. Initially. Then something happened."

The doctor prompted him when Aaron went silent. "What was it that happened, Aaron?"

"I . . . Rape happened, Doctor."

One female guard had tested the waters with him while he was in his early thirties, Aaron said. Aaron's unfinished, male-identified self had been the guard's reward to two female inmates, theirs for the night because they'd righted some wrong among prisoners while in the yard. A noisy dusk-to-dawn of supreme debasement, with two women so in need of a man that they'd earned some intense fun with Aaron, even as incomplete as he was, inclusive of the probative toys they'd brought along to enhance their enjoyment.

Aaron was stripped. Aaron was tied down. Aaron was ridiculed.

. . . Aaron was married. Aaron was a father . . .

Aaron was probed, licked, and sucked. Was burned. Was peed on.

Raped.

The one night was a dry run. It turned into additional nights, unannounced, at the guard's discretion. She liked to watch.

All told, Aaron lost count of the frequency. It stopped two years after it started, when the guard retired. Aaron made four trips to solitary during that time, and during every stretch he'd been violated in the same manner. He soon learned why he never saw his inmate perpetrators after he'd returned to the general population, where he might have been able to deliver some retribution: They'd been selected by the guard because of their short sentences in the prison. Once he was out of solitary, each inmate was already gone. In one respect, the guard might have saved Aaron's life by selecting inmates he couldn't exact revenge against, because he would have killed every one of them until someone killed him.

"Calm down, Aaron," Dr. Francine said, "you're hyperventilating. Take a deep, cleansing breath, then we can continue for as long as you need to."

He did as the doctor said and was soon able to mentally return to his bedroom, which allowed him to return to the debauchery of his prison cell, which again made him a prisoner of all his nightmares. Aaron had more incidents to describe, but the doctor stopped him.

"You're telling me something has turned this around. Have you put another lens to it, understood something about it?"

"Yes."

"What do you now understand? What did that for you?"

"It's about the power—always about the power. And I've taken the power back."

First the prison guard had the power. When she awarded Aaron to the two inmates, she gave the power to them, then to multiple inmates in succession. For Aaron, the power had remained in the cell even after the inmates left. It seeped into the gray walls, the ceiling, the floor, it did not relent, and it visited him day and night. The gray. It owned him.

"I'd given the gray the power. It's taken some time, but now I'm taking the power back."

"How?"

"I've embraced the overturned conviction. That crime—it was not my doing, it never was. Paperwork confirming my non-felon status is due to arrive any day now. I've got a bank account balance. I'm looking for a job. I'm learning to drive again. All of this, it's, ah, it's all helping to reestablish my self-worth."

Dr. Francine smiled. "And you'll be a VIP at the presidential debate in a few days, right? That's something, too."

"Yes. Right. I can't be forgetting that, can I, Doctor?"

Aaron, beaming, pulled himself up from the couch to a sitting position. He faced his analyst.

"These pieces, Doctor, they're pushing aside the melancholy, the self-pity, the depression. They're rounding me out, all helping me move forward. Which brings me to a request."

"I know," Dr. Francine said. Her eyes smiled from behind her glasses. "You want me to tell your surgeon you're ready for reassignment surgery."

"Yes. I need your approval."

Aaron watched her jot in her notebook, watched her face closely, analyzed her. These were happy notes, encouraging comments, breakthrough stuff, yes, she could only be writing positive things considering her expression. After she finished, she put her notebook on a side table and her pen on top of it.

She met Aaron's gaze. "I'm sorry, Aaron, but not yet."

"What? Why?"

"You're just not ready. You're closer, but not ready."

No blink, only a wide-eyed stare from him, the same in return from the doctor. It was a low blow, her analyst's face now losing its features, losing its color, his vision blurred, like Aaron was about to pass out. Something rallied him. "That's not right, Doctor. Please. *Please—*"

"What are you feeling now, Aaron? And it's important that you tell me the truth. Very important."

"Hurt. Lost. Like I've done my best but failed . . ."

"Tell me what you see."

Gray.

"I, uh, see you giving me more exercises, to get my arms around whatever deficiency you're still picking up in me. To keep me on track. To help me get there."

More gray, way too much gray . . .

"Excellent. No mention of color. Specifically, no mention of the gray. So here's the deal, Aaron. One more visit, and we'll go from there. I think you're in a better place. We'd still need to see each other for a bit afterward, if the surgeries become a go. I think—I hope—you'll be adjusted well enough to proceed. Stay the course, Aaron."

His disposition: On the outside, he was pulling it off. Her decision to delay her approval had added only one more visit to his sentence. He'd already done thirty years. He could do one more visit.

But on the inside, when she told him he needed more time, her face became the grayest face he'd ever seen, one that was raping him all over again.

NINETEEN

October 13
Saint Possenti's Bingo Hall, Rancor, Pennsylvania

Days before the final US Presidential debate: 3

Counsel and Andy met outside Saint Possenti's, there to bring their hard-at-work artist Sebastian Leone his special graduation dinner. A big day tomorrow, with Sebastian about to deliver on the fruits of his extended labor, and them then delivering said fruits to the Brandywine Museum of Art. They flashed their memberships and were buzzed inside the pistol range, Andy carrying a large, insulated food delivery bag.

"This is a bad precedent," Counsel said. She spoke over the noisy, target-shooting pop-pop-popping coming from members in their stalls. "Vonetta tells me she wants equal or better treatment for her and her husband when this deal is done." They passed the last stall, rounded a corner, and walked toward the rear of the building.

"And you shall get it for her," Andy said, "and maybe take *all* of us to dinner. A celebration. It'll be epic."

"Pizza and beer it is, then."

"Ah, no. Chateaubriand with crapaudine sauce and *tournedos villaret* and a kidney bean puree," Andy said. "Same as Sebastian is having tonight. It smells so good."

"I get the Chateaubriand steak part, but crappy tornados *what?*"

"Steak with a French sauce, stuffed mushrooms, and mashed kidney beans. And potatoes. He's been a good boy. We needed to bring him something special."

"We're bailing his ass out, and he knows it. Hell, I could have painted the Sistine Chapel in the time it took for him to crank out these few pieces."

They neared the last stretch of the gun range, passing the concrete wall baffle separating the range from the makeshift artist studio Sebastian was working in.

"Trial and error, Counsel. A few false positives before he was able to nail it, and nail it he has. Dody and I stopped by earlier today. We look to be a-okay good to go."

They turned the corner and entered the workspace. Andy put the dinner on the café table Sebastian used to eat his meals.

The lights, TV, and laptop were on, but nobody was home, in this room at least.

"Sebastian?" Andy called. No answer. They moved to the sleeping area behind the studio, also empty of Sebastian. Andy removed his handgun from its holster. Counsel removed hers.

"Sebastian," Counsel said, firmer, "show yourself, *now*."

Nothing. They neared the toileting area, closed off from the sleeping section. Counsel barked a command: "Make yourself decent 'cause we're coming in . . ."

She entered the bathroom first, then Andy, their guns raised. No artist. They retraced their steps to the studio section, guns still drawn, swinging them left to right and back. Messy brushes, floor, table, and multiple painting canvases leaning against the walls, also with stray paint. Which one was the finished product, the one that would replace the original, which of them were the trial runs?

"*Fuck-fuck-fuck*," came Counsel's sub-conscience rants, unadulterated words and near-words now leaking out rapid fire, no stopping her stoked disease.

"*. . . anal fuck-face cumsock klepto suckit suckit suckit bastard . . .*"

Andy holstered his weapon and called Vonetta on his phone. He put her on speaker.

"Fully functional," Vonetta said when asked about Sebastian's electronic anklet. "He's where he's always been, where he's supposed to be, at the bingo hall. Wait—hold a second—"

Counsel and Andy traded glances. An impatient Counsel yelled at the phone. "C'mon, Vonetta, you're killing me. What's wrong?"

"He left the building. The monitor tracked him. He didn't go far, a city block, maybe two, but he did leave. I . . . sorry, guys, I didn't notice any of that. It looks like he's stationary again."

"You see him?" Andy said. "Where is he?"

"He's—there. Where you are. Or at least the anklet is. Check the building. You want my help? I can leave now."

"No. Hold off while we sweep the studio again."

Back in the studio bathroom, they checked behind the toilet, in the toilet tank, all the fixtures, the under-the-sink cabinet, then around the bed, ripped off the bedclothes, then they searched his work area, still turning up neither the bracelet nor Sebastian. If he'd cut it off and left it somewhere, Vonetta's phone alert would have gone epileptic, so the anklet was probably still on him.

"Sonovabitch," Counsel said. "He's not here, and neither is the bracelet. Grab a bed pillow, Andy. We're going to need it."

They hurried outside the gun range. Counsel put her hand over her mouth, limiting a new Tourette's episode. She and Andy visually swept the vista that was small-town main street Rancor at dusk. Banks, a strip mall, a coffee shop, bakery, and a few hundred yards down the road, the bowling alley marquee ablaze in lights. In the distance, dusky daylight poked out from behind the camel humps of the Pocono mountains.

"No transportation, no money. He had to have someone pick him up," Counsel said. "Gone, damn it. I'm getting Fungo."

"Calm down, Counsel."

"This *is* me being calm. Me, dogs, and fuzzy keychain, pissed as hell, but calm." She leashed Tess. Fungo, her takedown specialist, was already accessorized. Her two K9 deputies jumped from the rear of the van and sat on their butts, attentive and waiting. "Pillow?"

Andy produced the bed pillow, the dogs slobbering over it while absorbing the scent. She handed Andy a leash. "Here, keep Tess company. Fungo and I are going for a walk."

Counsel grabbed her German shepherd Fungo's face and talked to him nose to nose, the dog's butt wiggling at hearing his name. "Well, Fungo, you get another crack at Mr. Leone. How's that sound, big guy?"

Fungo shoved his nose into the pillow again, the two of them now focused on finding their target. Counsel tossed the pillow into the van, let the leash extend, felt a taut tug come from her extremely motivated partner. She leaned back to restrain him plus balance herself against his need to run. They were off, at first returning to the gun range front door, then into an about-face that pulled Counsel back to the curb. Fungo sniffed the sidewalk and the gutter but went no farther than half a block up the street before he stopped, surveyed the gutter again, spun, and headed back to the gun range's front door. He now sat there, waiting to be rewarded.

Counsel eyed Andy, them both curious. She reached down and patted her K9 partner.

"You want inside the gun range? Fine. Good boy. No jute yet, bud, but soon. Andy, make Tess comfortable back in the van please, then we'll head back in." A shooting range was not a good place for working dog Tess, Counsel's explosives specialist. Too much gunpowder. For Fungo, not an issue.

Counsel again badged herself past the glassed-in entry and let Fungo guide them, her canine interested only in tracking the target. Andy followed, on the phone with Dody, who would engage her friends in Rancor's town watch, wanting to get the APB out.

Inside the range Fungo went berserk, pulling Counsel in all directions, soon heading down the hall to the studio. Inside the living space, Fungo pawed the mattress and a blanket and left dirty prints on the sheets on the floor. Another pirouette and the dog wanted out of the bedroom, back into the studio. They stopped at the table with the laptop. Fungo, his front legs on the chair, sniffed the laptop keys, did another spin, then pulled hard to leave the room.

"Andy—check the laptop's search history then catch up to us."

The dog was eager, Counsel needing all her weight to keep him from bolting into and through the pistol range and spooking the patrons. Attack dog versus people with firearms: As fearless as Fungo was around guns, and as good as he was at incapacitating fleeing adults, K9s were no match for bullets. Except, *whoa,* Fungo went right at one of the shooters in a stall, pulled him away from an instructor by the shooter's raised arm, then slammed him onto the floor. The German shepherd deputy sank his teeth into the man's fists, both wrapped around a handgun previously pointed at a paper target. She shook his fists with wild-dog abandon, liberating the gun—

"Fungo, no, heel, buddy, heel! Wait—*Sebastian?*"

"Ow, call him off, Counsel—*owww*. Stop. The hands!"

Counsel produced a piece of jute. Fungo released Sebastian to snatch his reward, then heeled at Counsel's side and chewed contentedly.

She looked closely at their captive, Sebastian now seated on a bench, whimpering and rubbing his hands. She saw no blood, no sign that Fungo had broken the skin, but the takedown had been savage.

"I do not like your dog, Counsel!" Sebastian said. "The other one, the smaller one, she is nicer."

"Believe me, the outcome might have been different had it been Tess. You'd have holes in your arms and hands now. What the hell are you doing out here?"

Sebastian grimaced as he lifted one hand to point at the far wall, his other holding the first steady. "See that target? I did that. Me, a world-class artist, put all those holes in John Dillinger, your Public Enemy Number One. I was bored. All these people with their weapons—they all are having so much fun shooting them."

A borrowed handgun, and after one quick lesson on gun handling and safety, Sebastian was shredding targets like the other "bingo" patrons. "I am hooked, Counsel. Can't we stay a little longer?"

Counsel eyed his paint-flecked shoes and smock. So incongruous an image, him covered in splotches of color while gripping a handgun. "No. Your dinner's here. Something special. You're lucky you didn't shoot yourself."

"Au contraire, mon ami. See, I am quite good. That Isis target now has no balls."

She hustled him back to his quarters where Andy was setting out the dinner—Chinet, white napkins, and mock stainless steel utensils in plastic. Andy removed the cork on some cabernet and poured it into a plastic tumbler. Sebastian sat, covered his paint-splattered, pleated lap with a napkin, and began eating.

Counsel checked the search history for the computer they'd let him use. Sebastian had left the building, that was a given. Maybe it would give something up about that. It showed nothing more than his interest in art museums, curators, and art dealers, etc., but also a search on the anklet he was wearing.

She grilled him. "You left St. Possenti's, didn't you? Researched the anklet, thought you could beat it. Where is it?"

"Yes, my lovely captor, I left the building, but it was not to run." He lifted his pantleg. "See, here is that abominable device, still on my ankle. It is easier to ask for forgiveness than for permission, right? I left to look for one of those marvelous sandwiches you fed me before. A hoagie. I purchased one, and I devoured it. Then I returned and learned how to shoot a pistol. And now, I am enjoying this incredible French cuisine for dinner. I am truly blessed."

Unconvinced, Counsel asked where he'd gotten the sandwich. He said the name of the hoagie shop. Andy legitimized his answer with a nod. "We'll check out your story, Sebastian, but you screwed the pooch here. We can't trust you now."

Sebastian chewed a sliver of his chateaubriand, rare, with some demi-glace, closed his eyes, and ignored Counsel while he let the enjoyment of the superbly prepared meal overwhelm his senses.

"My dear Counsel," he said, his knife and fork busy, "you cannot ruin my mellow. I can't address your mistrust, but please know that I am now completely one with this endeavor. I agreed to paint those cowboys for you, and I've kept that part of the deal. There is more we need to accomplish. I want to see this through, and I will."

TWENTY

October 13
Scranton Lace Company, Scranton

Days before the final US Presidential debate: 3

Mercer Crawford's armored Hummer limo left the city street, entered a short unlit stretch of alley between two buildings, both looking ghostly empty, all three of their stories the epitome of urban blight eyesore. The limo exited the alley and entered a courtyard interior bordered by more abandoned industrial warehousing. The courtyard was a mess, detritus and overgrown weeds covering much of the blacktop. It was nine p.m. The limo idled, its headlights illuminating a wall of glass panes, many broken. As bad as the enclosed area looked, Mercer couldn't have cared less. The only features of interest to him were its isolated location, its manageable proximity to the presidential debate, and that it needed to have more than one exit, which it did.

The limo doors opened. Mercer, Dagmar, and Renner climbed out. They walked a few crunchy steps on broken glass, the skeletal remains of the Scranton Lace Company surrounding them. Established 1890, the company had ceased doing business 112 years later in 2002, and after twenty-plus years of being shuttered, the facility's long buildings and grounds were already in irreversible, spiraling decay.

They walked the courtyard's perimeter, Mercer and Renner keen to the entry and exit points, Dagmar following them.

"Can they get the truck in and out of here?" Mercer said.

"The sellers and the buyers both said yes," Dagmar said. "It will be two eighteen wheelers. Large enough to handle the quantity."

"Then this will do fine. Tell them I'm good with it."

Gatling Arms, the sellers, would deliver the merchandise as agreed. Five thousand semiautomatic rifles, one thousand semiauto Uzi-knockoff handguns, additional magazines for each, all crated, plus ammo.

The buyers were an underground mercenary group known only as The Minutemen. Darknet players. They had found Renner, Renner turned them over to Dagmar, Dagmar vetted them. As a private military company American in origin, their specific physical American location, or headquarters, if there were any, was unknown. Mercer had never heard of them. If Gatling was satisfied that The Minutemen money was good, Mercer would earn his commission, and by extension downstream, so would Dagmar and Renner. The transaction was worth ten million dollars, and it included the trucks needed to deliver the merchandise. The incentive for Gatling was it moved stagnant, older inventory: firearms that performed well but had received bad press due to a few high-profile law enforcement lawsuits. For The Minutemen, equipping so extensive a group of followers would earn them huge respectability in the clandestine mercenary market.

A simple plan. Drive the trucks in, open their rear doors, and let the buyers inspect the merchandise by crowbarring open the crates, as many as they wanted. Hand over the keys for the semis. Dagmar and Renner would witness the transaction in person while Mercer was preoccupied in another part of the city.

"These Minutemen," Mercer asked, "for them to afford this, who are they?"

"Disgruntled veterans," Dagmar said. "Jarheads, grunts, flyboys, gunnery sergeants, Rangers, SEALs, and a few moneyed industrialists, all with axes to grind. Some retired low-level military brass. Every armed service represented. They say they want to saddle up and do some damage in South America, against the cartels. But hell, Mercer, I can't validate their intentions. They've got the money, and they could be any group of military malcontents bent on imposing their will, anywhere, anyhow, on foreign players or domestic, if they were so inclined. Might even be backed by a foreign government. Only time will tell. But what do you care?"

Labeling The Minutemen as mercenaries eased Mercer's mind, him drawing comfort thinking this large quantity of illegally acquired guns would leave the country and be used to defeat the filthy, foreign, different-skinned hordes, or a cartel, or whomever. It gave his conscience plausible deniability should domestic terrorist attacks come from any of these illegal guns he'd had a hand in putting on the street.

"I do care," he said. "A lot. Fighting the cartels. A valiant cause, Dagmar."

"Sure. However you need to rationalize it, Mercer."

Passive-aggressive again. Mercer was tiring of her attitude. So ill advised on her part.

She'd get one more chance from him, tonight, after this gritty visit here was over, where she'd be asked to audition for a larger role in the organization. The alternative, should she not cooperate, would be her retirement as an AEF officer in the shortest of order.

He moved to a more predictable assistant, his lead bodyguard. "Is the recon work done here, Renner?"

"Yes, sir."

The Scranton Lace Factory covered a large urban footprint a quarter mile long in the northern part of Scranton, paralleling the Lackawanna River. It once employed 1,400 people, boasting multiple attached buildings, a full-length interior basketball court with spectator seating, an infirmary, a barber shop, a cafeteria, and a small bowling alley, all of it now abandoned and deteriorating, including its massive clock tower.

" . . . and it's loaded with exposed asbestos, sir. We'll need to stay here, in this courtyard, and out of the buildings."

"Work it out between you two, I'll be elsewhere. Are we done here, Dagmar?"

"Yes. But I need to speak with you about another matter. I hear you're having the membership folks revise the application for new AEF members."

A perfect lead for Mercer. He'd address two issues—nay, opportunities—later tonight.

Number one, the issue she mentioned.

"Ahhh. Yes. There are some concerns that I took to the Board. A sensitive topic. Let's talk when we get back to the hotel."

Number two: "But not anywhere downstairs. Too many prying eyes."

***

Mercer opened the door to his Scranton hotel room for his guest. Dagmar was dressed the same as when they checked in, a tasteful, tan buttoned blouse under a rust-colored autumn-chic blazer, casual jeans, and flats. Mercer was in hotel slippers and gym trunks with a towel around his neck, his Nike tee a tight fit that advertised his gym membership was indeed benefitting his sixty-eight-year-old-body. His hair was wet. He twisted open a bottle of beer, its neck foaming. He palmed the cap.

"For you, Dagmar. Sorry, this was all there was in the fridge."

Who could decline a foaming bottle of beer? Not her, her slightly wide hips and full waistline attesting to this. She accepted it, eyed the bottle's foamy label. "Spoken like a true beer snob," she said. "I happen to like Yuengling."

"Like I said, the only thing in there." He grabbed a second open beer bottle from a ledge in the suite's hallway, then gestured at the sofa. "Have a seat. I ordered room service. Something stronger than beer is on the way up."

"What I'm drinking is fine, Mercer."

She sat at one end of the sofa, he at the other. "I'll get right to it, Dagmar. The membership is in a state of flux. The Board agreed to look at the changing demographics, and they liked my idea about strengthening the new member application process. To keep out the deadbeats, pretenders, and welfare abusers, that kind of thing. Become more proactive, more selective."

"In other words, keep out people who don't look like you," she said.

He took a gulp from his bottle, returned her stare. "Better stated, me *and* you."

"Oh. So no gender discrimination, only ethnic? That's still racist."

"The wrong way to look at it, Dagmar. Look, you're getting all upset. Not a good look for you. Relax, drink your beer—"

"Let me explain something to you, Mercer. We *are* seeing an uptick in non-white membership, and that's a good thing. Have you heard of the gun rights group GAS?"

"Of course. Brand new. 'Gun owners against something-something.' We're keeping an eye on them."

"'Gunowners Against the Slaughter.' Their officers include many people of color. A completely different view about the Second Amendment. A large portion of their dues goes to victims of gun violence. They're militant about responsible civilian gun ownership and weaponry."

"Dagmar—"

"They want more effective background checks, they prefer semiautomatic rifles be off the street, and here's the clincher, they agree to having a national gun ownership database. As far as they're concerned, President Lindsay isn't coming for their guns. She's a person of color; she has no problem if people of all races and backgrounds have legal guns. GAS doesn't view the government as an adversary, they consider the Feds partners in protecting this country. And we *should* be watching their organization, to maybe learn from them. What if the gun industry's future is GAS, not the AEF? Trust me, Mercer," she said, "you want people of color to apply here, to the AEF, rather than to GAS."

"You said 'the gun industry's' future, Dagmar. The AEF isn't the gun industry. It's a group of sportsmen and patriotic Americans exercising their Second Amendment rights. You're forgetting your own identity."

"And you're forgetting who you're talking to. Drop the pretense, Mercer. The least controversial aspect of our identity is we're a gun lobby.

The most controversial and realistic aspect of organizations like us is we're the gun industry itself."

Too philosophical, too blasphemous, too not-getting-him-a-piece-of-this-coveted-ass kind of comments for his temperament. A redirect. "Nice little speech, Dagmar. You done? Here's the problem. Those people are loading up the membership. I'm hearing about it from all the state chapters. Black, Latinos, Muslims, Hindis. They're not only joining our organization in sizable quantities; they're also showing up at gun shows and rallies in large numbers, and they're buying everything in sight, legal or not. Semiautomatic rifles, Dagmar, are selling so big now at the shows. AR-15s, AK-47s. I can only imagine what's happening online. These people are scarfing them up."

Dagmar, undeterred: "You're worried about groups of Black men cradling AR-15s, aren't you? Wandering throughout the Open Carry states with rifles on their backs, and holstered Glocks, or with concealed carry licenses. Those images scare the hell out of you, don't they? Dark-skinned men with guns. You're just so out of touch here, Mercer."

"Tell me this, Dagmar. How do you reconcile the deal we have with Gatling Arms? Putting guns in the hands of people who will actually *do* something about the bad guys? Pretty holier-than-thou of you, firing salvos from your glass house."

This quieted her, her squint indicative of her discomfort at what was a low blow. Mercer, still on the offensive, "How do you feel about what we're doing with *them*? *For* the people at Gatling, losing their jobs? And for these . . . Minutemen? These patriots who want these guns to neutralize some really bad people?"

"Mixed feelings, Mercer. Your agenda, not mine. We all have our reasons for participating. Mine is strictly monetary, and for me, the scale is tipped only barely in favor of going along with it."

"*Going along* with it? You arranged it!"

"I work for you. It's your deal, and as your employee, I'm nudging it along. Proud of some of the aspects, but not all of them."

"Dagmar. Listen to me. If we're not careful, the AEF will be overrun by the same terrorists this country is looking to eliminate around the globe.

The Board wants to slow down the membership numbers, not turn off the faucet completely. Guns are good for the American people, but the balance of power needs to be maintained by—"

"In favor of people who look like you and me," she said.

"That's the nature of things, Dagmar."

A knock at the door and an announcement through it: "Room Service."

"Dagmar, let's agree to disagree for the moment. The food is here."

A quick signature for the waiter, who left the tray on the coffee table. The seafood's aroma was pungent. There was also a bottle of Jim Beam.

"You won't want to eat this in that," Mercer said, gesturing at her suede blazer then laying his hands on her shoulders, going for the jacket's removal. "Here. Let me hang it up over—"

She leaned back, opening up some distance. "Hold on. What did you order, Mercer? Oysters?"

"No, not oysters. Mussels in a white wine sauce. I wanted oysters, they didn't have them. Your coat, Dagmar, please, else it will get—"

"You've got to be kidding me. Oysters and booze? This, this right here, this little seduction thing," some finger-pointing at the food tray, then at him, "it isn't happening, Mercer. We've got an incredibly busy schedule over the next few days. Two delicate business transactions, plus your expected attendance at the debate, and you decide to hit on me *again*? I am so outta here. Good night."

Mercer remained seated. "I'm sorry you feel this way, Dagmar. Truly sorry. My apologies. I—"

Dagmar closed the door behind her just short of a slam.

He moved some of the mussels onto another plate, grabbed a fork, sipped his beer, and decided the Yuengling wasn't bad. He would stay with it for tonight, would take the bottle of Beam home. He slurped a mussel from its shell, spoke with his mouth full.

"But I'm not as sorry as you will be, Miss Soon-to-be ex-AEF executive."

TWENTY-ONE

October 14
Lou The Image Maker Men's Store, Scranton

Days before the final US Presidential debate: 2

"Lou will get it done, Dad. Right, Lou?" Linus said. Linus continued poking at his phone, not waiting for an answer.

"I will," Lou the tailor said. Alongside Aaron, the two of them in a mirrored cubby toward the rear of the high-end clothing shop, the floor littered in thread, straight pins and fabric, the elderly tailor smoothed out the shoulders of the suit jacket. He lifted one lapel closer to Aaron's neck, assessing its coloring.

"Wool, in navy. Yes. This is the color. You look good in solid navy, and navy is good for TV. You'll need a solid light blue shirt and a solid maroon tie. They work the best for the camera."

Lou the tailor, owner of this locally legendary men's haberdashery, flicked repeated glances between Aaron's shoulders, arms, chest, waist, and legs, interspersing each glance at him in the flesh with a glance at him in his unaltered new suit in the mirror. Lou touched him everywhere—well, almost everywhere, in the way that a great tailor does without getting too personal—starting at the shoulders and moving south, recording measurements the old way, with straight pins, inseam tape, chalk, a nubby No. 2 pencil, and paper.

"You cut a fine figure, Mr. Aaron Pappas, sir," Lou said, the straight pin in his mouth not hindering to his speech. "You will look fantastic. I will have it done in two hours. Stop back then."

Aaron, a bit overwhelmed at the attention, remained silent, this whole TV thing a little too over the top for his comfort. Lou stepped between Aaron and the mirror and took measure of Aaron's apprehension, staring into his helpless eyes. Lou took the straight pins out of his mouth. In a clear and calm, elderly voice, he addressed his customer.

"As RuPaul once said, Mr. Aaron—"

Aaron perked up to meet Lou's stare. Lou's wink and nod were conspiratorial. With his professional resume, in business over sixty years, his touch sophisticated enough to get all the dimensions correct, how could this tailor not have figured it out?

"'Be yourself, know your proportions, and have a good tailor,'" Lou said.

He patted Aaron's chest, adding a smile. "Relax, if you can, and enjoy this time. I guarantee I will take good care of you, and that you will look every bit the part of an attractive, successful businessman. You will look *bellissimo.*"

Linus had choked on hearing the RuPaul comment, seeming only now to notice Aaron in the ill-fitting jacket and trousers assaulted by straight pins and white chalk. His smirk disappeared when he went back to reading and keying texts.

"Yes," Aaron said, exhaling. "Thank you, Lou."

Aaron investigated the contours of his suit, tucking his hands into various places around the jacket and the pants.

"You said you wanted pockets, Mr. Aaron. This jacket, those pants, the pockets in both, they are all functional. Now, remove your jacket, go to the dressing room, and step out of your new pants so I can get to work."

Aaron changed out of the trousers and back into his jeans. He needed a bio break and found the restroom where Lou pointed.

Linus burst into the bathroom, his face pained, his phone in front of it, ranting. "Dammit. Can you believe this? The Feds! They want to talk to you—they want to *clear* you—"

One toilet, and Aaron was sitting on it, jeans at his feet, his relief in progress. "Uh, privacy, Linus?"

Linus continued through Aaron's verbal stop sign. "This is harassment, Dad, pure and simple. You're trending with the media now, mostly positive. But don't worry. I'll take care of this with Mary. She'll get Senator Hudson involved and make them stand down from their request."

Linus's eyes opened wide at this person sitting on a commode, suddenly aware of the impropriety. He looked over his shoulder at the open door behind him, just now seeing the painted admonition "*WC.*"

"Oops. Sorry, Dad, my bad."

Aaron covered up, a red-faced Linus leaving Aaron to his privacy.

***

Linus remote-started his Volvo. With them both inside, he updated his father.

"Senator Hudson fixed it already. Secret Service, the FBI, they're now all on the same page. Sometimes law enforcement can be idiots. You're golden now, Dad, like me. It was agent overreach. No interview needed. The agent got her hand slapped."

Aaron, uncomfortable with the notoriety, pressed. "They wanted to interview me about what?"

The Feds' interest was something Aaron thought could happen. Blowback from the Bethlehem shooting, a connection to *Doodlemy9erdandy* maybe, who was gone, *dead*, but the guy's internet identity, his trail . . . could it have identified Aaron? Their chats were over the darknet. Something called "encryption" should have made tracking user locations and identity impossible. But he was new to all this technical crap. Maybe it was all BS. Or maybe he was in trouble.

Thoughts ran rampant in his head, but everything came back to one thing: guns. He'd researched them, tried to buy them, bought gun parts, and had them shipped to the condo. And, of course, there was *Doodlemy9erdandy*, his ghost gun machinist. How long before they discovered their discussion?

"An agent and her team out of Philly," Linus said, a start to answering Aaron's question. Linus negotiated the Scranton streets in the Volvo, one hand on the steering, one on his phone, him sneaking glances at texts. "She'd heard you would be in the audience for the debate. They wanted assurances. Senator Hudson, diplomat that he is, explained you'd been through hell. One law enforcement overreach was one too many. It already cost you thirty years in prison. A few calls to the right people, poof, the harassment was gone."

The darknet thing. If it, or any other incriminating lead, gave them a reason to look at him, the rest would fall like dominoes.

Two days. Just two more days.

"Dad?"

"Yes?"

"Apologies again for my poor bathroom manners. It'll be something, won't it, the day I use the bathroom after you, and I see the toilet seat already up?"

The comment made Aaron sad. Too cavalier, too light; a benign throwaway. Insensitive, and almost rude. Men born into the sex that matched their psyche would never understand what a simple task like being able to pee standing up could mean to a transitioning male. Or how it so repulsed some women born into the wrong sex to see, day after day, male genitalia, their own, dangling between their legs. For them, it was an everyday assault on their gender mis-identity.

Linus. Too casual about Aaron's lifelong struggle, but also too cavalier about a clandestine connection to him that might be close to being outed.

And too confusing.

"Yes, son, it will be epic. For sure."

TWENTY-TWO

October 14

St. Possenti's Bingo Hall, Rancor

Days before the final US Presidential debate: 2

Counsel and Andy stood with their heads tilted, absorbing the oil-on-canvas piece with critical but inexpert eyes, the piece now on an easel sitting free of any encumbrance, a spotlight on it. Next to it on another paint canvas was an opaque projection of the original from a close-up photo, the best example of the paint-by-numbers method Counsel had ever seen. They hadn't the foggiest idea how to analyze what was on the canvas—how to grade this forgery versus the original. They would need Sebastian to tell them what they should think about it.

"Do not be concerned," Sebastian said, admiring his work. "It is perfect in every way it needs to be. I have copied several of N. C. Wyeth's pieces over the years—other Wyeth artists, too—and a few more than once. American art collectors are less discerning, which is in direct contrast to their willingness to spend outrageous sums on stolen art, more than collectors in other countries. I say this not to offend you, but that is my belief. It's what I call the American blowhard quotient."

"America likes its cowboys," Counsel said, raising an indignant eyebrow, "and no Bolivian BS con artist will tell us what we can and can't like. Let's get it ready for transport."

Sebastian covered the front of the painting in glassine paper, placed a foam board against the back of the canvas, and tucked the glassine around the edges. He bubble-wrapped it twice over, then enclosed it in two foam boards sized a little larger than the canvas to protect it. He taped the boards tightly, length and width wise. Counsel and Andy slipped the painting into a special flat cardboard box and taped the end shut.

"Ready," Sebastian announced. He grabbed his coat, threw it on over his hoodie and pulled a slouchy beanie onto his head. Andy and Counsel lifted the package. They exited Saint Possenti's through a back door.

With the rear door of the van open, Fungo barked but remained crated. Tess faced them, panting, her dog grin encouraging them, her legs spread for balance. She gave them room while they leaned one edge of the package inside the interior, upright.

Counsel climbed in and directed Tess to the front seat. Andy pushed, Counsel pulled, until the tall, flat box was side-by-side against the other identical packages. Multiple bungee cords secured their cargo tightly against the van wall.

Sebastian, alongside Andy now, peered in the van at their cargo, Counsel squatting next to the packages. "No slide or shift?" Sebastian asked.

"They're snug as a bug in a rug," Andy said.

Counsel's affliction, unfortunately, did not miss a trick.

"... *huggy-bear, bugaboo, boogaloo, bibbidi-bobbidi-boo, booby bug in a rug—*"

Tess padded forward, stuck her nose into Counsel's armpit from behind until her face pushed through to greet Counsel's waiting hand, which stroked her deputy's fur to short-circuit the rant. She and her dog nuzzled. Sebastian gawked.

"Don't," she warned Sebastian, with him looking ready to comment.

"Oh, on the contrary, Ms. Fungo. You are an enigmatic, principled, attractive, yet filthy-mouthed woman. I am in awe of you. You have my utmost admiration."

"Huh," she said, slack-jawed, then, "Compliment accepted." Counsel willed away the blush she knew her cheeks now displayed. "So, are we done here then? Finished loading our prize?"

"We are," Sebastian said.

"Super. Andy is driving and I'm shotgun. Grab yourself some jump seat pleather and buckle up, Sebastian. Let's go make a special delivery."

***

They arrived at the entrance to the art museum a little after four p.m., which was closing time. "Be there in thirty seconds," Counsel said into her phone, the van negotiating the rolling hills that paralleled the Brandywine River.

"Follow the signs for deliveries," came from a male security guard. "There's a large cart waiting for you at the loading dock."

"Is she here?" Counsel asked, avoiding names and titles.

"Yes."

It took ten minutes to unload their cargo, another ten to push the encumbered cart inside the museum's bowels, into a small storeroom secured by a metal door but poorly lit, with dust bunnies kicking up under the cart's wheels as they pushed it into the center of the open space.

"Do *not* open anything in here," Sebastian directed Counsel. "It is too dusty. It could ruin the product." But it could stay here in its packaging for the time being if it was under lock and key, they decided.

Wherever the painting would be unpacked, it would need to be in a controlled, well-lit, clean, and sealed area, one where the photographers typically worked their magic when creating promotional materials for the museum. Also an area where art photographers from around the world would play with the lighting and the climate when creating tributes to the more heralded pieces of the museum, such as this one.

Click-a-clack, click-a-clack. A woman in high heels crossed the concrete floor behind them, arriving before they realized it. Short, in large dark sunglasses, her top was a black sequined punk rock tee under a slouch beany like Sebastian's, and it covered her auburn hair. She put her finger to her lips and took out her phone. Counsel's phone pinged, as did Andy's. Somewhere in the distance, voice echoes emanated from a larger space, an auditorium. A text came through.

There's a presentation to museum donors in progress in a nearby auditorium. Do not talk

More keying from her.

The piece stays here until the original is removed from the museum exhibit for photos in two days. Original and replacement will move down the hall for that, to a clean studio area, our media room. No dust, no grime

Counsel glanced at Sebastian before responding.

Fine. But our artist needs to see that space

Their hostess nodded. She walked them through two rooms to the doorway of a third, the room dark. She swiped at a few wall switches that turned on the overhead lighting. Voila: a windowless photography studio with floodlighting, tripods, backdrops, prop walls, assorted umbrella lights, softbox lighting kits, and three of the museum's landscape paintings in various stages of photographic exploitation.

Counsel and Andy eyed Sebastian eyeing the room's contents, the floor, the walls, the suspended ceiling. In one corner, a clothes rack held one item on a hanger: a gold blazer, the museum's orange crest sewn onto a chest pocket along with the name of their hostess, *Adamsky.*

Sebastian stepped farther into the room and swept his hand across a table to check for dirt.

Their punk rock T-shirted emcee keyed into her phone again.

Are we good?

Counsel dropped a hand onto Sebastian's shoulder to get his attention and offered him a thumb's up as a question. He looked at his fingers, clean of dust, and nodded. Counsel keyed.

We're good. We'll be back in two days to get the show started.

TWENTY-THREE

October 16

Time left to the final US Presidential debate: 5 hours

"You stand next to them when they take it off the wall," Mercer Crawford said. He sipped his wine, chewed his rib eye in between delivering phone instructions to Renner. The Scranton restaurant waiter arrived alongside his table with a water pitcher. Mercer waved him off.

"Watch them carry it out. Watch Dagmar validate that it's the original with that chemical. Watch them package it for transport. Stay on top of this, Renner. Do not let that painting out of your sight."

"Yessir, Mr. Crawford. Still waiting on Ms. Bystrom."

"Dagmar texted that she'd be at the gallery in a minute. Are you ready, Renner?"

Large, plain-suited Renner. His jacket was buttoned tightly but showed no hardware bulge. The agreement was that Mercer's players would have no guns. Renner and his troupe were in the exhibit area where Wild Bill Hickok still confronted a card cheat with his drawn Colt in the back room of a saloon, the $2.2 million original oil-on-canvas painting hanging under multiple spotlights. The museum was locking up for the night. Outside the door to the room, an attendant placed a placard on an easel announcing EXHIBIT CLOSED. The room with the popular N. C.

Wyeth painting was shutting down, its doors locking, its lights dimming, the Muzak turned off.

"Yes, I'm ready, Mr. Crawford. The exhibit is closing now. We're a go."

"Good. Stay on the phone with me, Renner. Is the art broker there yet?"

Another door opened in the rear of the room, Renner eying the entrants. "He just walked in."

Ricardo Lopez entered with a walking stick, an Australian bush hat over his wild hair, and sunglasses out of Breakfast at Tiffany's. Behind him, a woman in a gray jumpsuit carried photo equipment: cameras, more tripods, lenses—all of it as cover for the photography ruse. A second woman in a jumpsuit carried a large cardboard shipping container stuffed with packing material.

"Who is there with you, Renner?" Mercer asked.

"Mr. Lopez and two women. His photographers."

"The curator?"

"Ms. Adamsky is here also, yes. Here comes Dagmar."

Dagmar Bystrom entered wearing flats, jeans, a jean jacket, aviator sunglasses, and a fanny pack. She removed her shades. No introductions, the entire room quiet save for Renner speaking in a low voice on the phone.

"I think we're ready to get started, sir."

"Tell them to wait," Mercer said. "I'm going to my car for privacy. I will call you back on FaceTime. Two minutes."

Renner's phone rang. Mercer's face filled the screen. "I'm in my car. Change the phone's perspective so I can see the room."

The press of a key flipped the camera's picture around. Mercer could now see art broker Ricardo Lopez, still a flamer, plus his jump-suited women photographers and the smartly dressed Ms. Adamsky in her gold blazer. "Okay. Good. Let's get on with it."

Dagmar, hands in her rear pockets, arrived alongside Renner. She spoke directly to her boss, his visage at the end of Renner's arm. "You ready, Mercer?"

"Indeed, Dagmar. How about Ms. Adamsky?"

Dagmar eyed the curator. "You good?"

Ms. Adamsky raised her eyebrows in Ricardo Lopez's direction, referring the question. Mr. Lopez nodded at her.

"Yes, we're good," Ms. Adamsky said. "Two hooks hold it to a custom-sized metal strip fitted to the wall. Lift the piece off the hooks, place it on one of those two easels. It doesn't matter which one."

"Okay, here we go," Dagmar said. "Take the painting down, Mr. Lopez."

The two women photographers pulled on nitrile gloves then lifted and separated the painting from the wall. They walked the heavily framed piece ten feet and placed it on the easel, both easels under spotlighting.

"Mr. Lopez, your assistance please," Ms. Adamsky said.

The art broker stood face-to-face with the painting on the easel, stared it down for a moment, admiring it. "Quite a theatrical endeavor, don't you think, Ms. Adamsky? Melodramatic."

"That was N. C. Wyeth's style," she said. "In his paintings, things happened. Drama and sensationalism, in color. That was Mr. Wyeth."

"Yes, indeed. That's why I, too, like to paint him."

The gloved Mr. Lopez reached inside a camera bag and produced a putty knife and a Phillips' head screwdriver. His helpers leaned the painting forward on the easel to give him access to the top of the wooden frame from the rear, exposing two metal latches that kept the painting inside the frame. He unscrewed one retaining latch, careful to let the screw and the latch fall into his gloved hand, then the other. He inserted the putty knife gently between the top edge of the canvas and the underside of the frame, separating the canvas from the frame inch-by-inch as he advanced the putty knife along the inside, wary of it sticking, careful not to force it.

"Zero bonding to the frame," Mr. Lopez said. "Excellent."

His helpers lifted and rotated the painting on the easel to the next edge so he could do the same with the next two latches with similar success, then he did the remaining two edges. They held the canvas in the frame until he could free his hands of his tools.

"I'm ready to remove the canvas from the picture frame, ladies," Mr. Lopez said. They let the top of the painting tilt into his waiting hands on one corner and the curator's waiting hands on the other, lifting it out of the frame. The frame out of the way, they leaned the canvas back against the easel, again admiring it.

Ms. Adamsky produced her phone and keyed in a few digits. "Ms. Bystrom and company, would you care to see what I'm about to do?"

Dagmar arrived alongside, ushering Renner with her.

"See that black dot on the rear of the canvas, bottom right, on the edge of the frame? It's the security tag. It's also a GPS tracker. With a few strokes—"

She punched a few digits, Dagmar looking over Ms. Adamsky's one shoulder, Renner with Mercer on Facetime looking over the other. Her phone's search bar returned a message: "*Security Disengaged. Tracking Disengaged.*"

"Free as a bird now, Ms. Bystrom. It's all yours."

"Thank you. Mercer," Dagmar said into the phone screen, talking at Crawford's attentive face, "are you ready to watch me do this?"

"Yes. Do it."

Dagmar zipped open her fanny pack, retrieved a small, smoky amber eyedropper bottle. She stepped up to the painting. "Mr. Lopez, turn the painting around and on its side and place it back down on the easel, so I can get near the bottom edge."

The back of the canvas was now completely visible. No stray paint, no marks, its only knock a slight yellow dinge due to its age. With the painting balanced on the easel edge, the bottom edge also visible, Dagmar loosened the bottle's screw top. She gave the rubber tip a gentle squeeze to prime the eyedropper with the chemical. A full twist of the top and the eyedropper was out of the bottle, the tube nearly full, ready to be squeezed onto a Q-tip, to reveal an invisible mark made by an art collector looking to validate his newest acquisition as genuine, the one he had agreed to buy.

Renner moved in close to look over Dagmar's shoulder again. He spoke to his onscreen boss. "Can you see the edge of the painting, sir?"

"Yes. Dagmar, please get to it."

A swipe of the swab with the purple-colored chemical applied to one inch of dull yellow canvas un-hid the mark like magic. An instantaneous reaction, two characters now visible: *2A*, in deference to Mercer's Second Amendment reference. "We have a winner, Mercer," Dagmar said. She reinserted the eyedropper and tucked the medicine bottle back into her fanny pack.

"Renner?" Mercer asked, wanting another opinion.

"Yes, Mr. Crawford. '2A' is clearly visible, sir. I think we're good, sir."

Mercer stayed emotionless, but he was anything but. He barked into the phone, almost giddy. "Get it packed up and get it up here for me to see it in person, Renner. Then, Ms. Adamsky, we'll consummate the deal financially."

"Not so fast," Ms. Adamsky said. "It's not going anywhere until I see what the broker brought the museum in trade. Mr. Lopez?"

Mr. Lopez lifted his walking stick, gestured at a hunk of flat cardboard standing in a far corner. "Bring it over to that table, ladies, please."

Two pair of scissors in the hands of Mr. Lopez's photographers liberated the wad of double-wrapped, taped canvas sitting inside the cardboard, lifting the unframed forgery from the table to the open easel, placing it side-by-side to the original.

"Inspect it at will, Ms. Adamsky," Mr. Lopez said. "Here, you may use my magnifying glass."

Ms. Adamsky descended with a magnifier upon what would be her newest addition to the museum, a replacement for the valuable N. C. Wyeth painting there on loan. She called over to someone in the shadows. "Gavin? Come here, please."

The security guard emerged from a dark corner. Horn-rimmed glasses, heavyset yet light on his feet, as he got closer to the canvases he retrieved something from his pants pocket. After a quiet click, a razor blade emerged from inside a dull gray box cutter, the metallic blade glinting.

Someone might as well have yelled *Gun!*

Mr. Lopez started forward in protest, about to intercept the guard. "Put that away now, you brute!"

Renner tossed his cell phone at Dagmar, the toss not connecting, and reached for something strapped to his ankle under his pant leg. He came away with a small caliber handgun that he snapped up and at the security guard. Too slow. Renner was greeted with a large .45 that appeared in the hands of one of the female photographers, who held it to his temple. "Don't—take—a breath," she said through clenched teeth.

The second photographer was on top of the security guard, one-handing him back a step with a push while straight-arming her gun at his face, stopping him in his tracks.

"Stop! Everyone stop!" Ms. Adamsky pleaded. "Mr. Lopez! Have your assistants put their guns away. Do it. I will clear this up. Gavin," she said to the guard, "stay where you are, no false moves."

Mr. Lopez was shaking, almost in tears, but collected himself enough to give the word to his gun-toting photographers to comply.

Except one stood her ground, the barrel of her gun still at Renner's head, Renner's gun still raised at the guard. "Your peashooter, jackass. Put it gently on the floor. *Now*, tough guy."

Renner gritted his teeth, looked about to swallow his assailant whole, his face reddening—a "maybe, maybe not" response.

"Renner!" Dagmar scolded. "Don't do anything stupid—it's not worth it—give it up . . ."

The standoff lingered, three guns aimed with deadly intentions, one exposed razor, four chests heaving until—

A phone voice startled them. Mercer on speaker, the phone screen facing up at floor level, a tantrumming, furious voice, him hearing the action, seeing nothing but a blurry white suspended ceiling on his end. "Someone talk to me, goddammit!" he screamed.

Dagmar raised her voice. "Tell Renner to back off, Mercer. We need to trust Ms. Adamsky. If this goes south, she doesn't get paid either. Do it, or it's going to end badly for all of us. Mercer? Mercer, *please*. Call Renner off . . ."

One second, two, three seconds, then, "Renner, stand down," came through the phone's speaker. Renner placed his small caliber pistol on the floor, the photographer scooping it up.

One gun, one razorblade remained in play.

From the phone's speaker, Mercer's bluster continued. "Someone tell me what the hell is happening." Renner's assailant gestured for him to retrieve his phone from the floor. He held it facing out again.

Ms. Adamsky spoke, hers a nervous anger. "We had a deal, Crawford. Our people armed, yours not. I should pull the plug on this right now—"

Mercer's speakerphone voice was panicky. "No! It was a poor choice on the part of my assistant, wanting to protect my investment. We all understand each other now, don't we, Renner? Give your phone to Ms. Adamsky, Renner, so I can talk with her."

"Yessir, Mr. Crawford. Sorry, Mr. Crawford."

Ms. Adamsky, to Mercer and to the room: "Fine, Crawford, we're back on track. Gavin here is not really a security guard, he's an art authenticator. I want him to, shall we say, keep Mr. Lopez honest and evaluate the quality of the forgery. I want to know what I'm getting in return. Gavin? Please get on with it."

Gavin retracted the razor blade and returned the box cutter to a pocket. He showed his empty hands, then he retrieved a keychain with an illuminated magnifying glass from a different pocket. He neared the easels, careful to make no false steps toward the original.

"What I will do is visually inspect the forgery closely, then the original. I will then check the forgery's layers of varnish. Do you understand, Mr. Lopez?"

Ricardo Lopez nodded.

"Good. First, the inspection of the forgery."

Ms. Adamsky spoke into the phone, Mercer visibly annoyed but listening. "Gavin is my two-birds, one-stone authenticator for N. C. Wyeth pieces, Crawford. First, he'll handle the connoisseurship of the work, then the science."

Whatever, Mercer thought, aware of her approach. *I just want my painting, damn it.*

Connoisseurship was long the gold standard of art authentication. It relied on an authenticator's ability to recognize a specific artist's hand, which also allowed him to recognize a forgery. Regardless, to Mercer, it was just taking too damn long.

Ten minutes became fifteen, with Gavin moving back and forth between the paintings, studying different sections on all quadrants, the canvas edges, the margins, the signature, the personal dedication to Elva Corson, the painting's reverse side. He straightened up, signifying a finality to his inspection. "You might also take a black light to it soon as you can," Gavin said to Ms. Adamsky, "to look more closely, when time permits."

"Yes, Gavin. When time permits."

Gavin nodded then addressed Mr. Lopez. "Do you know the artist who reproduced this?"

"We all play our part, sir. I remain at arm's length regarding these transactions. Names, faces—it's best to keep to one's own business in the chain, especially involving the darknet. Healthier that way."

Gavin continued, disappointed. "Pass along my kudos to him—or her. This is an extremely good reproduction of N. C.'s work. The best I've ever seen, actually. And now," he glanced at Ms. Adamsky, "the science side of it. Everyone remain calm, please, while I retrieve my utility knife. If you'd like, sir," he addressed Renner directly, "you can stand between me and the original while I now tackle a particular aspect of the forgery for reasonability, per Ms. Adamsky's request."

Renner didn't hesitate, lumbering into position between the two paintings.

Both paintings had a gray-yellow tint, from the wall behind the hatless Hickok to the card table, the rogue player's hat, and the back of his vest, the original piece painted in 1916, the forgery over the last few weeks. But they also both had a yellowish hue that pervaded the rest of the painting as well, settling even on Hickok's midnight green coat. It was something that could have gathered on an original as it aged, and something that would have needed duplication on the reproduction for it to be convincing.

Gavin inspected the top edge of the forgery where the canvas was stretched taut. The edge would not be visible after reinsertion to the frame. He gently scraped the underside of the razor blade against a thick layer of varnish, shaving off the thinnest of layers into his palm. He inspected the shavings then slid them into a white business envelope, out of the way. He scraped a second time, then a third, sliding the shavings into the same envelope, which went to his pocket.

"Yellow, all the way through," he said to his audience.

"That's good, right, Gavin?" Ms. Adamsky asked.

"Yes, that's good."

"Will it pass?"

"It's an incredible forgery. I can't tell it from the one next to it, so in my opinion, yes. I am keeping the shavings."

"A fair trade for your opinion," Ms. Adamsky said. "You're welcome."

Gavin again eyed the art broker, an appreciative smile emerging. "Again, my compliments to the chef, Mr. Lopez."

"I will tell him, sir."

TWENTY-FOUR

Time left to the final US Presidential debate: 4 hours

The museum's media room released a collective breath. Ms. Adamsky, the curator, addressed the small group of clandestine art enthusiasts.

"Folks, this has been special, so don't take this the wrong way, but I'd really like you all to get the hell out of my museum right now, please."

She raised her voice in Renner's direction before he closed out his Facetime session. "Tell your Mr. Crawford he has six hours to come up with my money, otherwise I report the painting stolen."

The voice and face on the phone became agitated again. "Renner! Give your phone to Ms. Adamsky," Mercer demanded. Renner did as instructed.

"Ms. Adamsky. Christine, I believe it is?" Mercer's grin showed he was making nice, then his lips flat-lined. "If the painting arrives unharmed, you get paid. Everyone gets paid. If you do *any* such thing like report the painting stolen, I swear to God, you best remember who I am—"

Dagmar grabbed the phone to interrupt him. "No threats, Mercer, please, she gets it. Relax. We'll all settle up when we get the painting upstate. I believe we're done here, Renner. Mercer, it needs to be goodbye for now."

At the loading dock, Lopez's female "photographers" loaded the repackaged painting into a passenger rental van, Renner hovering for the entire trek from museum media room to vehicle, Dagmar trailing. They closed the van's rear doors.

Renner objected. "Wait. Open the doors back up. We're not going anywhere yet. Mr. Lopez," Renner pointed, "*who* is *that*?"

Renner eyed the sole vehicle idling at the end of a loading dock. Dodge Durango SUV, deep charcoal exterior, tinted windshield dark enough to be illegal, the rest of the windows the same, all limo-like. The engine thrummed like a road hog, the SUV's lights off.

Mr. Lopez answered. "My return ride from the Poconos. They will meet us in Scranton. I will travel with you and the painting in the van for delivery to Mr. Crawford, to keep my word that there will be no monkey business. Then I will take my leave and return south with them."

"Hold on a minute." Renner held up his hand to the photographers standing sentry at the van's rear, Dagmar next to them. "Keep that door open so I can see inside." He then right faced and closed the distance on the Durango, his face grim, glancing back frequently at the passenger van. When he arrived at the SUV, he tapped the driver's side window. "Open up."

No movement inside, no reaction from the driver. Seconds passing, the engine remained throaty in its idle.

"I said," his fist pounded the tinted glass, "open up your goddamn window—"

The driver's window stayed closed, but the window behind the driver opened six inches for Renner's benefit. He shielded his eyes with one hand and leaned close enough to get a look inside the darkened interior.

"Look, hotshot, I wanna know who the hell is following me—"

Two sets of snarling dog teeth crammed into the six-inch opening looking to rip off Renner's intrusive nose. He backed away quickly, their mouths still snapping at him. The passenger window powered closed, choking off the barking.

The driver's window opened an inch.

"So now you know," the male driver answered from the SUV's shadowy interior. The window eased closed.

Renner retreated to the van and growled at the gathering there, still pissed. "Close these doors, now. We're wasting time." Dagmar, Ricardo Lopez, one of the photographers, and Renner all buckled themselves in. Renner floored the van away from the loading dock.

The Durango continue to idle. The second photographer climbed in back, was accosted all familiar-like by Counsel's working dog Tess while she buckled up, the dog looking for a head rub.

"Hi, sweetie," Dody said to Tess, accommodating her. Tess rolled onto her back, shaming Dody into giving her a belly rub. Fungo was back in his crate.

Counsel spoke from her seat up front next to Andy, the driver. "So Dody, spill for us. How'd it go?"

Dody exhaled. "What a rush. A little tense inside, but all's well that ends well. So far, Crawford's people are happy, the museum people are happy, and I was happy I got to put a loaded .45 up to that baby-faced bodyguard's temple when he overreacted to the art authenticator doing his thing. It felt good seeing him squirm."

"So he pulled a weapon," Andy said.

"Yep," Dody said.

Counsel put her hand out. "Pay up."

Dody pulled a wallet from her hip pocket, placed a twenty into Counsel's wiggling fingers next to the twenty Andy had already dropped in. "I honestly didn't think he'd be that stupid," Dody said.

"Not that stupid," Counsel said, "that *loyal*. Tuck it away for future reference. Get some rest during the drive. Big night tonight."

***

Dagmar tapped her nails on the van's console, Scranton's city streets descending into dusk, her eyes peeled for parking. "There," she said, pointing. "It says 'Overflow Parking for Hannigan-McMaster Center.'"

The center itself, an old, repurposed Baptist church that oozed gothic charm, was a showpiece for the school of music for the university. And in a few hours, the church would be rocking as the site of the US presidential campaign's final debate, Democratic nominee vs. Republican nominee. Local, national, and world-wide coverage. A city on political-pundit overload, which was why they had to park two blocks away from the music center itself. They approached a concrete entrance ramp for a multi-floor parking garage. The circular ramp was one of four, each attached to a corner of the garage, the ramps corkscrewing their way upward from street level, the one-way ramps having dual purposes. For now, two ramps were entrances, two were exits.

"Dumb idea meeting here," Renner said, his bitchface back on, steering the van onto the bottom of the ramp. He grabbed a ticket from the machine and waited for the arm to rise. "We should be somewhere closer to the debate."

"Scranton's kinda busy tonight," Dagmar said, her sarcasm oozing, her *we've been through this already you idiot* suffix in abeyance. "Nothing closer to the venue has the covert space we need. The debate's strangling the city. Mercer's limo, your security team, and a place where we can circle the wagons while the prize moves from vehicle A to vehicle B—this garage will handle all of it fine. Plus, Mr. Lopez, don't you have something to add?"

She strained and gave a supplicating look in Mr. Lopez's direction in the jump seat behind them.

"My people rendered the garage's security cameras non-operational for the evening," he said.

"See, Renner, all under control. This is the last parking level under roof. It happens here."

The floor spread out before them, a poured concrete prairie half a city block long with cement columns hop-skip-jumping its length and width, two adjacent sides walled off. Less than half of the spaces on this level had parked vehicles in them. The van's headlights sought the farthest corner, closed in on two sides, dark and empty save for three sedans that the van's lights illuminated, Mercer's security detail positioned to take up six parking spaces. Renner goosed the gas a little then suddenly stopped short after the cone of the lights gave more definition to what was in another corner, making him upset. He jammed the gas pedal and lurched toward it, fishtailing the van to one side, its tires screeching. The lights now showed the other corner.

"Those losers with you, Mr. Lopez?" he grunted.

Parked there was the charcoal Durango SUV from the art gallery, a man standing in front of it, leaning back, his butt against the grill. He acknowledged the passenger van's headlights in his face with a small wave and a relaxed, friendly smile. Renner clicked on the brights. The man didn't flinch, instead lowered his sunglasses from his hair to his eyes. A shorthaired woman exited the SUV. Brown pixie cut, her sunglasses were already in place. She joined the guy in front of their ride and leaned back same as him, crossing her ankles then her arms. All they needed was popcorn.

"Indeed," Mr. Lopez said. "Good. My return ride is already here. Excellent."

A newly confused Renner stared them down before powering the high beams off. "She look familiar to you, Lopez?" he asked.

"A nameless acquaintance of no consequence, hired to do a job," Mr. Lopez said then changed the subject. "Mr. Renner, it would please me immensely if you could find me a men's room."

Renner wheeled the van around, reversing direction. They arrived alongside his security detail in the other corner. He exited the van, slamming the door.

"Take care of that piss you need to take, Lopez. Down two levels, first floor. Make it quick, then get the hell back up here. You need to stay with Mr. Crawford's painting. I'll leave two men here with you. But you and I, Dagmar—"

"I know, we have business at the lace factory. First, I need a restroom visit just like Mr. Lopez does. Mr. Lopez," Dagmar said, "shall we?"

TWENTY-FIVE

Hannigan-McMaster Center, University of Scranton

Time left to the final US Presidential debate: 90 minutes

Linus stopped his Volvo inside the parking garage next to the music center, its first floor cordoned off for VIP parking. He lifted the event badge tethered around his neck and slid it over the window ledge to let a Secret Service agent zap the bar code with a reader. On the passenger side of the car, another agent did likewise with Aaron's pass. The agents waved the Volvo forward.

"Senator Hudson needs to sharpen his responses, toughen some of his positions," Linus was saying, "so the true conservatives of the party can get more comfortable with him. They're backing him, of course, but the real money always comes out when the party moves away from moderate positions, keys more on . . ."

Blah-blah, blah-blah-blah. Aaron was hearing that the senator apparently had a softer, more likeable disposition nowadays, or so the media was saying, and Linus was validating this but sounding a bit peeved about it. Aaron's mind was made up, remaining unconvinced that a person could make so dramatic a change to their core being. Especially the person responsible for sentencing him to a prison hellhole for thirty-plus years. And yet—

"Mary, er, Congresswoman Inkster, now *there's* someone who's on top of her game. She'll hopefully help Senator Hudson sort out some of his inconsistencies when they're in office. The ticket's in great shape with her as the VP nominee. Did you see her during her debate with the current VP? She kicked his butt. Wow, she . . ."

Aaron grunted a few uh-huhs where they seemed appropriate, accepting that Linus had a significant bias about the congresswoman. He kept his seatbelt buckled until the car came to a complete stop. He hadn't been in a suit in over thirty years and was now dressed in the nicest suit he'd ever worn. Navy blue wool. Solid light blue shirt, solid maroon tie. Everything the haberdasher had suggested. The jacket was on a hanger behind him, and he kept an eye on it with glances over his shoulder as the car negotiated each of the turns on its way from the condo to the debate, the coat's lapels and pockets occasionally flapping against the window.

"Ready, Dad?"

"Sure. Ready."

Suit jackets on, their walk from the garage was short, passing under the overhang to a small line of people awaiting entry at a special single back door akin to ones used by people with back stage passes at events. Inside, the next line was longer, leading to a combination walk-through metal detector and body screener, with downstream agents in tactile gloves patting down every guest where their 3D screened image showed anything out of the ordinary in size, shape, or unascertained metallic content.

Aaron's palms were moist, a physical reaction to what was in store for everyone in line, him included. In his head, however, there was no real panic, the sweat a visceral reflex only, manifesting latent anxiety at the sight of equipment he'd been subjected to all those years during his incarceration. He followed closely behind Linus, as directed, with Linus bypassing the scene in front of them by stepping out of line.

"Dad. Over here." Linus pointed to the far left, at a curtain. "We go in here. There are VIPs, and there are VIPs," he said, winking. "We'll get to mingle with other special guests before the debate."

Behind the curtain, another Secret Service agent stood with a handheld metal-detecting "super" wand. He wanded Linus first and found a money clip in his pants pocket. With the clip removed, Linus was ushered forward. Aaron stepped into place.

Linus's advice to him before they'd left the car: *"No keys, no pens, no coins, no chains. Nothing metal. Leave your phone in the car, too. Everything metal stays in the car."*

Do as I say, not as I do, Aaron thought regarding Linus and his money clip.

The first pass of the wand, Aaron's arms were at his side, his legs spread—up, down, in, out. No beeps. The second pass, his arms were raised. Again, no beeps.

"Next," the agent said to the person behind Aaron.

It was the outcome Aaron had expected.

Inside a special suite, he did some superficial mingling. He stayed shy and reserved when meeting Congresswoman Inkster again, feeling undeserving of the attention the other guests and news media were paying to him, with him in the company of so many hard-luck folks like victims of gun violence, military gold star families, and families of law enforcement killed in the line of duty. He felt like an imposter; in fact he knew he was, and on more than one level.

Mingle time was over. Linus and the congresswoman led him out of the suite.

"I need to use the restroom," he said.

"You need any help, Dad?" Linus said. "I can run interference for you." An unnecessary reminder of the occasional bathroom challenge a transgender person faced.

"Ah, no, Linus, I think I can manage."

"Good. Look, out there." Linus pointed. "The first row is where we'll be, with space reserved for you between Congresswoman Inkster and me when you come out. We'll still have some time to mingle out there, too, but I'd get back here ASAP after the restroom visit, okay?"

"Will do, son."

Ten stalls in the restroom. Aaron chose the one against the right wall. He closed the door and latched it.

Exhale.

Too much gray in here. Too much soul-sucking gray . . .

He took a few more deep breaths to calm himself, allowing him to catch the second wind he hadn't known he needed.

Better.

From his left inside pocket he removed the gun frame, a black resin piece that included the housing, the trigger, the lower receiver, and the grip. The right inside pocket gave him the long, black resin cylinder pin needed to keep the cartridge housing in position inside the frame. The same inside pocket gave him the taut elastic band that would act as a spring.

From a flap jacket pocket he retrieved the cylinder, also a composite. Six bores for six cartridges, but he would have only three, one from each of the trumpet's three pistons. He snapped the piece into the frame, inserted the ramrod-like resin pin into a bored hole, which kept the cylinder in place while allowing its rotation, then he fitted the elastic band into the space reserved for the trigger spring.

He turned the assembled gun over and over in his right hand, admiring it. It was light, like a plastic toy. The space in the handle meant to house the legally required amount of detectable metal was empty.

Three pieces of 3D-printed resin composite and a rubber band, snapped together and engineered to deliver multiple .22 caliber bullets at the tickle of a trigger, with a force that would be deadly if the range were close enough.

He'd been gone, unsupervised, too long. Aaron checked all his pockets. They were empty of anything and everything. He lifted a flap pocket, slipped the ghost gun in. He was good to go. Linus, Congresswoman Inkster, the debate audience, and the debaters, awaited him.

At a TV commercial break, he'd retrieve the cartridges.

TWENTY-SIX

Scranton Lace Factory, Scranton

Time left to the final US Presidential debate: 75 minutes

Less than ten minutes from the music center by car, the abandoned Scranton Lace Factory facility loomed ominous in the mid-October dusk, a full city block of late-nineteenth to early twenty-first century manufacturing decay. Dagmar and Renner, in the back seat in a Buick sedan, circled the property's periphery in search of the paved entrance. Two all-beef members of Renner's protection team sat in the front as driver and shotgun. The deserted acreage was covered with crippled brick and concrete structures, a clock tower reaching to eight stories, and many broken windows, some of the windowsills still with air conditioners. Red and orange brick façades had massive bites missing from collapsing in on themselves, others clawed by steam shovels and other demolition equipment. The clock tower's label as "historic" was keeping it from the wrecking ball. Nature contributed to the repurposing, reclaiming the site with small, leafy trees and other foliage growing from windowsills and the roofline as well as at ground level.

The car turned onto a driveway on the property.

"We stay in the courtyard," Dagmar said.

Tablecloths, napkins, curtains, and other lacework. Parachutes and camouflage netting. The factory's thousand-plus employees came to work one day in 2002 and were told their shift would be the last one the 112-year-old factory could manage. The city block's worth of dead space had a coliseum vibe to it, and the vibe for the courtyard itself felt Shakespearean.

Something entirely different was on tap for the factory grounds tonight, loosely borne of American patriotism, and more directly associated with American enterprise and entrepreneurship. The Buick braked, its tires grabbing the scrabbled cement beneath it, kicking up dust particles that swirled in the headlights, the car coming to a scratchy but uneventful stop. Visible ahead was one other paved road that led out of the courtyard, into the night. Dagmar and Renner and their front-seat brawn exited the car.

"When do they get here?' Renner said.

"The buyers," Dagmar checked her watch, "any minute." She looked over her shoulder. "Same entrance we used. Multiple vehicles that will look like rejects from a law enforcement resale lot, or so I'm told. When do the trucks with the goods get here?"

Renner checked his phone. "ETA ten minutes."

"Truck-wise, what are we going to see?"

"Two Stop and Shop eighteen-wheelers. Also an RV for Gatling Arms's security team. Trucks first, RV second. They'll all enter through that separation next to the clock tower," Renner said, adding a chin point. "How many buyers?"

"An army of them," Dagmar said, now chewing gum. "They're dropping ten million on this transaction." She offered Renner a piece of gum; he declined. "But they're good for it. Or they will be. If not, no deal."

Renner reached into his suit jacket, removed a handgun from a shoulder holster, no pretense of being discreet. He checked the clip, was satisfied; he shoved the clip back into the gun. "If there is no deal," he said, "that won't be a good outcome. For any of us." He returned the gun to its holster.

Dagmar inhaled another piece of gum, enjoying the rush of flavor. She threw a pointed question out there, trolling. "How much for you, Renner?"

For Dagmar, it was $50K.

"None of your business."

Renner would get less, maybe only half that. There was this bromance going on between Mercer and Renner, but it was mostly one way, and Dagmar knew Mercer had probably taken advantage of it.

"When those trucks arrive, it's going to get crowded in here," she said. "My advice is to keep your head straight until it's over. No need for any fireworks."

Renner sneered, the sneer's message being *You're pathetic, Dagmar.*

She'd follow her own advice. She'd rely on the fact that she, too, was carrying, a loaded small caliber Colt under the back of her blouse, the holstered gun sitting just above the crack in her butt and feeling kind of erotic in there, her seeing no reason to check on it at the moment.

Headlights entered the courtyard behind them, from multiple vehicles creeping their way in. Her recon was right. Three beat-up Ford sedans, all full-size four-doors, all law enforcement-like.

"Christ, could they look any more like Feds?" Renner said. "Ballsy."

Doors slammed. The exiting occupants kept their distance, shadowy men with long rifles resting against their chests, their fingers trigger ready. Dagmar counted eight including one, maybe two women. A ninth occupant exited a back seat, a flashlight in his hand, no weapon visible. He barked orders, making one car move until its high beams shined in Dagmar and Renner's faces. After another order, the brights retreated to low beams.

The man with the flashlight approached them, stone and glass crunching under his boots, his flashlight off, his silhouette backlit by the car headlights. When he arrived alongside, the headlights from their own car gave him up. Caucasian, bushy beard, green and black camo tee, beer belly, black leather vest. A caricature, Dagmar opined.

"Hello, friends. Ma'am. I go by Paul Revere. Nice night. Which of you is 2A-yada-yada with all them silly symbols, from the darknet?"

Smooth, easygoing, congenial, low-key, direct. Dagmar was told to expect this when she'd done the vetting. The Minutemen, they called themselves. As clichéd-looking an assembly of male American mercenaries as she'd ever seen. Or rather not able to fully see, considering the encroaching darkness, save for one and only one woman, she was sure now. Regardless, from the buyer's side, this was Renner's show, so—

"That's me," Renner answered. "The trucks will be here any minute."

No small talk, but also no time for it. Rumbling up the paved lane in low gear, a dieseling semi approached the courtyard, crushing the crusty coat of detritus that layered the passageway. The truck's advance slowed, the cab feeling its way over discarded brick and stone in the courtyard like a moon rover over rough terrain, the debris surviving until the truck's trailer heavy with its payload compressed it into dust. The truck stopped in the center, belched exhaust above the cab through its vertical pipes, then the diesel engine idled. The driver stayed inside.

A second semi inched forward, same MO, arriving alongside the first. Pulling into the courtyard behind them both, an RV. The RV's occupants piled out like frat brothers arriving for Spring Break. Five men in sweats and athletic jerseys and gym shoes and ball caps, beer bottles in hand, other bottles and cans spilling out as they descended the RV steps. They assembled alongside the vehicle in a crooked line, one man not facing forward because he was relieving himself on the pavement.

"These are corporate officers?" Renner said not quite under his breath, squinting at them. "They're all drunk."

"Not all of them," a sixth one said correcting Renner, in gym gear also, and now rounding the indistinct line of revelers. "A designated driver. Me. I'm the company's CFO. The person who will confirm that the financial terms have been met. These guys are—"

The line of men was now boot-camp straight and much steadier than a moment ago, their feet squared, their shoulders back, their postures balanced.

" . . . sober when they need to be, and here as assurances. Let us proceed. Which of you will be master of ceremonies?"

Renner stepped up, Dagmar trailing. "I represent the broker," he said, and summoned the two groups together. Stepping forward from among their charges, the CFO gun manufacturer seller and the Paul Revere buyer shook hands. The CFO led them to the rear of the first eighteen-wheeler, a man with a crowbar following. The CFO keyed numbers into an eye level pad on the truck exterior, next to the truck's rear doors. The doors swung open on their own power, and an electric tailgate lowered itself to ground level.

"After you, Mr. Revere," Mr. CFO said. All five people stepped onto the gate and found their balance. The gate raised them to payload level. "And now, the reveal."

He switched on the semi's payload interior lights, dull, but bright enough to discourage stumbling. Paul Revere lit his torch of a flashlight, led the troupe down the middle of the truck's interior, small pallets of rectangular wooden crates lining both sides, reaching almost to eye level.

"Let's see. This one, that one, and that one," he said, his finger-pointing random. "Open them up."

Crowbar in hand, Paul Revere's associate complied, the metal nails on the crate lids groaning then giving way, the lids popping. Paul pulled one crate lid out of the way and removed a long gun. An AR-15 with a tan frame and a sixteen-inch barrel, with a push-button release for a thirty-round clip.

"Not loaded?"

"Not loaded. The ammo is separate. But I have a bonus for you, Mr. Revere. All have bump stocks. That makes you pretty much fully automatic. No extra charge."

"Really?" Paul said. Paul's crowbar guy held Paul's flashlight for him. He ejected the bullet clip into his hand, checked it to make sure it was empty, then snapped it back into place. Lift, aim, a trigger tickle, then he relaxed his finger. "Thank you, Mr. CFO, for the bump stocks. Nice of you."

He put the gun back into the chock, wiggled his fingers for his flashlight. Paul sought and found the gun's serial number.

The CFO leaned over his shoulder. "Like we agreed. All are serialized with bogus number strings not recorded anywhere. At Gatling Arms or anywhere else. These weapons don't exist."

Nineteen more guns in the crate were in the wood chocks, two rows of them, cradled inside. He moved to another crate and did a similar inspection on the PM15-22 handgun order, an Uzi facsimile, then to a third crate that was all ammo.

"When I check the next truck, what will I find?" Paul said.

"Loaded to the ceiling with palleted weapons, same models as these, the counts per our agreement. Five thousand long guns, one thousand handguns, ammo for both."

"Then let's open it up."

Paul, Renner, and Mr. CFO did a walk-through with the next truck, Dagmar abstaining, texting on her phone.

Almost done here Mercer. Smooth as silk. Everyone happy so far. Ready for some financial activity. Confirm with Renner when you can

Dagmar, at the rear of the second truck, listened to Mr. CFO's oration as the deal moved closer to consummation.

"Here. My business card," the CFO said. "It's legit. Count the boxes in both trucks and do the math, but please don't insult me by checking more than a few more crates and kicking the tires on the trucks. If you need to find me, call that number. And I'm in the company directory. All you'll need to do is get past my executive assistant. Not easy, by the way, he's ornery, but I'm sure you'd somehow manage."

A shared chuckle. Ten more minutes of validation. The bystanders on both sides remained encamped near their vehicles, everyone behaving. Paul and his crowbar guy emerged from the payload area of the second truck, all smiles. At ground level—

"I suppose we're ready, Mr. CFO. Let's return to our corners and finance ourselves silly, shall we?"

With Mr. CFO and Paul retreating inside their respective vehicles, Dagmar and Renner did likewise, their phones beeping and a-blazing in the backseat of the Buick, a computer on Renner's lap making rat-a-tat-tat noises like a semiautomatic handgun followed by a woman moaning each time an additional transaction crossed the transom. Renner's darknet ID was on overload, Dagmar observing the transactions on her phone.

"Cute, Renner," Dagmar said, needing to project her voice loud enough to better the female sound effects. "That's getting me all hot," she said, a headshake negating her comment before she'd finished it.

"I bet it does," Renner said.

Mr. CFO emerged from his RV the same time as Paul Revere emerged from his car. Renner perked up, fist-pumped once, and keyed a text to Mercer and Dagmar.

You see it on your end sir?

Indeed I do Renner. The finder's fee is now in my wallet. Nice work. Sending your bonus now

Renner's laptop rat-a-tat-tatted then moaned. "Yes-s-s," Renner said under his breath. He sent a return text to Mercer, with Dagmar still in the thread:

Thank you sir! Thank you!

Smooches, kisses, hearts should have suffixed the text, Dagmar felt. She waited for a similar text from Mercer plus a similar transaction to appear in her darknet wallet. Waited, and waited, and waited.

You sonovabitch, she thought.

Beeeep. She opened her online wallet inside her darknet ID.

Sixty grand received from Mercer's account. Ten grand more than expected. A pleasant surprise. No accompanying text from him, no return text from her, instead, radio silence. Dagmar moved the money out of her wallet to different banks in increments small enough to not trigger money laundering alarms.

Renner exited the car and hoofed it to where the two clandestine pseudo-titans met again in the middle of the courtyard. Dagmar trailed him, for her a casual walk.

"Mr. Master of Ceremonies," chief Minuteman Paul Revere said addressing Renner, "Mr. CFO and I are satisfied with the progress of our transactions, are we not, Mr. CFO?"

"Indeed, sir, I am. The transfers are progressing forthright. ETA for the rest of it," he looked over his shoulder at someone in the RV sending hand signals, "maybe another twelve minutes."

"I trust your benefactor is in receipt of his brokerage fee?" Mr. CFO said.

"Yes," Renner said. "He says thank you much for your confidence in him and his team."

"Excellent. In that case," he turned to Paul Revere, "here are the keys to your new eighteen-wheelers. Drive them in good health."

Trucks with guns, delivered. One-point-five million broker's fee transferred to Mercer Crawford's darknet wallet. The transfer of ten million more was in progress, moving from The Minutemen to Gatling Arms' wallet. Renner turned, moving uncomfortably close to Dagmar's face.

His grin was large, threatening, his face red, his bust-his-buttons attitude about to swallow her whole. "Give me your ID, Dagmar."

"Excuse me?"

"Your AEF badge. Give it to me. Right now. You're terminated."

Her phone beeped with texts from Mercer.

AEF no longer needs your services Dagmar. Today's your last day. Do as Renner says. BTW that extra ten grand you received is your severance

I'm firing you for insubordination. Per Legal, insubordination negates the terms of your contract. You're lucky I'm giving you the extra ten grand. Good-bye.

TWENTY-SEVEN

A parking garage two blocks from the debate

Mercer's stretch limo stopped at the automatic ticket dispenser, his driver grabbing the card. The car rumbled up the winding turret entrance, on its way to the third level. Behind the limo were two cars with two men each. Mercer texted Renner and asked for an update on Dagmar. Renner responded.

I have her ID sir. She's not talking. I think she's on the phone trying to get a cab

Let her go Renner she's dead to me

Renner's next text was a thumbs up plus rolling laugh emojis.

"Moron," Mercer said to himself.

Parking garage level three. The two cars peeled off and stopped short in front of the two stairway entrances to the garage, blocking them. The men positioned themselves facing the stairwells, advertising their semi-automatic rifles.

The armored Hummer limo slowed on its approach to the far corner, creeping toward the passenger van, their rendezvous vehicle, the van's engine running, its parking lights on. All parts of this garage floor were illuminated, LED floodlights protected by metal mesh screens meant to discourage mischief by BB guns, other guns, or rocks, all doing their jobs. The limo's engine shut down. Mercer exited the back seat dressed in a business suit looking TV camera ready, prepared to attend the presidential debate, which would begin shortly.

Across the way, Mr. Lopez left the van, the two large AEF babysitters bookending him. He took a few aristocratic steps, his walking stick echoing. One of the babysitters grabbed his elbow, stopping him in his tracks. He placed a hand on Mr. Lopez's chest that said wait here.

Mercer closed the distance, buttoning his suit jacket. He walked past him, leaving a deadpan glance at Mr. Lopez in his wake. He disappeared behind the rear of the van, leaning back out.

"You coming, Mr. Lopez?"

"Oh." A stroke of his beard went with the tilt of his head. A jab of his cane pulled him forward. "Certainly."

Mercer eyed the two ceiling cameras in each of the corners. Mr. Lopez followed his eyes.

"No need to worry," Lopez said. "They're functioning, but they're not recording. The garage attendant has been paid to look the other wa—"

Mercer gestured to his driver then pointed at the cameras. The driver trotted to the closest one and separated it from the wall with a baseball bat, then crushed it with multiple smashes from the bat's barrel, the camera dying with a small spark.

"Oh dear," Mr. Lopez said.

The driver stomped across the floor to the other corner, past the parked Dodge Durango SUV that was Mr. Lopez's ride home, Counsel and Dody seated behind the windows' heavy tint, but no Andy. Three swings of the bat connected with the second livestream garage camera, its pieces tinkling then settling onto the floor.

"That will give us more privacy, Mr. Lopez," Mercer said.

"Indeed."

"Open the rear doors to the van," Mercer said to his driver. "Let's see what our art broker has brought me."

The doors opened. He barked at his driver to remove the flat cardboard container and place it on the floor of the parking garage. "Give me your X-Acto knife."

Razor blade exposed, the tangle of wrapping tape surrendered the cardboard carrying case's contents. Mercer sliced through the triple-wrapped bubble wrap and peeled all the layers back.

"Oh my God. It's beautiful." He eyed Mr. Lopez. "Now let's make sure it's the right one." He wiggled his hand at his driver. "Help me turn it over."

A purple swish, bottom right, exposed tiny letters also in a deeper purple on the rear of the canvas. Mercer clasped his hands over his mouth in appreciation.

"Excellent! One moment. I now need to make a phone call."

Across the floor from them in the parking garage—

"Can you see what he's doing, Counsel?" Dody asked. The tint of their windshield kept their anonymity, their SUV fifty feet from the van.

Counsel still had her binoculars raised. "Crawford's on the phone. Are you logged into our ID?"

"I am."

"Let me know when you see the money hit the wallet."

"You know I will, honey."

"Purple it is, Renner," Mercer said into his phone, referencing the color on the back of the paint canvas. He'd spoken loud enough for Mr. Lopez to hear him, and exaggerated enough for Counsel to lip-read. "We have a winner. Go ahead, release the rest of the funds. Everyone gets paid. Let's wrap it back up and move it to my trunk. Mr. Lopez, nice doing business with you, but we really must go."

"Likewise, Mr. Crawford."

Counsel spoke to Dody, her binoculars still raised. "Anything yet?"

"Patience, doll. It needs to climb some darknet firewalls and get through a clearing house before we'll see it."

Counsel gripped her furry keychain, the tension stoking her affliction, needing to will away a tongue-twister. "C'mon, Renner, get it done already ..."

"Whoa," Dody said. "I'm seeing numbers queuing up. Big numbers. We're looking for what again?"

"Seven fifty and three zeros."

More seconds passed, then a full minute. Across the way, they watched Crawford answer his phone. He put his phone away then mouthed a comment. His driver and another bodyguard got back into the car. The men guarding the garage entrances saddled up in their separate vehicles.

Dody confirmed the transfer's full amount. "Wowzers. Hoo-*eee*."

"I wanna hear it's the largest jackpot you've ever seen, Dody."

"It is at that. Good stuff, honey. Is our art broker on his way over here?"

The Crawford limo peeled out, two cars in its wake, all heading toward the exit. Mr. Lopez stood leaning on his cane, the chinstrap for his Australian bush hat resting under his bearded chin. As soon as Crawford's limo left the floor, he tossed the walking stick. It skittered on the floor, underneath another car. He sprinted toward the Durango and hopped into the back seat. Once inside, he began grabbing at his face.

"Thees beard—it is giving me a rash—"

He peeled it off, tossed it in the back, into Fungo's cage.

"Not a good place for that, Sebastian," Counsel said. "Fungo will think he's supposed to track you. You already know how that will end."

"But I am a good guy now, Ms. Counsel. You would intervene, correct?"

"Maybe."

Another of their SUV's doors opened. Andy in an orange hunting vest hopped in behind Dody and gave her shoulder a friendly squeeze. He leaned forward for a peck on Counsel's cheek.

"Well?" Counsel asked.

"No issues. Perfect exchange one level down, with happy customers. Anything yet, Dody?"

"Checking, Andy, checking, just stay calm."

The other back door opened and Vonetta squeezed in, huffing, puffing, coughing, in a tracksuit and sneakers. "Three sets of cement stairs," she said, still catching her breath. "Don't y'all say nothing, Counsel. I can still beat you on the course in full riot gear, so you can just shut your diarrhea mouth the hell up." Vonetta's head swiveled at the SUV's occupants, three women, two men, two K9s, no casualties. "We good, y'all? Someone tell me we all did good."

"If your exchange was good, then we all did good, Vonetta," Counsel said.

Andy spoke from the rear seat. "Great. Let me drive. It's my SUV rental."

Counsel and Dody traded humoring glances.

"Let me see," Counsel said. "We're about to make our getaway, so who gets to drive? The state trooper who chases bounties for a living, as in me, or the state trooper who's now a bail bondswoman, as in Vonetta, or the former sheriff, as in Dody? Or should we go with the mansplaining nurse saying he should drive because he rented the car?" A delightful glance at Andy. "How about no, lover, you're not driving, I am."

Counsel put the SUV in gear and they drifted slowly out of the parking space while she looked both ways. She headed for a different exit than the stretch Hummer. "Soon we'll be doing even better, right, Dody?"

"I'm working my way down our list, Counsel," Dody said, her fingers blazing. "The money's all gonna go where it's supposed to go, just be patient, I'm keying as fast as I can . . ."

TWENTY-EIGHT

The stretch Hummer found one of the two exit ramps and eased into the circular concrete tower, the tires squealing at the severity of the corkscrew turn.

"Slow down," Mercer said to his driver.

Mercer was beside himself, a little unhappy that he couldn't be in the back with his newest acquisition. Wild Bill Hickok, Mr. Aces and Eights himself. Goosebumps. He'd already set up a shrine for it in his Virginia home pending its arrival, to go on a wall with other highly coveted western and American frontier art pieces by the likes of Frederic Remington, Charles Marion Russell, and W. Herbert Dunton. His gallery of masterpieces. All expensive reproductions, he'd boasted, something he was up front about when he entertained all those genuflecting captains of industry, politicians, and corporate CEOs.

Except that was all a ruse. He had a secret. Something that could never be shared in the circles he traveled, at least not while he was alive. And that secret was, many of the pieces *were* the originals. He'd had people steal them, just like this one.

He was giddy with anticipation. He'd arrive home tomorrow with his new acquisition and have it take its rightful place as the crown jewel of his collection.

Yes, life was good.

The Hummer slowed its descent to fall in line behind another car using the exit ramp from the second garage level. A silver Bentley.

Mercer stiffened, leaning forward to get a closer look. He glared at the car's bumper. On it was a state of Virginia license plate that was a vanity tag: *ART-GUY*.

"Bosco," he said, thinking aloud before he could stifle himself. "That's Bosco Horvath in that Bentley."

Mercer found his phone, searched for a saved number, and listened as it rang. "Answer your phone, Bosco . . ."

"Horvath here."

"It's Mercer. I need to know where you are right the hell now, Bosco."

"And why is that, Mercer?"

"Tell me where the hell you are!"

"Okay, if you must know—I'm in Scranton."

"Turn around and look out your back window, you sonovabitch."

The Bentley stopped. Mercer saw its rear-seated passenger squint at the headlights from Mercer's Hummer shining in his face.

"Yes, that's me behind you. What have you done, Bosco?"

"I, ah, had an opportunity present itself that I couldn't refuse, so I—hey, wait a minute. What are *you* doing here?"

"Exactly, asshole. Now do you understand?"

They shouted at each other, friends now screaming death threats into their phones, their vehicles advancing down the ramp in fits and starts, finally reaching the bottom, falling in line behind the exit gate, one car ahead of their two vehicles.

"Pull over when we get on the street, Bosco, you bastard! We need to talk."

Mercer hung up, dialed Renner, and started in on him. "Where are you?"

"Still at the lace factory, sir, in the courtyard. The transfer from the buyers to Gatling is almost done."

"Look, dipstick, I don't know how you did it, but you screwed the pooch royally with this Wyeth painting. Something's not right. The painting . . ."

He verbally wailed on Renner, blasting him about Bosco double-crossing them, pulling the same heist, tonight of all nights, how *dare* he, until—

Mercer stopped in mid-sentence to crane his neck outside his car window, looking ahead of their two cars. The person leaning out of the car first in line, paying a garage employee to exit the garage—high and tight gray haircut, square jaw matched by bulky, square shoulders, the car with a bumper sticker that read *Semper Fi*, that person was—

"Christ. That's . . . that's Colonel Jammer."

Mercer hung up on Renner, dialed another number and calmed himself to keep from spitting all over the phone. "Jammer. Mercer Crawford here. This will be an odd question, but where are you—physically—as in right, the hell, now?"

"None of your damn business, Crawford, but because I like you so much, I'm in Scranton."

Three separate transactions, maybe more. Which meant the masterpiece in the rear of Jammer's car was—

" . . . a forgery too, Colonel," Mercer explained. "They're probably *all* forgeries. Park on the street. You, and I, and a former art-authenticating friend of mine, we all need to compare notes right *now*."

He ended the call and repeatedly punched the back of the front seat, F-bombs punctuating the pounding.

He let the phone drop into his lap, his hand hurting, him screaming threats that stayed internal to the car. His phone beeped. It was a social media notification addressed to *@AEFHeadHoncho*, his Twitter, or "X" account, which was followed by over 800,000 people. He pulled the tweet up.

Dominic Lucatelli here. All my Mummers brothers died a senseless death in Philly. I survived. Someone just put $50K in my GoFundMe acct in your name, Mr. Mercer. TY & God bless you

He looked blankly at his phone, stunned. He stomped out of his car, got in Bosco Horvath's face, finger pointing and blustering, then went at Colonel Jammer as well, who grabbed him by the lapels and was about to plant a right cross on Mercer's chin if he didn't calm the hell down. Their phones were all ringing, dueling ringtones that bettered the noise on the street. Horvath answered his phone and put up his hand for Mercer and the colonel to calm down. He covered his other ear so he could hear. He mouthed "my secretary."

"Horvath here. I did *what*? Thirty grand in my name went to someone's *crowdfunding account*?"

Jammer let go of Mercer, checked his Twitter account on his phone. His face pinched, straining to read the entry, about to explode. Their phones rang and beeped again and again, the thank-you calls and tweets and Facebook posts all similar, coming from gun violence victims, anti-assault-style rifle groups, and liberal politicians, plus they'd each, apparently, made large contributions to PACs that promoted bans against assault-style weapons. One phone call more than the others made Mercer's heart jump into his throat.

"Darville Washington here, Mr. Crawford. I'm the CEO of the gun rights organization knows as GAS, short for Gunowners Against the Slaughter. I must say I'm a bit overwhelmed by your generosity, especially considering our organization and the AEF don't quite see eye-to-eye."

The donation: $100,000, to a competing gun rights organization with radical anti-gun lobby and gun ownership ideas, made in Mercer Crawford's name. Mercer was about to throw up.

None of the calls to them had come from their banks, with good reason. This money, the wire transfers, the electronic deposits, it was all coming from bank accounts other than their own. Charitable donations made in their names that could never be recovered and would never be returned, originating from anonymous accounts, all coincident with their recent purchases of a certain iconic painting by N. C. Wyeth.

The darknet art brokers, damn it—they were donating their earnings.

The three blustering men compared their exchanges. Crawford's contact was flamboyant Ricardo Lopez. Horvath's contact, a large, track-suited woman who went by the name Moms Vermillion, was a street artist with connections. Jammer's contact, "Coal-man" Coleman, was a male Philly graffiti artist turned deer hunter banished to the Poconos, or so Jammer had been told. Real people or fake personas? Regardless, they were each unloading their spoils, doing the social awareness thing, and were being benevolent with their ill-gotten funds. They all had consciences, dammit. The media would have a field day unraveling this.

Someone had to have the original painting, but chances were it was none of them. Mercer, Jammer, and Horvath each opened the trunks and tailgates of their cars and had their drivers pull out their paintings and remove the nearly identical packaging. Inside their packages was N. C. Wyeth's *Hickok at Cards*, now in triplicate, the painting edges resting on the tops of car bumpers, the cars double-parked on an open-air Scranton boulevard under exterior parking-garage floodlighting and flashing storefront marquee neon. They looked like street-hustling starving artists with velvet Elvises for sale.

Mercer barked at Horvath, the three men staring at their spoils. "Well, Bosco, you're the art expert. Start talking."

"Extraordinary pieces to the max," Horvath admitted. "If none of these is the original, I am beyond flabbergasted."

"Turn them around," Mercer said, knowing where he was going. "The backs might tell us something."

Each had already seen the backs of their acquired canvases, each had decided that they had the original. Except Mercer's "original" looked different. It had marks on it, on the bottom right corner, exactly where he'd made them.

His hopes rose. He was the only one of the three to brand his purchase ahead of time.

Jammer stared Mercer down. Mercer was about to gloat at this as a reveal, then—

"Mercer," Horvath said, "it looks like someone spilled something on yours, down here where I'm pointing. Right over those two handwritten letters? They look like the number two and the letter A underneath the spill."

Yer damn right someone spilled something on it, Mercer thought. *A special chemical. That's because it's the real deal, assholes. Those are MY marks . . .*

Horvath's pointer finger inched closer to the rear of the canvas, ready to poke at it.

"Hey! No, Bosco. What are you doing? HEY. Back off—"

Too late. Horvath touched his finger to the purple stain, then to his mouth.

"Like I thought. Grape. Probably grape juice. The old grade-school science invisible ink experiment. Spoon of baking soda, spoon of water, dip a toothpick or a cotton swap in the mixture and voila, you can write a message. When it dries, the message is invisible. The acid in the grape juice lets you read it."

Mercer's jaw dropped.

"What? I said something wrong?" Bosco said. "You didn't know that trick?"

A fuming Mercer backed off, called Renner. "You jackass! You and Dagmar cost me a fortune, dammit . . ."

"It wasn't me, sir—the branding—it was Dagmar's idea . . ."

"Where the hell is she? And where—in the bloody hell—is the original Hickok painting?"

A few more berating sentences into his tirade, Mercer froze. The Dodge Durango they'd done business with cruised out of the parking garage's other exit tower, stopping at an intersection under a streetlight a half a block away, waiting for the traffic light to change.

"Get that painting back inside my car, *now*," he screamed at his men. "Get in and drive, dammit. Renner! Where arc you? We found the bastards. I'm about to get my money back."

TWENTY-NINE

"Counsel," Andy said. Their SUV waited for the traffic light to change. Andy had a clear view from the back seat of the nearly empty downtown street that intersected with theirs. "Ah, Counsel honey? Dody? You guys see what I see?"

All eyes looked right. A black stretch Hummer barreled down the city street, its engine accelerating, on a collision course with their intersection.

"Is that—?"

"Crawford's car. Run the light," Andy said. "Buckle up, everyone."

"Tess—?"

"I've got her," Andy said and pulled her in.

The Durango's tires smoked, the rear fishtailing then grabbing enough asphalt to evade moving traffic in the intersection. They sped up the city block. Behind them, the Hummer entered the intersection, screeching around the corner.

"You know the way, Counsel?" Dody asked, riding shotgun, her phone in hand.

"No—key in the address."

Dody's phone started shouting GPS directions.

"Turn right onto Mulberry Street, fool, then turn right onto Wyoming Avenue, hahaha. Proceed one mile, but don't you be speeding, you ain't no A-Team driver, fool, hahaha."

"What the hell, Dody? Mr. T is your GPS voice?"

"Shut up, Counsel, he speaks to me . . ."

***

Mercer was still on the phone reaming Renner, his voice having to better the Hummer's massive V8 that was gulping air and gas and breathing fire, pushing the vehicle up the Scranton street's blacktop at a high rate of speed.

"The gun deal done yet? I need you, dammit—where the hell are you, Renner?"

"Still at the lace factory, sir, trying to get out of here. The buyers say they're done with the transfer on their end, but Gatling doesn't have all the money yet."

Mercer threatened him with genital dismemberment and financial ruin, with Renner protesting, pleading his innocence and begging for forgiveness, until Mercer heard something he wanted to hear. "Say that again, Renner."

"They put a large package in the back of their car at the Brandywine museum that looked just like the other packages. It could be the real Hickok painting."

Mercer was out of ideas and panicky, his eyes on the Durango SUV that screamed through Scranton's downtown streets half a city block ahead of them. He didn't want his money back, he wanted the Wyeth painting. The goddamned original. If they had it with them, he'd get it back at gunpoint if he had to, then he'd also get them, at gunpoint, to reimburse him for trying to cheat him. The best of both worlds.

"Stay on the phone, Renner, I'm not done with you."

***

"Slow down, fool, and turn left half a mile ahead, hahaha."

Counsel shouted at the GPS voice. "Really, Mr. T? Move your cheeks, soccer mom!"

Intersection ahead, the traffic light red, the cars three deep. They needed the sidewalk so Counsel steered the SUV onto it, climbed a low set of steps, no people, and roared down a slate breezeway for half a city block.

The SUV launched a corner litter basket into the street then a trash compactor, then careened off a bike rack. They dropped back down the steps and found room on the blacktop again on the other side of the red light. Counsel accelerated.

"Fool! You're speeding, slow down, slow down, slow down, turn right a hundred feet, then left three hundred feet, onto Larch Street, speed limit thirty-five, hahaha, slow down, fool."

The red light in their wake turned green. The Hummer rocketed though the intersection stopping a UPS truck from entering. The Hummer was gaining on them on the straightaway.

"One mile to Larch Street, fool."

Honda dealership, Mazda, McDonald's, another red light—

"Left turn two hundred feet."

Green light. The Durango squealed into the turn. Storefronts on either side gave way to open space on unoccupied land parcels, dark and deep, empty construction lots, no streetlights—

"Point three miles to Sanderson Street," Dody barked, "soft right, stay on the gas . . ."

"On the horizon, Dody," Counsel said, "look—there's the factory."

"I see it. They're gaining, Counsel. Faster, lady, faster."

Counsel's foot went to the floor, the SUV lurched, eighty-five, eighty-seven, ninety, right turn coming . . .

Andy, Vonetta, Dody, all leaned right, their guns unholstered now, gripped tightly in their laps.

"Five hundred feet turn right, slow down NOW, fool!"

Darkness reigned on Glenn Street, a two-lane speedway, high beams on, past an empty bus stop, a public transit bus on the move ahead of them, they needed to squeeze past it—passing a closed beer warehouse, a stone supply company . . .

"Meylert Avenue, Counsel, coming up, last turn on the GPS, point two miles, there's the lace factory, slow up, honey, find an entrance."

The Scranton Lace Company, foreboding, shadowy, with chain link fencing surrounding it in spots, the speeding SUV paralleled the fence, the Hummer gaining.

"Find a way in, Counsel, there are only two entrances—"

"I'm trying, Dody."

Around a corner there it was, an entrance overgrown with foliage, no better than a back alley, no fencing across it, with construction equipment straddling the blacktop, but no obstructions. She hit the brakes, slid into a hard right, slammed the accelerator again, and steered at the dark, abandoned, three-story red brick and tan building ahead of them with a deep gash in the middle of it front to back, where a section had been removed. It wasn't a road, not an entry, debris scattered at ground level, with chunks of stone and wire and rebar sticking out in all directions, all tangled. Past it was open space, or what looked like open space: the factory's courtyard, lit at ground level by vehicle headlights that sluiced through rising car exhaust.

Dody grabbed Counsel's arm. "No, Counsel—it's not wide enough— the rebar—it'll spear the frame—"

"Sorry, Dody. Andy, hold Tess tight. Hold on, everyone!"

The Durango slammed the jagged groundcover at sixty, rammed its way through chaotic rebar, loose bricks, and leftover window frames, caught some air under it then came down hard inside the courtyard, the brakes screaming as Counsel stood on them to keep from slamming into the side of an eighteen-wheeler. She cut the engine, looked behind her. The Hummer screeched to a stop before the building's carve-out the Durango just bested; the Hummer's doors flew open. Whoever was in it would need to walk through jagged building fragments that looked like 9/11 ground zero to follow them.

"Get out," Counsel said. "Everyone out. Re-holster your guns."

They climbed out of the damaged Durango, the engine coughing but maintaining its idle. In front of them was a crowd, many men with assault weapons, their fingers trigger ready. Nobody spoke, all remained focused on the Durango and its five former occupants next to it. Someone emerged from an RV and heads turned, the guy oblivious to the addition of so road-weary a vehicle to their gathering.

"Hey, where's Mr. Revere? Paul? There you are. The transfer's done, sir. It's in our wallet. It's all good, dude. I believe everyone can saddle up and skedaddle, folks. Wait. What did I miss? Who are these people?"

All eyes returned to Counsel and her friends, their hands by their sides, her dogs barking furiously from inside the SUV. All the other hands in the courtyard now had weaponry in them.

Mercer Crawford answered the question from a distance, shouting to be heard while he tread delicately, disdainfully through the prickly debris trail the SUV had vaulted. "Who these people are, are people I have business with…"

His flashlight blazing, Crawford watched where he tread, dust kicking up, onto his suit, his driver helping him over the loose brick and stone. "I'm Renner's boss. No need for introductions. Ignore us, finish what you're doing."

Dramatic entrances, major intrusions. Still, no one else moved.

Crawford arrived at the rear of the Durango SUV, regained some composure, and pulled at the tailgate. Locked. He banged on it with a fist. "Open this goddamn tailgate. Open it!"

"Back off, Crawford," Counsel said, her fingers on her furry talisman. "Two dogs are in there. One's crated, but the other one will attack. Let me leash her. No funny business, I promise."

Counsel opened a passenger door. Tess was on the seat, waiting. Counsel leashed her and led her out, gripping the leash extra tight. Straining, she pulled Counsel to the rear of the SUV. Crawford's driver had his gun drawn.

"Really?" she said, her eyes on the gun. "That's where we are, Crawford? You think we don't have guns, too, for a deal like this? Put the gun away, asshole. Someone might get hurt."

"Open the goddamn tailgate," Crawford said.

"Why should I do that?"

"Open it!"

She pressed the key fob. The tailgate lifted. Inside was Fungo, one pissed-off German shepherd, barking, jumping, and baring his teeth, his crate bouncing against the side window and the ceiling. Lying flat on the floor next to the crate was a cardboard box.

Renner, next to Crawford now, spoke. "See, sir, there it is, that's another painting—"

Nearby, at the edge of the factory's courtyard, the RV's ignition caught, the rest of the Gatling Arms men inside, its interior lights on. They were busy still high-fiving themselves, popping open sudsy beer cans, some of them visible through the large windshield. The RV idled, waiting to follow the semis out of the courtyard, except the eighteen-wheelers weren't moving. No engine ignition, no revving gas pedal, no exhaust overhead from dieseling pipes, because there were no drivers inside either semi's cab.

"Hey, Mr. Revere," Gatling's CFO called, about to climb up into his RV's driver's seat. "Don't tell me you forgot to bring people who know how to drive these rigs. Ha! Sorry, only kidding. Mr. Revere? Hello? Where'd you go? Mr. Revere?"

The Minutemen stayed in formation, but Mr. Revere was no longer available. One of the mercenaries, a woman, stepped out of line and moved to the front. She approached one of the semis, her disciplined associates drifting forward with her.

Crawford, still fuming, ignored the other gathering, stayed focused on Counsel and her friends, all at the rear of the Durango. He barked an order. "Pull that box out and open it, Renner."

Renner and another bodyguard slid the cardboard carrier into a standing position and leaned it against the bumper. Renner's switchblade snapped open. Counsel's K9 deputy Fungo banged against his crate, snapping and snarling. Tess pulled hard at the leash Andy held.

"Ready, sir?" Renner said.

"Open it. Be careful . . ."

A few careful slices eliminated exterior packing tape. Unfolding a flap, they removed a framed painting heavily bubble wrapped. Renner's switchblade was out again, waiting for Crawford to join him.

An impatient Crawford grabbed the knife and gently started at the top, slicing through the bubble wrap. After six inches of the painting was exposed, his eyes bulged. He spit out his displeasure. "Nooooo . . ."

Dogs Playing Poker, or better known by its actual title, *Poker Game,* a painting by Cassius Marcellus Coolidge.

"It's an early Christmas present, Andy," Counsel said, beaming. "I guess I should say, 'Surprise!'"

Crawford turned the knife around in his hand and raised it at the painting. Andy's relaxed grip on Tess gave her wiggle room. She catapulted out of his grip and sank her canines into Crawford's wrist, wrestling his arm to the dirt. Renner and both bodyguards went for their pieces, as did Counsel, Andy, Vonetta, and Dody.

All armed, all with bad-ass bluster, all stalemated, the seconds ticking until—

From a bullhorn came a woman's voice, undercover as one of The Minutemen. "This is the FBI! Drop your weapons. All of you. Now!" Additional vehicles skidded into the periphery of the courtyard, slamming their brakes while plugging up both exits.

"This is Special Agent in Charge Escobar speaking," the bullhorn voice announced. "You!" she shouted, then used her shouldered M4 carbine to point at faces around the courtyard, "and you and you and you, and everyone in the RV camper—we're taking you all into custody for illegal arms trafficking. Hands up, everyone. Do *not* do anything stupid. We will use whatever force is necessary . . ."

The "yous" did not include anyone from the Durango, but their weapons still went on the ground.

Mercer Crawford objected, refusing to raise his hands. Around him, plainclothes FBI began handcuffing people.

"I have nothing to do with this! These people . . . they've stolen a large sum of money from me, from my bank account. I followed them here. Do you know who I am?"

A voice came from the periphery. "Yes, they do, Mercer."

Dagmar Bystrom. She took her time passing through the headlights from the obscurity of the courtyard's unlit perimeter. She held up her phone like an exorcist with a crucifix as she neared her former boss, the voices from a recorded call on a loop, cutting through the cacophony of clicking handcuffs and agents Mirandizing their alleged perps.

Dagmar's recorded voice: *"Buyers are good for a ten-million-dollar order to Gatling. Untraceable AR-15s, semiauto handguns, ammunition. You want me to place the order, Mercer?"* Crawford's recorded voice: *"Do it."*

Agent Escobar grabbed one of Crawford's wrists, pulled it behind his back, grabbed the other, and clicked the handcuffs in place. "Mr. Crawford, you are under arrest for illegal arms trafficking. You have the right to remain silent . . ." She walked him to one of the cars, tucked him inside.

Dagmar asked the agent to open the window of the car with Mercer in it. She leaned in and spoke to him in a calm, low voice.

"A few more things, Mercer.

"One, in case you didn't work this out in that misogynistic head of yours, I set you up here with the Feds, but I also set you up with the art scam. Branding the painting with 'special chemicals'?" she said, smiling and using air quotes. "That was my idea. Two, all the people at the museum, and all these people here? They were in on it. You didn't brand the original, you branded an unpainted canvas that was behind the original in the frame. See those lovely people over there, staring at you now?"

She pointed. "Yeah, them, the ones in that SUV. The woman with the dogs, waving at you, and that short Hispanic guy—the scam was all their idea." Dagmar was beside herself, beaming. "Whew. This was so much fun, I might just wet my pants. Plus, get this, Mercer, there's more."

She reached into her fanny pack and retrieved a folded paper.

"I am thrilled I'm getting to read this to you in person. I'm having a copy of it signed by Darville Washington himself so I can frame it for my new office. This releases to the media tomorrow, Mercer. Ready?" She cleared her throat.

"For immediate release. Gunowners Against the Slaughter, also known as GAS, is proud to announce the creation of a new executive position for the growing organization. CEO Darville Washington revealed today that GAS welcomes the appointment of Ms. Dagmar Bystrom, formerly an executive with the gun manufacturers' lobby Arms Equal Freedom, commonly referred to as the AEF, as the new president and newest member of its Board of Directors, effective immediately.'"

Crawford's jaw tightened. "They're nobodies, Dagmar! They have no chance in this environment. The AEF is the premier gun rights organization in the US . . . the world! The AEF will crush them . . ."

"The AEF is a good ol' boys network on the way out, Mercer," Dagmar countered. "Half the membership doesn't agree with your take on all the gun violence. And those people of color you don't want in the AEF? Every one of them has a home with GAS. Hell, many of them have already become GAS members. Your personal conduct here, this Gatling Arms illegal gun sale fiasco—how the hell do you think this is going to play to gun rights advocates who prefer that their spokespeople *not* be felons, hmm?"

Dagmar dropped the press release into Crawford's lap and flashed a big smile in response to his red-faced silent bluster. "Headlines are already queued up for tomorrow from news agencies. Something Darville orchestrated: *'New Exec Gives Gun Rights Upstart Immediate Credibility.'* These GAS execs, I love them already."

She tapped the roof of the vehicle signifying the driver could now close the back window. Dagmar tossed a parting sentiment at her ex-boss as the glass powered upward. "See you and the AEF in civil court, bitch, for my wrongful termination."

Nearby, the federal agent gripped Renner's wrist. "Renner Merkler, you have the right to remain silent . . ."

Renner shook free. "No. This was Mr. Crawford's idea, not mine. He threatened me into cooperating. I'm not involved—"

Agent Escobar told her arresting agent to stand down. She took the agent's place in confronting Renner face-to-face. "You were here acting as an illegal gun broker for this transaction. You will be arraigned, and you will go to jail. You own an illegal handgun. I'll finish Mirandizing you. You have the right to—"

"You have no proof—"

Escobar stopped speaking to assess her detainee. "Really? You want to go that way? Okay. Let's revisit the probable cause aspect. Ready? Take your pants off, and your shirt."

"What?"

"You heard me, Mr. Merkler. Your pants and your shirt. That ID you use on the darknet is cute. Original. It took us a bit to match you up. The *2A* Second Amendment part was simple enough to figure out, but the gobbledygook that followed it took a bit more imagination. Your *2A* ID fronts the word *palindrome* in cryptic letters and symbols," she said, air-quoting his name, "*'Renner.'*

"Back to you dropping your trousers. We've got you on video, lover. So lift your shirt and drop your briefs right here to prove it wasn't you in those photos you sent over the darknet, otherwise let my agent cuff you. Go ahead, impress us with what you don't have in your pants. We'll wait."

Counsel, speaking to Andy: "Jeez, will you look at the time. Can you give me and Tess a lift to you-know-where?"

The presidential debate was expected to start in twenty minutes, the venue at least ten minutes away by car.

"Not enough fun for one night already?" Andy said. "What am I supposed to do while you're at the debate?"

"You drop me off in this battered SUV and find somewhere to hide its abused remains while you wait. You and Fungo then get some alone time with your new doggy painting. It's not just any street art reproduction, mind you, Andy. It's a Sebastian Leone original."

"Original *forgery*."

"Potato, po-tah-to. The guy's still an art genius. Plus you get to tell great stories about it at parties."

"Indeed, I will. Fine. Let's go."

"One other thing, Andy."

"What?"

"Go talk to your daughter." Counsel chin-pointed at Special FBI Agent in Charge Escobar.

Andy, in full deflection mode: "I . . . I can't, Counsel. She's busy if you haven't noticed. Plus you'll be late to the debate."

Counsel leaned in, pulled him into her, put her arms around his neck, and kissed him lightly. "I'm not worried about the debate. You guys need each other. Make the effort. She's your daughter. Go."

A chastised Andy, with Counsel in tow, caught up with Special Agent Theodora Escobar, who excused herself from a conversation to greet him. "Dad. Hi. Hello to you too, Ms. Fungo."

Counsel nodded.

"Hi back, Teddy," Andy said.

"We need to stop meeting like this," Teddy said. A slight attempt at humor, although they each knew it took a lot of effort for her to do even that. Their last encounter had closed out the elimination of a mass murderer. It also earned him one large step in the right direction: Teddy's decision to call him "Dad" again. There'd be no further father-daughter public display of affection today, however. Still too early in their reconciliation.

"So proud of you, Teddy," he said. "Very impressive."

"Yes. And I appreciate your help with this. A high-profile bust that will get some national attention. I've got an outstanding team here, Dad. Good, dedicated, law-abiding, law enforcement professionals."

She met his gaze, them both knowing a specific point she'd just made: "law-abiding," as in not vigilante. For her, there could be no going back. No reopening of the Pandora's box that was the town of Rancor, Pennsylvania. Her appointment to the Bureau had been the best thing that had ever happened to her. Her willingness to overlook what she'd left behind was the best she could do for her relationship with her father, and for her hometown. Or so she'd said to him five times or more over the past ten years of their estrangement.

Andy stayed away from the flashpoint. "You're welcome. Glad we could help, and glad to have stayed out of your business. Glad you stayed out of ours."

She handed off her FBI-issue long gun to another agent and shook her head free of her baseball cap, her dark hair spilling out, falling just short of her shoulders. Her straight-lipped stare was confirmation of an unspoken agreement: *I don't want to be in your business, Dad. With me in the Bureau, I can never acknowledge your business . . ."*

Andy's was a stone face, Counsel knew, that he'd had to chisel for himself after years of navigating around the chasm that had formed between them.

"A cup of coffee is all I ask, honey. Sometime when you're free."

"Maybe. I'll need to get back to you."

THIRTY

Inside the former Baptist church turned college concert hall, the lights lowered. What remained was studio-quality illumination that focused on the debate stage, the PBS moderators, and the two empty podiums. The TV cameras first captured the moderators busy announcing themselves, the debate's format, the rules, and the decorum expected of the in-person audience. The second focus became the stage. The third was a quick scan of the debate audience sitting shoulder-to-shoulder in dark, wooden pews with worn red cushioning, church capacity 650. A moderator introduced both presidential candidates in close to the same breath, incumbent US President Alfreda Lindsay, the Democratic nominee, and Senator Quinn Hudson of Pennsylvania, the Republican nominee. The debaters entered from different wings with photo-perfect smiles and advanced quickly to shake hands. They proceeded to their places behind their podiums.

"Our first topic, and the first question," the female moderator said, launching into the debate, "goes to Senator Hudson. Senator . . ."

Aaron, seated thigh-to-thigh between Linus and VP candidate Congresswoman Inkster, feigned his interest as the debate progressed. Ms. Inkster's admonition that the TV cameras would find Aaron often was ringing true, especially when the topics were prison reform, discrimination, and how some laws continued to negatively impact the already marginalized LGBTQ community. Aaron didn't know when exactly it happened, or why, but a part of him began listening, *really listening* to the responses, in particular Senator Hudson's. If the senator wasn't sincere about some of these difficult topics, Aaron decided, he was doing a great job faking it.

Ms. Inkster elbowed his arm, interrupting his concentration. "See that suit, Aaron? The senator's suit? I picked that out for him, the color, everything. I talked him into it. Looks great on him, doesn't it?"

The comment was a trigger. It redirected him, refocused him, and put him back on task. The senator's suit was a blue-gray number, and he did look good in it, but the blue-gray was morphing, fading, losing its blue-ish tint, losing all pretense of the blue, turning all gray.

The debate moderator spoke, trying to wrap up the senator's answer. "We'll need to leave it at that for the moment, Senator. Madam President, Senator, we need to take a break here. We'll be back in a bit with the next round of questions, the topic global warming."

The TV cameras went dormant, cutting to commercial. Aaron stood, announced that he needed another bio break badly, left the front row in a near trot, and headed for a hallway. He found stairs leading to the ground floor. At the bottom he quick-stepped into the storage area and zeroed in on the lockers. The area was empty, quite a difference from his prior visit. He rounded a corner of the room and neared a particular locker.

The combination lock he'd used to lay claim to it was hanging loose. The lock's curved shackle had been snipped then reinserted back into the locker latch.

Nooooo …

He ripped the lock from the latch and opened the locker door. The trumpet case was still there, in the back. A quick look up at the locker's interior ledge. The finishing nails sat loose on the metal shelf. Minor relief. Now, with him about to throw up, he stared at the upright instrument case again. He lifted it out and found a worktable.

Deep breath. He snapped the case open.

The trumpet was still nestled inside, all in one piece, but had it been disassembled? He raised it, eyed it closely, wary of the little time he had left, minutes only before the debate would recommence. So far he was no worse off, just startled by this bump in the road, this violation of his personal space. He hand-loosened the first piston valve, then the next, then the next. Hands sweaty, his forehead beading up, he unscrewed the first valve all the way, did the same with the second and third, and turned the trumpet upside down on the table.

The pistons fell out, and behind them, the three .22 caliber brass cartridges.

The authorities had been in the locker, which meant inside the instrument case, which meant they'd examined the trumpet, maybe even security-wanded it, but had noticed nothing out of the ordinary.

Exhale.

Aaron felt energized now, invincible, unstoppable.

He scooped the cartridges up and shoved the disassembled trumpet and its case back inside the locker. He grabbed a loose finishing nail from the ledge and slammed the locker door shut. In less than five seconds he loaded the ghost gun with the cartridges and inserted the nail as the firing pin. The assembled plastic handgun went inside his jacket pocket.

He sprinted up the steps, pushed through the SRO people on the periphery of the concert hall stage, and returned to his seat. He straightened his tie and exhaled.

"Everything come out okay, Dad?" Linus said, smirking at his lame joke.

"Yes. Everything's fine."

Back from TV commercial, the debate continued.

THIRTY-ONE

"This is not how I saw this playing out, Tess, honey."

Counsel rubbed Tess's head, her dog's paws resting on Counsel's knee. She eyed an ocean of moving cars on the street in front of their banged-up SUV rental, Andy driving, Counsel riding shotgun. Fungo rode out the traffic jam crated in the back. Bumper-to-bumper, taillights a-blazing, the drivers tickled their brakes from city block to city block, corner to corner, circling the music center looking for nonexistent parking spaces.

"Andy, I blame you for not finding a way around this mess."

"Of course you do. After all I'm, like, only a nurse."

"Exactly."

The parking garage nearest the music center debate venue said *Full*. The parking garage two-plus blocks away, where they had done the art swap, was now full as well. No parking spaces were open on the street anywhere, with other parking lots all full, too, some cars even double-parked with their flashers on. She would be late to the debate, and was now also worried that the debate organizers wouldn't let her and her working dog partner inside once she got there, even though she had a ticket.

Last minute adjustments she was taking care of now: her two handguns went to the glove box, and she tucked a few dog treats into a fanny pack in case she needed some rewards.

"Forget parking close, Andy. Let us out anywhere near the front of the building. Find a coffee shop or a bar or something and watch the debate from there. I'll call you when I'm ready."

Counsel and Tess on foot blended into the crush of people hovering near the main entrance to the former church, now university music center. Twenty minutes past the scheduled start of the debate, they stood in line to be wanded, screened, patted down, and released into the church ante room, people according them a wide berth worthy of Tess's Psychiatric Service Dog designation and bull terrier breed. The pews holding the audience were packed, downstairs and up. The debate was in progress. Counsel received accommodating looks when she showed her super-golden-Willy-Wonka-ish debate lottery ticket to ushers and audience runners, but no one would seat her. She tightened the leash and leaned down to talk to her working dog.

"I see prime real estate near the side of the stage, sweetie. Let's go in for a closer look."

The lights around the venue came up, returning to full strength for a television commercial break. She and Tess made their move.

A sympathetic female Secret Service agent responded to her service dog card, state trooper ID and VIP ticket, letting her and Tess hover on the perimeter of the security contingent off-stage, behind other security people. From what Counsel could tell, there were no other working dogs in the concert hall.

"Guess you and me are on duty, Tess honey," Counsel whispered, happy, "just like the old days." She patted Tess, the two of them liking this vantage point.

Stage-level behind the podiums for the two candidates, and raised, was the music center's massive pipe organ. In front of the podiums were fifteen feet of open space that fronted the desks and chairs for the moderators. Behind the moderators, a few steps down, were row after row of the audience, people moving in and out of the church pews during the TV commercial. The lights in the church building dimmed, the debate was about to start back up. The candidates returned to their podiums. Empty front-row audience seating was filling in. There, in the middle of the first pew, was Hudson's running mate, VP candidate Mary Inkster.

"Wow," Counsel said to herself. Congresswoman Mary Inkster was quite an attractive woman. Counsel reached for Tess and stroked her head, heading off a Tourette's episode stoked by female envy. A straggler speed-walked his way back to the seat next to the congresswoman, squeezed himself in and sat. Counsel sharpened her stare.

Wow again. The straggler was the media's recent darling, Senator Hudson's personal guest Aaron Pappas, newly released from prison. The press coverage, the news stories—Counsel remembered it all. Decades behind bars, exonerated of multiple murders, and now the presidential candidate senator's personal reclamation project. A transgender ex-con. Pappas looked good in his suit, having cleaned up really well.

But Counsel's antennae went up, seeing him there, this close to the stage.

Back live, the moderators went to work, the debate audience now in television-prescribed silence.

***

Aaron was here, was stoked, was ready. Quinn Hudson, Pennsylvania senator, the prosecutor who'd ridiculed his sexuality during his murder trial thirty-plus years ago, was less than fifty feet away. The man who had put him in prison and destroyed his life. The man who had earned political stardom on Aaron's transgender back. The man who was now in head-to-toe gray, on a gray stage, behind a gray podium, his hair, suit, shoes all gray now, his skin morphing from its salon suntan to a pale, gray ash.

But here also was a moderate presidential candidate committed to prison reform who had pushed for the overturning of Aaron's conviction, and had owned up that the wrongful felony conviction, by the senator's admission yet again tonight, was "a grave miscarriage of justice." In Aaron's mind, here, on the stage, the senator was a changed man.

Aaron's mind, analyzing this, was now a hot mess.

Sitting with his son Linus, the wheels were turning. Linus had only recently become—suddenly, and oddly—his new cheerleader. He'd provided little support during Aaron's incarceration, but at a some point he became Aaron's champion. He'd helped him with money, housing, transportation. Ran interference for him. Eliminated the red flags when the Feds showed interest in him. Enabled his return to society, enabled this evening, enabled his attendance at this event.

On Aaron's other side, Ms. Inkster, the steaming-hot congresswoman. Second in line on the ticket. Mary Inkster was more conservative than the presidential candidate, also seemed more ambitious. There'd been laughter at Aaron's expense, mocking him, demeaning his sexuality—she was humping his son, was controlling him . . .

Linus and the congresswoman, a manipulative team, able to champion Aaron's front row appearance at the debate, and with only cursory security wanding, not full-body screening . . .

The gray, everything around him, all of it was so gray . . .

***

Counsel focused. Across from her, in the front row, former convicted felon Aaron Pappas seemed stiff, intense, agitated, looking uncomfortable in his seat. Her law enforcement sixth sense spiked. There was something, a trigger, or maybe a landmine about to set Pappas off, with Counsel's own body language alerting her working dog Tess. Tess assumed the position, was now barely controllable, her ass on the floor, wiggling in anticipation, watching her master's face, waiting for a command—

***

Aaron unbuttoned his suit jacket. His right hand reached into the inside pocket.

The ghost gun emerged, all toy-like and unthreatening because it didn't look like a gun, it looked like a square hunk of black walnut on top of a plastic handle. He extended his arm in full, his target Senator Hudson.

Mary Inkster and Linus recoiled into defensive postures on each side of him, their hands raised, surprise overwhelming their faces, except—

The congresswoman showed a momentary giddiness, a facial hallelujah with a praise-the-Lord chaser, a barely noticeable high she converted into fright on the fly. Linus's animation was momentary but equally revelatory: laugh lines emerged, the corners of his mouth contorting, first curling up, then turning down, soon mimicking shock, terror. These reactions—

Aaron's subconscious glimpsed them. Something was gravely wrong with their reactions.

Senator Hudson's face—Aaron's second pass at him revealed a warm, tanned hue, some rose in his cheeks, the gray gone.

He swung the gun away from the senator. Aaron's line of sight and the plastic gun barrel now glided toward President Lindsay.

Counsel in the wings shouted "Gun!" like all the other security types. She let go of Tess's leash, the only command Tess needed. Her dog deputy sprinted across the stage.

The podiums and people and props and papers all became a blur, bodies scrambling everywhere, diving at the candidates, tackling them, covering them—

Aaron continued swiveling his ghost gun. It now faced Mary Inkster.

The trigger pull yielded a soft sound, *pffft*, like a dart from a blowgun. The quiet bullet zipped past her protesting hand, into her temple. Aaron made a swift one-eighty turn, his son Linus now staring into the square barrel.

Aaron panted while speaking, his eyes tearing: "You see me as a monster, Linus, a freak, a means to an end—"

"No, Dad, nooo!"

Another trigger pull, another *pffft*, the bullet slamming his son's gray forehead, parting the flesh, and punching through his skull into his brain, his body collapsing, the entrance wound dripping red.

" . . . just not the end you expected."

Aaron stuffed the barrel into his own mouth.

Tess reached the end of the stage and went airborne. The dog clamped her mouth onto his wrist and pulled his arm down, became ferociously violent, her teeth shredding skin, the force of her ragdoll shake breaking Aaron's arm and slamming it and him to the floor, the ghost gun bouncing, sliding away. Secret Service agents pounced on him. Counsel arrived, there to control her dog.

"Tess! Heel, Tess, heel . . ."

The crush of agents held down the assassin, manhandling him in search of more weapons. Counsel picked up the ghost gun and disengaged the revolving cylinder. One cartridge was left in one of the plastic chambers, a small caliber. Counsel's snap assessment—the attack, with this caliber, needed to be at close range, no farther away than the front row. An agent ripped the gun from Counsel's hand without apology, but also with no protest from her.

They pushed Counsel back, Tess barking, protesting loudly, but heeling with her, Counsel still able to see the writhing shooter on the floor. Aaron Pappas's wrist, his eyes, his face—it all showed the agony of Tess's takedown plus the severity of the agents' physical responses, the assault on him getting worse, him dishing to the agents during his beating, them all tuning him out.

"They were using me! Senator Hudson—he's a decent man. My son, he used me—"

The agents gripped his head, muzzled him with their hands, muffling his words, and they hustled him off the stage.

Chaos continued, on the floor, the stage and backstage, with a worldwide TV audience in shock. Multiple ambulances arrived, soon leaving the venue with two dead, one injured. The presidential debate candidates, as shook up as they were, remained protected and off camera.

***

Outside the music center, Counsel hit the bricks with Tess next to her, leashed and heeling, a good girl, Counsel feeding her treat after treat as rewards, hustling them both down the sidewalk, their destination a rendezvous with Andy and Fungo. Neither the media nor the Secret Service had discovered their absence yet, and Counsel was happy for that small favor. They'd be hailed, more like hounded, as heroes; she wanted no such treatment. She saw the rental SUV two streets away in the middle of the block, the meeting spot prearranged by text with Andy. He exited the vehicle and sprinted up to meet her, his rib-crushing embrace transcendent, as congratulatory as it was a relief.

"Let's get you two out of here, Counsel. Things are going to be nuts for you going forward."

No argument from her as they trotted back to the SUV. Inside, their sumptuous kiss was invigorating, but Counsel cut it short.

"Take me home, Andy. I need a bubble bath with you, we can drink some wine, you can hold me, we can get creative in the bubbles, and we'll have no mention of what just went down.

"Just get me out of here now, please."

THIRTY-TWO

Brandywine Museum of Art, Chadds Ford, Pennsylvania

Two days prior to Presidential Election Day

The museum's pre-opening crowd extended out the entrance, down the sidewalk, made a right turn at the Brandywine River, then wended along the riverbank parallel to the art museum a hundred feet and still counting. Today N. C. Wyeth's painting *Hickok at Cards*, missing from public view for weeks, would return to the exhibit space after its lengthy absence. Where it had been, and for what reason, had already become the stuff of speculation, legend, conspiracy, and fantasy, chronicled and mis-chronicled by national news agencies, art enthusiasts, and political pundits around the country.

From the haven of the museum's media room, with a gently twisting, glass-window-view of the winding river, Counsel and friends watched as the line outside continued extending itself into a copse of trees. The museum would not open for another half hour, the entrance line showing no quit, looking as busy as the grand opening of a blockbuster movie.

All told, the painting had been somewhere other than part of the museum exhibit for a total of forty-six days. What had been reported about its absence, its travels, and the personalities involved, was fast approaching infamy:

It had been sold to a new Wild West theme park in Michigan.

It had been stolen by a Russian oligarch and would go to the highest bidder on the darknet.

It sat in as the target for a new heist movie being shot in Ecuador.

Eventually, however, the media attached its absence to gun activist Mercer Crawford and the AEF, rumored to have been scammed out of a large sum of money with an elaborate scheme that put dirty AEF funds into the hands of victims of gun violence. A grand jury had already convened, indicting Crawford for brokering illegal weapons sales. The indictment lent this rumor the most credence, bolstered by indictments of multiple executive officers at troubled gun manufacturer Gatling Arms.

The collateral damage: AEF members were renouncing their memberships in large quantities. In contrast, the membership of advocacy group GAS, Gunowners Against the Slaughter, was spiking.

On day forty-seven after its disappearance—today—the original painting would return to the public eye as part of the museum exhibit. To the heartiest of the conspiracy theorists out there, all of them wrong, the museum had lost the original and would be rehanging an imposter.

The painting's travails rivaled those of the most iconic art masterpiece in history, the *Mona Lisa*, stolen from the Louvre in 1911 and not returned until 1913. Like the *Mona Lisa*, the painting's appraised worth had skyrocketed from the notoriety.

All of it was common knowledge to the small group gathered in the museum media room: Counsel, Andy, Vonetta, curator Christine Adamsky and her museum security guard Gavin, and Dagmar Bystrom. With glass flutes filled with champagne in their hands, they were ready to toast the unveiling of the missing masterpiece as soon as Dody Heck arrived with art counterfeiter Sebastian Leone in tow.

Christina the curator spoke. "Shall we have one last look at Mr. Wyeth's pièce de résistance before its adoring fans swarm it this morning?" She ushered them forward, through a Staff Only door, to the exhibit.

They formed a semicircle around it, keeping a respectful distance, their champagne flutes notwithstanding. Silence, until Counsel spoke.

"I love it, but let's be honest. I've seen enough of this masterpiece that I think I could paint it myself with my eyes closed. So let's do this."

She raised her flute to the group. In her other hand were the leashes for Tess and Fungo, both sitting on their haunches. "A pre-toast toast," she said. "Where should I begin?"

She cleared her throat.

"To the victims of gun violence. So many communities affected, for so many years. Decades. For me, the worst were the victims of the Wissinoming String Band slaughter. An indiscriminate annihilation of a social club, done not by the indiscriminate firepower of military weapons, but in the name of it. The deaths, the surviving families, the outrage at blaming the victims—for too many lobbyists, this has been business as usual, a what-else-you-got kind of response. Not this time, buckos.

"To Dagmar Bystrom. Dagmar, thanks for having a conscience, and for reaching out to GAS. Thanks for cooperating with the Feds. Thanks for staying in your boss Mercer Crawford's ear the whole time. I know that proximity made your skin crawl. And many thanks for that little baking soda and grape juice paint-branding trick. Ingenious. Good luck to you, Dagmar. Good luck to GAS.

"To Mercer Crawford in absentia. Thank you for your $750K in donations even though we had to scam the money out of you." A chorus of chuckles ricocheted then died off.

"To the infamous journalist Karl Decker, deceased. Your 1932 *Saturday Evening Post* story about the *Mona Lisa* theft, true or not, with players real or imagined, showed us the way.

"To Christina and Gavin, our museum accomplices. You guys followed Karl Decker's lead and pulled it off. Inserting a blank canvas behind the original, and having Crawford brand it—so clever, Christina. Wonderful.

"And to my deputies here."

Counsel was teary-eyed. She scratched Tess behind her ear, then Fungo. She struggled some, was emotional in voicing her appreciation.

"I don't know where I'd be without my beautiful deputies. Probably in jail, or maybe under the long-term care of a psych nurse. You, my puppies, have been my salvation."

She regained her composure. "Speaking of psych nurses. To Andy. You believe in me—you *love* me, despite all my flaws, something I still have trouble processing. I love you, hot stuff. And to your daughter, Special FBI Agent in Charge Theodora Escobar. Teddy is on top of her game, Andy. You should be proud.

"To Vonetta. My state trooper homey. A vocal gun control activist looking to effect change from the inside. The biggest heart to go with that larger-than-life body of yours . . ."

"You calling me fat again, Counsel? You keep it up, no more bounty business to you."

" . . . and someone who thinks she's my boss.

"To Sebastian, who will be here shortly, but I'm on a roll so I'm not waiting. The lynchpin. The ringer. The chameleon. The man who gets my vote as the greatest con man I have ever met, certain to make the all-time list of one of the greatest reproduction artists in history as well. A student of the art forgery game who put us onto the *Mona Lisa* sleight of hand.

"And finally, to Dody Heck, now just arriving, our front to our AEF marks—"

Counsel raised her voice in Dody's direction. All eyes turned as she wandered in, dark blue blazer, gray skirt, white blouse, and pumps, looking movie-premier worthy. She grabbed two champagne flutes, one for her and the second, apparently, for her, too. She guzzled one glass then quick-stepped over to the group to wait for Counsel to continue her kudos, except Counsel didn't.

"What?" Dody said, her head swiveling, absorbing the interest. "Spinach in my teeth?"

"Where's Sebastian?" Vonetta said.

"What do you mean where's Sebastian? He's with you."

A headshake no. "The deal was, Dody dear, you haul him from your wonderful Rancor bingo hall-slash-police station where he's been living, and you and he drive down here to the museum to celebrate. Then I take him back north to face the judge where he pays off what he owes his creditors, with all of us, including the FBI, as character witnesses, so he maybe gets released with a suspended sentence."

"I'm agreed on all of that," Dody said, "except one part. *You* were supposed to pick him up, not me. You bonded him. I expected you to take him in."

"Wait." Vonetta fished out her phone, punched up the GPS app attached to Sebastian's electronic anklet and checked it. "Okay. Good. The app says he's here. Somewhere."

After multiple head swivels in all directions, Counsel spoke, sounding resigned.

"Everyone check your pockets and bags. Vonetta, I thought there'd be an alert—"

"No alert," Vonetta said, "and the GPS, it's still operational . . ."

The champagne glasses found table space. Clothing and accessories searches commenced. After a few seconds—

"Damn it," Dody said.

She removed her hand from her blazer side pocket. Hanging from her fingertips was a black electronic ankle bracelet slick with petroleum jelly. Size-wise, Sebastian was on the smaller, wispy side as far as men went. "Christ. A conman *and* a contortionist. He pulled me in for a hug this morning. This is why."

"Fine, but it makes no sense," Counsel said. "The largest chunk of the bounty was going to him, or at least to his creditors. He doesn't have his money yet."

Within seconds, a few of their cell phones beeped. A group text that was a selfie of Sebastian and another man drinking wine in an anonymous airport lounge.

Hi all. Eduardo de Valfierno and me, waiting to board.

"Where have I heard that name?" Counsel said. "I know. One of the Google searches on his laptop when we thought Sebastian was AWOL—"

Christine spoke. "I know the name. It's the name of the person who supposedly masterminded the *Mona Lisa* theft. Except he didn't actually exist. The plot that *The Saturday Evening Post* reported was deemed not credible."

Beep went their cell phones with another text.

I shall fill in some blanks. Eduardo not his real name was my accomplice at the Longwood Gardens art exhibit. He stole the cameo, Counsel

Beep. Yet another group text.

And he's been a busy salesman

Additional photos hit their phones in rapid succession.

De Valfierno with another man holding Wyeth's *Hickok* painting, the painting standing upright in a car trunk. Another photo, this one with the *Hickok* painting and de Valfierno with a woman at an NRA rally. Another snapshot with a man at a monster truck event, another one with a hip-hop diva backstage at a theater in NYC, then one with a female art collector at a New Orleans gallery . . .

The next beep was all text.

Remember the forgeries that weren't up to my standards?

Surprise! We sold them all. Mr. Wyeth's "original" exquisite painting that so captures the drama and tension of America's wild west now sits in eight personal art collections, and Eduardo and I have been compensated royally for our efforts in procuring them for our clients

BTW sorry to disappoint you all, but if you haven't figured this out yet, I will not be returning

"Sonovabitch," Vonetta groused. "I'm out the bond I posted with the court for that little weasel. I'm in deep shit."

"Not so fast, honey," Counsel said. Another beep had followed the last text. "Check your phone."

To Miss Vonetta. Use my share from the sting to replace the bond forfeiture. Whatever is left over, give it to my creditors

But please do not send Ms. Fungo and her nasty demon dogs looking for me. I like Ms. Fungo, but I do not like her dogs

***

"Here they come," Christine the curator said, wary of the excited horde hustling down the museum corridor.

Their group stayed huddled in a corner to the side of the art exhibit as the crush of art enthusiasts, reporters, photographers, conspiracy theorists, and other fans hustled through the cordoned path no doubt reminiscent of opening day at the Louvre a hundred-plus years earlier in 1913, when the *Mona Lisa* returned to the public eye. Today, and today only, museum management and the painting's anonymous owner agreed to allow the painting to be photographed. The only change to the current display of N. C. Wyeth's *Hickok at Cards* versus its prior showing was it now sat behind a piece of glass.

"Bulletproof?" Counsel asked Christine.

"Yes," she said. "Renewed interest, the increase in popularity, the increase in its appraised value—the painting's owner wanted additional protection similar to what was accorded the *Mona Lisa*, so the museum has provided it."

"When do I get to meet him?" Counsel said.

"Who?"

"The owner of the painting. Andy, you'd like to meet him, too, right?"

"Hell yes."

"First," Christine said, "very presumptuous on your part, Counsel, that it's a man. And second, that will never happen. Too private a person." She gestured in a direction away from the crowd. "Shall we?"

She took Counsel and Andy by their arms and escorted them out of the display area, the others following. They exited the rear of the building and stayed together for a lazy walk along the bank of the Brandywine River, a bite to the November air, with tree branches swaying, leaves swirling, dogs sniffing, and discussion topics that turned away from art and settled more on politics.

THIRTY-THREE

A prison in Carbon County, Pennsylvania

Presidential Election Day

The prison hospital's visitation room opened earlier than normal. Armed Pennsylvania State Police troopers stood guard, shoulder to shoulder, at the room's entrance. Two large Secret Service agents also stood sentry, their backs to a special visitor seated on a stiff chair outside space that was glassed in like a bank teller's. The visitor picked up the phone.

Five a.m. Republican presidential nominee Senator Quinn Hudson, dark suit, white shirt, wine-colored tie, was here to see patient-prisoner Aaron Pappas. For the senator, this was an early start on the busiest and most consequential day of his career, one that his political party hoped would end with a victory rally as US president-elect at whatever late-evening or early-morning hour was necessary.

Aaron, in bright orange and behind bulletproof glass, picked up the prison phone. The senator was across from him.

"Surprise," Senator Hudson said.

The only gray on or around the senator was his hair. For Aaron, this was not a reimagining of the senator's appearance, it was only a change in Aaron's assessment of it. His doctors would call this progress.

"Hello, Senator."

"Hello, Mr. Pappas." Senator Hudson absorbed the hard, unflattering visage of Aaron in handcuffs and leg irons. "I'm sorry we couldn't tell you ahead of time about my visit here. My campaign people strongly advised against it, so it's hush-hush. If word got out, it would only confuse people. But my heart and my conscience said I had a responsibility to see you. May I call you Aaron?"

"Yes."

"So tell me how you are doing, Aaron."

Aaron felt squeamish—stomach unsettled, hands clammy, his mind a bit anguished—but he did not feel frightened or overwhelmed. Small doses of anti-anxiety drugs had tempered his fear while not impacting his ability to reason.

"I'm not at the top of my game, Senator, in case you hadn't noticed." Aaron concentrated, cutting through the slight drug haze. "But I understand why I'm here. What I don't know is why *you* are here, Senator."

"Fair enough." The senator cleared his throat. "I'm here because I want to help you. I didn't help you before; I didn't *want* to help you before. I wanted to convict you, and I did. It was a mistake."

"But now?"

"Now I do want to help you, despite what you've done."

"So you're here, on Election Day? I don't know what to say."

"Yes. Election Day." He paused. "I know, 'Intended victim visits his aspiring assassin' is the stuff of urban legends. Except this visit won't remain anecdotal. After the election, I will substantiate it."

"But I wanted to kill you, Senator."

"You wanted to, but you didn't. I'm alive today, and here, because you changed your mind. You were confused. I'm here to understand."

Aaron struggled with this, some with where he was, some with where he would be going, but mostly with this unexpected visit.

His therapist, in the days just before the debate, had reneged on her promise. She had not cleared him for the surgery. Clearance would have been the last thing Aaron would have needed to keep him from attempting the assassination. The hope that he could live his life as he saw himself: as a man. With that hope gone, Plan B was to go through with it. An action that had fostered multiple death warrants. Two successful, one that was not. Still so incredibly tragic.

But what he didn't struggle with was what no longer invaded his thoughts, his consciousness, day in, day out: the gray. Previously so pervasive. Oppressive. Incarcerating. But now it was gone. Dead. It died with his son Linus and Mary Inkster. And the senator, the man who had originally portrayed Aaron as a heinous monster for all the world to see, wanted now to show the world that Aaron was not that person.

"My son Linus, Senator—and Ms. Inkster, your running mate—their agenda—I was the perfect pawn."

"Yes, you were. The FBI has their laptops and phones and is looking at their exchanges. You were being manipulated. It was a very sad day for our country."

"I'm so sorry, Senator."

"No less sorry than I am," he said. "You will be indicted for the homicides. There's no getting around that. But you'll have a good defense team, and there's a lot to be said about your change of heart. I will be in your corner for as much of it as I can, Aaron. I will speak on your behalf wherever necessary."

Tears rimmed Aaron's eyes. The senator raised his left hand, made a fist, and touched his knuckles to the glass for a bump. Aaron reciprocated.

"Senator, if I may, I have a different favor. I don't know how to ask this, but—"

"I already know, Aaron. It's about your reassignment surgery." The senator leaned in, adding a nod.

"When you are well, regardless of where you are—regardless of the outcome of the election, and regardless of my party's position on this topic—you have my word that I will do everything in my power to make that happen. That's a promise. Peace to you, Aaron."

END

America is a Gun by Brian Bilston

England is a cup of tea.
France, a wheel of ripened brie.
Greece, a short, squat olive tree.
America is a gun.

Brazil is football on the sand.
Argentina, Maradona's hand.
Germany, an oompah band.
America is a gun.

Holland is a wooden shoe.
Hungary, a goulash stew.
Australia, a kangaroo.
America is a gun.

Japan is a thermal spring.
Scotland is a highland fling.
Oh, better to be anything
than America as a gun.

ACKNOWLEDGMENTS

This one took more time to find a publishing home than my other novels. It includes material that some deemed too third-rail political, plus it includes a prominent character from a marginalized population. I appreciate the folks at Black Rose Writing for taking a chance with it.

Thank you, Brian Bilston, X's (Twitter's) unofficial poet laureate, for granting permission to include your memorable poem "America is a Gun" as a postscript to the novel. Brian, I pushed back big time to have the title of this poem become the title of the novel, but I lost the argument. Sigh. I still refer to the novel by that title in my inner circles.

Bucks County (Pennsylvania) Writers Workshop, chaired by author Don Swaim, which recently celebrated its twenty-fifth anniversary.

Authors Bill Donahue and Natalie Zellat Dyen, for their kind words after their close review of the manuscript.

Rebel Writers of Bucks County members past and present, including Rusty Allen, David Jarret, Kathleen Madigan, Jennifer Giacalone, Martha Holland, Jackie Nash, plus founding members Marie Lamba, Damian McNicholl, John Wirebach (RIP), and Jeanne Denault (RIP).

#1 NYT and Sunday Times bestselling author Clare Mackintosh for choosing the novel's first sentence as a Best First Sentence winner in the International Thriller Writers 2024 Thrillerfest Masterclass "Best First Sentence" contest. ("A major award." Ha!) The win garnered Clare's feedback on a partial for the novel's first few chapters. Whatever doesn't work here, Clare, is probably where I thought I knew better.

Author Etheljean (Ef) Deal and husband Jack Deal, trumpet aficionados and marching band legends. (How could I forget Doc Severinsen?)

Richard Condon (1915-1996), author of THE MANCHURIAN CANDIDATE.

Jeff Maguire, screenwriter, who wrote the screenplay for *In the Line of Fire* (1993) for Columbia Pictures.

Severn River Publishing, Andrew Watts in particular, for help in creating and shepherding my brand, which is whatever the hell I feel like writing in whatever the hell genre I feel like writing it in, with and without the profanity.

Our pittie-boxer Maeby Fünke Bauer, the best squirrel-takedown artist EVER, and the inspiration for Counsel Fungo's working dog Tess. RIP Maeby April 2024. Maeby also starred as herself in my political thriller JANE'S BABY. Good girl, Maeby. I'm sure it's beautiful where you are.

ABOUT THE AUTHOR

Chris Bauer has ten published thrillers: crime, horror, espionage, political. He's a subject matter expert in none of the following, although his fictional characters are: guns, billionaires, aviation, NASA, geology, law enforcement, crime scene cleaning, Hawaiian mobsters, US senators, or the Supreme Court, nor does he have six fingers on either hand. Chris wouldn't trade his Philly upbringing of street sports played on blacktop and concrete, fistfights, brick and stone row houses, and twelve years of well-intentioned Catholic school discipline for a Philadelphia minute (think New York minute but more fickle and less forgiving). He's a member of International Thriller Writers. You can find him online at chrisbauerauthor.net. He currently resides in Doylestown, PA.

NOTE FROM CHRIS BAUER

Word-of-mouth is crucial for any author to succeed. If you enjoyed *I Heard You Paint Cowboys*, please leave a review online—anywhere you are able. Even if it's just a sentence or two. It would make all the difference and would be very much appreciated.

Thanks!
Chris Bauer

We hope you enjoyed reading this title from:

www.blackrosewriting.com

Subscribe to our mailing list – *The Rosevine* – and receive **FREE** books, daily deals, and stay current with news about upcoming releases and our hottest authors.
Scan the QR code below to sign up.

Already a subscriber? Please accept a sincere thank you for being a fan of Black Rose Writing authors.

View other Black Rose Writing titles at www.blackrosewriting.com/books and use promo code **PRINT** to receive a **20% discount** when purchasing.